LESSON FROM A LORD AND MASTER

"I cannot answer for other women, but it does not seem right to me to leap into bed," Lady Olivia informed Sir Noah.

Noah spoke softly. "I shall endeavor to respect your sensibilities, my dear. But you must do your part to promote our marital well-being."

"I am not sure precisely what you mean, Noah," she said hesitantly. "You want me to kiss you?"

"Definitely that. But I will ask a great deal more of you." His voice was bland, and his eyes were unreadable.

"You are frightening me. Tell me what you mean," Olivia pleaded.

Noah rose to stand before her, an imperative hand stretched out to her. "I will show you, Olivia. I see no reason why I should not teach you all I know."

LAURA MATTHEWS was born and raised in Pittsburgh, Pennsylvania, but after attending Brown University she moved to San Francisco. Before she sat down to write her first novel, she worked for a spice company and an architectural firm, and on a psychology research project.

A
BARONET'S
WIFE

Laura Matthews

A SIGNET BOOK

SIGNET
Published by the Penguin Group
Penguin Books USA Inc., 375 Hudson Street,
New York, New York 10014, U.S.A.
Penguin Books Ltd, 27 Wrights Lane,
London W8 5TZ, England
Penguin Books Australia Ltd, Ringwood,
Victoria, Australia
Penguin Books Canada Ltd, 10 Alcorn Avenue,
Toronto, Ontario, Canada M4V 3B2
Penguin Books (N.Z.) Ltd, 182–190 Wairau Road,
Auckland 10, New Zealand

Penguin Books Ltd, Registered Offices:
Harmondsworth, Middlesex, England

Published by Signet, an imprint of New American Library,
a division of Penguin Books USA Inc.

First Signet Printing, January, 1992
10 9 8 7 6 5 4 3 2 1

 REGISTERED TRADEMARK—MARCA REGISTRADA

Printed in the United States of America

For Diana and Kathleen,
with thanks.

A
BARONET'S
WIFE

Chapter One

"My brother said I was not to ride this morning?" Lady Olivia asked incredulously.

The embarrassed groom shuffled his feet and mumbled, "Said as how you was to spend the day greeting his guests, ma'am. Begging your pardon."

"He might have told *me*," Lady Olivia retorted coldly with an annoyed flick of the riding crop she held. More gently she said, "Very well, James. It is not your fault, heaven knows."

Nonetheless she felt disgruntled that her brother should have chosen such a shabby way to restrict her movements. She returned to the house to change from her riding habit into a morning dress, knowing it was highly unlikely that any of the Earl's guests would appear for several hours. There would have been time for a leisurely gallop across the estate, but it would only be perverse of her to disobey her brother, and would undoubtedly provoke his sharp tongue.

Olivia moved restlessly about the Gold Drawing Room, at one moment thinking to start a letter, at another drifting to the harpsichord. The Earl's extravagances were all about her in the room's gold silk and cotton damask covered walls, cut glass chandeliers, Carrara marble chimney-piece, carved gilt pine sconces and Aubusson carpet. The guests, when they started to arrive, were no less elegant than the room, and were not in the least put out that the fifteenth Earl of Bolenham was not there to greet them. Peter, intent on a day's hunting with the guests already in residence, was granted an eccentricity usually reserved for the elderly; the fact that his friends and relations were arriving to celebrate his coming of age witnessed to their easy tolerance, or total indifference. Olivia judged them all to be intent only on their own pleasure, and they were likely to be well repaid for their journey, as Peter had ordered a celebration which would last a week, with plays in the theatre, dinner parties, balls, and a staggering variety of other entertainments fit for royalty. The only relief offered her in the arranging of the festivities was that the Prince of Wales had been forced to decline at the last moment.

Although the number of guests had already exceeded those recollected by her brother in giving her notice of who was to attend, she had well prepared for his oversight by ordering an additional dozen rooms made ready. There were few occasions on which his memory had served correctly in the past, and she expected no improvement in the future. A sigh escaped her as she glanced into the pier glass with its large ho-ho bird perched high above her on the cresting. She shared with her three brothers the raven-black hair of the Fullertons, the aquiline nose and pointed chin, but her eyes were set more widely apart and were a softer gray. Fortunately her complexion had escaped the swarthiness of theirs, and her reflection assured her that the printed linen with its trailing flower sprays in red, blue and green was becoming. With all the dignity of her recently achieved eighteen years, she imitated the haughty sniff and lifted brow of her aunt, who had just left the room.

"Excuse me, Lady Olivia," a voice spoke from the doorway, startling her out of her mimicry.

Olivia turned, flushing, to the young man who stood there. "I did not hear you enter, Mr. Evans. May I be of some assistance?"

James Evans advanced into the room before commenting, "I realize you are busy today, Lady Olivia, and I have no intention of imposing on your time, but Lord Bolenham left this morning without directing me in my cataloguing. He made some mention of a secondary library but did not indicate its whereabouts." He spoke respectfully but there was a hint of amusement in his eyes.

Olivia responded with a rueful smile. "How unlike the Earl to forget such a detail, Mr. Evans. He must mean the book room adjacent to the master suite. I will have Hawker take you there," she offered as she gave a tug on the pull. Olivia was not unaware of the admiration in Mr. Evans' eyes as they dwelled on her and she could not but be flattered by it. After spending a day greeting old men who chucked her under the chin like a child; middle-aged men who ignored her; and young men who leered at her because she was her brother's sister, she was more than ready to approve of the quiet, respectful admiration Mr. Evans showed. His situation at Stolenhurst just now was particularly awkward. Before the guests had begun arriving for Peter's birthday, he had taken his meals with the family; now he was no doubt relegated to his own room or the housekeeper's, and Olivia determined to speak with Peter about the matter as soon as he should appear.

When Hawker arrived in answer to her summons, she watched Mr. Evans out of the room with a little disappointment. She would miss his amiable company when he finished his work and returned to London. It had become her habit to wander into the library while he worked; and, perched on the high stool there, she would hand him a volume as he needed it.

Only yesterday she had asked, "Do you ever see a volume you want particularly to read?"

"Often, and when I have the time I read it while I am in residence. But if not, Mr. Whittaker can usually run it down for me later. It has become my custom to do a quick survey when I first arrive. Then I have something to keep my evenings from boring me to tears," he laughed.

"And did you find anything here?"

He had reached down a volume from above her head and opened it. "This is James Thomson's *Castle of*

Indolence. Most people are familiar with his *Seasons*, but I like this better, especially for reading aloud. Listen to how it flows:

> *Joined to the prattle of the purling rills,*
> *Was heard the lowing herds along the vale*
> *And flocks loud bleating from the distant hills,*
> *And vacant shepherds piping in the dale:*
> *And now and then sweet Philomel would wail,*
> *Or stock-doves 'plain amid the forest deep,*
> *That drowsy rustled to the sighing gale;*
> *And still a coil the grasshopper did keep;*
> *Yet all these sounds yblent inclined all to sleep.*

or

> *Full in the passage of the vale above,*
> *A sable, silent, solemn forest stood,*
> *Where nought but shadowy forms were seen to move,*
> *As Idlesse fancied in her dreaming mood."*

He abruptly closed the book with a self-mocking grimace. "I should not bore *you* with my enthusiasms, Lady Olivia."

When he had moved to return the volume to its place, Olivia had stayed him. "No, if you please, I should like to take it with me. If I have read it before, I have forgotten it, and I should like to do so again. You read extremely well, Mr. Evans."

"It is not my reading, I assure you," he protested. "The poem itself is the melody of a lazy summer day."

Olivia toyed with the volume as she murmured, "I should hate to think of Peter selling the books. The thought of generation after generation adding to the library, and benefiting from it, is somehow important to me. That people should come and go, live and die here, and leave these treasures behind is reassuring. Then it does not matter so much that one Earl is a rake and a spendthrift while another is kindhearted and generous, for each succeeding generation has the opportunity through these works," she declared with a wave at the volumes on

12

the shelves, "to learn again the nobility of the spirit." Olivia flushed at her own sentimentality and did not meet Mr. Evans' eyes.

"Yes, it is encouraging," he replied kindly. "Tucked away in many a library is the volume which will help shape a life and mold it into something better than it would otherwise have been."

She had smiled gratefully at him for his understanding. "Books seem so permanent. The race horses will grow old and die, and the little theatre will one day fall into disuse and be pulled down, but the library will be here. Or I hope it will." Olivia frowned thoughtfully, for she could think of no reason her brother would go to the expense of having the library catalogued if he were not contemplating using it as a ready source of money. His debts were so great that even now, when he came into his inheritance, he would not be able to meet them. If he had not insisted on building the theatre, or adding so extensively to his racing stable, or entertaining his friends so extravagantly, he would not be in this fix. "I do not understand how someone can spend so much more money than they have! This perpetual, frantic race to throw one's money away on trifles is madness!"

Cautiously, Mr. Evans agreed. "Searching for pleasure is an expensive pursuit, ma'am. And a wearing one, for what was new and interesting yesterday no longer holds appeal today. You are blessed with a more practical outlook on life than many, Lady Olivia," he remarked admiringly. "I could not tell you the number of young ladies I have met in my work who care nothing for how much they spend, so long as there are balls to attend and parties to be given."

Warmed by his praise, Olivia had confided, "I sometimes think that I am alone in my viewpoint. All the rest seem determined on extravagance, and here am I making my little economies like a drop in the bucket. I am a fool to butt my head against such a wall." For indeed, she thought, there was no countermanding Peter's prodigality. No amount of reasoning, pleading or anger prevailed against his total lack of concern for his excesses. And her brothers Charles and Samuel were no less distressing than

13

Peter, in fact probably surpassed him in mischief and profligacy.

Mr. Evans was sympathetic, but avoided any comment which might be construed as a criticism of the Earl. "You cannot go against your own inclinations, Lady Olivia, especially when you know they are right."

"Well, I could," she had laughed, "but I am too stubborn to do so." Determined to interrupt his work no longer, she had excused herself. And now, as she watched him leave the room, she sighed. The cataloguing of the small book room would take him no more than a few days, and when he left she would miss their conversations. Miss Stewart, her companion, was too familiar and too timid to provide the easy interchange Olivia had enjoyed with Mr. Evans. Shaking off an oppression of her spirits, she turned with a welcoming smile as Lady Elizabeth Blake and her cousin Mrs. Lila Dyer were announced.

Lady Elizabeth floated into the room and over to Olivia with outstretched hands. "You are grown into a woman since last I saw you, Lady Olivia, and Peter has not said a word." Her blonde hair peeked out from under a charming pink high-crowned bonnet, and her smile was determinedly cheerful.

"It is a pleasure to see you again, Lady Elizabeth, and you, Mrs. Dyer. I have put you in the East Wing in adjoining rooms, and will have you shown there immediately if you wish to refresh from your journey."

"Yes, for the roads were vile. Nothing but ice and mud," Lila Dyer complained cheerfully. Olivia noted that she was no longer in mourning for her husband, but dressed in a cream woolen dress, with a rose-printed stripe, cut alluringly low over her bosom. Undoubtedly the costume was strikingly suited to her perfect figure, but could not have provided much warmth against the cold January day.

"Is Peter not here to welcome us?" Lady Elizabeth pouted prettily. "He promised he would not spend a moment from my side."

"He has not returned from hunting as yet, but I am sure he will not be long now." Olivia glanced at the long case clock in the corner. Lady Elizabeth's steadfast pursuit of her brother both amused and upset her. There was no telling if Peter intended to take her to wife, but Olivia could not imagine how the two of them would manage if he did. Lady Elizabeth's extravagance was quite as well known as the Earl's. She was every bit as beautiful as her cousin Lila, however, and Peter was obviously not immune to her flattery and coquetry. Olivia had the two women shown to their rooms and was on the point of seating herself when Hawker arrived once more this time to announce Sir Noah Lawrence.

Olivia turned in surprise to the door where the baronet, impeccably dressed as always, entered with his customary proprietary stride. At her expression his eyes gleamed wickedly and he murmured, "I see Peter did not inform you of my attendance at his festivities, Lady Olivia. I hope it will be no inconvenience."

Olivia regarded him coolly. "I assure you, Sir Noah, that he specifically advised me that you would *not* be at liberty to attend."

"That was indeed the case until a week ago, ma'am, but fortunately matters have turned out otherwise, and I sent him a letter indicating my ability to join his party some days ago."

"Doubtless he forgot to apprise me of the change in your plans, sir. It is no matter; there is a room in the West Wing which will suit you admirably."

"Any closet will do, Lady Olivia."

She rang for a footman and turned to him again. "I trust your mother is well."

"Quite well, thank you. She sent her regards to you and your brothers." His eyes sparkled with mockery, for he was aware that Lady Olivia would not believe his mother had done any such thing.

Olivia considered Lady Lawrence somewhat of a harridan, who had no affection for Olivia and her brothers; the Earl, along with Charles and Samuel, had made Lady Lawrence the victim of one of their pranks some years previously. Although it did not seem fair for Lady Lawrence to tar her with the same brush, it was a matter of indifference to Olivia, for she did not often see the

15

older woman. Sir Noah's home, Welling Towers, was situated some thirty miles away, and though there was a distant connection between the two families, Olivia was not familiar with its intricacies. Nor did she have any desire to explore it, as she considered Sir Noah responsible for leading her three brothers astray, through their mutual interest in the turf. Not that her brothers had been paragons even as youths, but Olivia felt they might never have become so involved in their expensive pursuits had they not associated with Sir Noah, who was half a dozen years older than Peter and a confirmed rake, in Olivia's eyes. She had herself heard Peter say . . .

"I do not mean to interrupt your thoughts, Lady Olivia," Sir Noah said lazily, "but I wonder if you could inform me if Lady Elizabeth Blake and Mrs. Dyer have arrived."

Olivia reddened slightly to have appeared so inattentive to her guest. "Yes, sir, but half an hour ago, I should say. Peter has not returned from the field as yet, but I expect him shortly."

"Ah, no doubt Lady Elizabeth was distressed that he should not be here to welcome her," Sir Noah suggested laughingly.

Olivia could not stifle the grin that lightened her features immeasurably. "Yes, the subject was mentioned."

When a footman arrived to show him to a room, Sir Noah murmured, "Perhaps one day Lady Elizabeth will lift the burden of managing Stolenhurst from your youthful shoulders." He acknowledged Olivia's flashing eyes with a solemn nod and strode out of the room as imperiously as he had entered it, his athletic form graceful for all the controlled energy it bespoke. He was well aware that he left Olivia fuming about his derogatory reference to her age; there was no comment more surely calculated to raise her spleen, and he enjoyed watching the color rise to her cheeks and the gray eyes glitter with annoyance.

In the hall he allowed himself a chuckle which she would not hear, but upon entering the bedchamber to which she had authorized the footman to conduct him, his amusement faded. The little hussy! It was very nearly the closet he had so rashly offered to accept, and nothing like the room he was usually given when he came to visit Peter.

"Tell Lady Olivia that this room will not do," he rasped to the footman, who obediently departed, leaving Sir Noah threateningly blocking the doorway of the tiny room.

Olivia calmly accepted the footman's apologetically delivered message. "I will see to the matter, Thomas," she replied staidly, her eyes sparkling with mischief. There was no haste about her journey up the branching oak staircase and through a maze of corridors to the furthest end of the West Wing. She found Sir Noah where the footman had left him.

"I understand there is some problem, sir. Is the room not to your liking?" Olivia stood on tiptoe to gaze over his broad shoulders into the freshly-cleaned room, a bewildered expression on her face.

"It might do for my valet," he remarked dryly, continuing to block the passage into the room. "I think Peter would not be pleased were he to learn that you had put me in such a . . . closet."

"I dare say Peter will return shortly and you should not hesitate to speak with him if you wish."

Noah glared uncompromisingly at her and lifted a hand to point to the short French bed at the south end of the room. "You can hardly expect me to fit into that thing."

Olivia's eyes opened wide with surprise. "Well, of course I would not expect you to fit into it, sir. Had you some intention of sleeping in your own room on this occasion?"

"I *will* speak with Peter," Noah threatened, his brown eyes snapping with anger, while his hands clenched at his sides.

"Certainly, if you think it necessary. However," she offered generously, "if you wish to have a room where you can sleep, I shall show you to another one which is prepared. Follow me." Olivia glided regally down the corridor without a glance behind her to see if he followed.

His boots were nearly soundless on the carpeted hall floors but she could hear the impatient drumming of his fingers on his gold-headed cane. She stopped before a door midway toward the front of the wing and dramatically swept open the door of a large bedchamber with an enormous half-tester bed, remarking pleasantly, *"More* than enough room for you, I think."

Noah stomped past her into the room and nodded a curt dismissal, which Olivia acknowledged with a mock curtsey before retreating happily to the Gold Drawing Room, where further guests awaited her. The encounter had improved her outlook on the house party, and she hummed cheerfully when she was once again alone, only to be interrupted immediately by her brother.

Chapter Two

Lord Bolenham had succeeded his father to the earldom at the tender age of eight and had not allowed anyone to forget his status from that day forward. He was willful and extravagant, charming and handsome. Although his mind was quick and it had taken him no time at all to learn how to raise the wind from the age of seventeen, he had no interest in the fact that his expenses far outstripped his income, even now that he was to be in charge of his own estate. His dealings with moneylenders made Olivia shudder with apprehension; his affairs must eventually lead to his arrest for debt if he did not curb his spending, but there appeared no likelihood of such a drastic change in his character.

"We had a good day's hunting," he told her now as he seated himself comfortably on a carved walnut armchair covered with a Soho tapestry which illustrated Aesop's fables. He had acquired the set of armchairs just a month previously, informing his sister, when she had exclaimed at their appearance in the room, that there had seemed no reason *not* to purchase them. "Has everyone arrived?"

"I should hope so," she replied dryly, "for I have only a further two rooms prepared."

"No matter." He waved a careless hand. "Did I tell you that Noah was able to come after all?"

"No, but he informed me so when he arrived. Lady

Elizabeth was not pleased that you were not here to greet her."

Peter screwed his face into the semblance of an old man and croaked, "She will be the death of me yet. Such a persistent woman could hound a man to his grave."

"She wants only to hound you to the altar, Peter," his sister retorted.

He sighed hugely and gave a theatrical gesture with one long white hand. "I have not as yet determined if I shall have her. There is a goodly dowry, of course, but she is not everything I could wish for upstairs," he remarked with an illustrative tap on the forehead. "Still, she is a ravishing creature and not to be discarded without considerable thought. I should like to bed her but she has just barely enough sense to insist on a ring first." He ignored the painful blush which stained his sister's cheeks and continued, "Now her cousin is another matter altogether. No demure miss there! But Noah has the inside track, and I should not like to find myself facing him at dawn with a loaded pistol. On the other hand, I doubt Lila is above a little double-dealing. Perhaps I should see what I can get in that direction."

"Please, Peter, I do not wish to listen to your lascivious plans," Olivia said coldly, the blush still on her cheeks. "You should change for tea."

"You really are a prude, Olivia," he snapped, well aware that he had no business speaking as he had in her presence. He rose leisurely from his seat and said cuttingly, "You will find scant sympathy for your fastidious views at *this* house party."

"I never do with you and your friends, Peter." She reached over to pick up her embroidery, her eyes not lifting to his contemptuous gaze. "Some brothers would feel otherwise."

"More fools they," he laughed and left her.

Olivia attempted to concentrate on her needlework but her mind kept returning to the scene that had taken place some months previously in her bedchamber. There had been a large house party at Stolenhurst and she had retired after the play, taking the usual precaution of locking her door. After dosing over her book for a while she had fallen soundly asleep, only to be awakened by the sound of a key turning in her lock. Her amazement had almost eclipsed her fright. When she had managed to light a candle, she called in a quavering voice, "Who is it?"

Peter had appeared in the doorway then, with a shadowy figure behind him. His voice was slurred with drink when he spoke. "Told him you'd still be up."

"I was not up, Peter. What is the meaning of this?" Olivia's icy tones did not sound as firm as she had hoped they might.

"Bet him your door would be locked, but that I could get in." Peter had to lean against the door frame for support.

"Well, you have won your bet. Now get out."

"Noah wished to congratulate you on your performance as Mrs. Sullen this evening, didn't you?" Peter, with a giggle, had asked of the figure behind him.

"Indeed. Most remarkable. Miss Richards could not have done better had she been able to perform," a rumbling voice had issued from the blackness of the hall.

"I am not interested in your congratulations, Sir Noah, and especially not at this time of night. I had no wish to take part in the play and did so only at Peter's urgent request when Miss Richards could not do so. There is no excuse for the two of you to be in my room, and I want you out of it this instant." Her eyes flashed in the candlelight and the hands holding the bedclothing to her chin tightened.

"No need to get in a huff," Peter asserted boldly as he reached behind him to draw Sir Noah into the room. "You should be flattered that Noah was impressed with your performance. He had said no child like you could carry off such a role. Had to have him up before the court to make him admit his error. Counsel for the Prisoner couldn't get him off and he was sentenced to apologize to you without delay." Peter swayed as he giggled again. "Rawlins thought the whole court should come, and he was Crier of the Court tonight, but your cherished brother Charles would not have it. Spoil sport. Told him he shall not be Lord Chief Justice next time," Peter declared sullenly.

Sir Noah never took his eyes from Olivia during this rambling discourse and at its conclusion said, "I apologize for my doubt in your acting ability, Lady Olivia. You did a remarkably fine job."

Olivia eyed him with disdain. "I would prefer, Sir Noah, that you apologize for entering my bedchamber unbidden."

Peter slapped a hand against his knee and yelped, "Unbidden! As if the Ice Maiden would ever bid anyone to her room. That's a good one!"

Thrusting Peter out the door, Sir Noah had bowed to Olivia with mock penitence and murmured, "You have my apology, child. I had no wish to distress you."

As he closed the door Olivia heard Peter mumble, "You know where you *are* bidden, Noah. I give you good-night."

The incident had embarrassed Olivia considerably, especially when she realized that all those attending her brother's mock court of justice would know that her bedchamber had been invaded in the middle of the night. Fortunately the house party had dispersed the following day and she had not had to endure the knowing glances of his guests, for she had not put in an appearance until late in the afternoon. Today most of the same people were present; but their memories were short in their constant pursuit of novelty, and she was newly emerged as hostess, rather than maintaining the background role she had played until her eighteenth birthday. Not that any of her brother's friends would have cared if she had put herself forward; but they would have assumed the worst in that case, and she had no desire to make her life less comfortable than it already was.

As the guests began to drift into the Gold Drawing Room for tea, she pushed her thoughts away from her and assumed a manner of sophistication which would be acceptable to them. Her brothers Charles and Samuel were among the first to enter, with off-handed greetings to her. They were enough alike to be taken for twins, and their enthusiasm for their day's hunt was loud and long, encompassing as it did their delight in a friend's fall and another's avoidance of a comparatively simple fence. Olivia no longer blushed for their ill-bred manners; if their guests accepted them, who was she to feel the discomfort of the situation?

Lady Elizabeth entered with a swish of her rose-colored velvet gown and approached Olivia with an offer to assist with the tea tray. There was no denying her as Olivia realized that Lady Elizabeth had a desire to have Peter enter the room to find her mistress of the engraved silver teapot. Lila Dyer arrived on Sir Noah's arm, laughing up at him as she playfully tapped his arm with her fan. A procession of bewigged and liveried footmen followed them into the room, bearing trays laden with cakes and tarts. Olivia called one of them aside and sent him to the small book room for Mr. Evans, annoyed that she had not remembered to speak with Peter about him.

It was some time before James Evans stood in the doorway, interestedly surveying the chatting groups scattered about the enormous room. He caught Olivia's eye enquiringly and she beckoned to him. "I did not wish you to miss your tea, Mr. Evans, simply because the house is full of guests. I trust you found the book room."

The young man grinned engagingly. "There was not the least difficulty, Lady Olivia, though I think Lord Bolenham was surprised to find me there."

"Do not say Peter actually went into the book room," Olivia protested, laughing. "I cannot imagine what possessed him."

Evans' eyes danced with amusement. "I believe he intended to exhibit its merits to the young lady who is now pouring tea, but he thought better of it when he found me there. Perhaps another time he will be more successful."

Olivia shook her head exasperatedly, but made no comment. "Will your work keep you here much longer, Mr. Evans?"

"I should think only three or four more days, unless

there are further book rooms of which I have not been advised." He looked at her enquiringly, but she shook her head. "Your brother has quite a valuable library and a very interesting one."

"It is a chief source of delight to me and I hope Peter will not contemplate disposing of it, but I am afraid he may. Is it difficult to sell an entire library?"

"No. Mr. Whittaker has had gentlemen walk into his establishment and ask for just that. They do not care about the content particularly, you understand, just that it is the sort of library that a gentleman might have in his home." Evans waved an encompassing hand to indicate the whole of Stolenhurst. "The library from an estate such as this, which has taken years to accumulate and includes many rare works and first editions, is in demand, and those who can afford to pay for such a thing pay very well."

"You do not think that the library might be as much a part of the Bolenham entail as, say, the furnishings?" Olivia asked diffidently.

Evans considered her thoughtfully. "It is as likely as not. Your brother would have to indicate that it is not, in order to sell the volumes. He should consult with the family solicitor, or perhaps he already has."

"I would doubt it, but I will make a point of suggesting it to him." Olivia considered the people milling about the room and said abruptly, "Forgive me for discussing your work when you are at your leisure. Allow me to introduce you to some of my brother's guests." Olivia took care to introduce the young man to those members of the party who could advance him in his profession and who would not disdain his acquaintance. She was aware that Peter's eyes followed her mockingly as she went about the room, but since he made no attempt to intercept her, she paid no attention. Charles and Samuel probably did not even remember who the young man with her was, and they would not have taken the trouble to question her in any case. Although they were both older than she, and as determinedly self-indulgent as their older brother, they were not so immune to Olivia's remonstrances as Peter was. However, Mr.

Evans soon excused himself with a grateful smile to his hostess and returned to his cataloguing, while Olivia continued to circulate among the house party, avoiding only Sir Noah.

Chapter Three

Seventy-five people sat down to dinner that evening at Stolenhurst, and Mr. Evans was not one of them. Olivia had approached her brother about his issuing an invitation for the library cataloguer to join the rest of the house-party, but Peter had been disobliging. "There is no need to include Evans at dinner, Olivia; he would be out of place." Olivia had thought it more likely that she herself would feel out of place with his friends, but had made no further comment.

As she had had the arranging of the seating, she put the doleful Mr. Carson on her right and the Stolenhurst chaplain, Mr. Winkles, on her left. The soft wood floors shone after their scrubbing with silversand, and the sand-colored walls with their stippled panels glowed in the profusion of candlelight. Conversation filled the room until the din gave Olivia a headache. She watched the servants in their crested livery pass an amazing variety of dishes amongst the company and noted that Peter had once again sent to London for another service of plate. An involuntary sigh escaped her—there was no end to his extravagance—but perhaps it was allowable for his coming of age. There really had been no need for the new raw silk ruched curtains, though, as their predecessors had hung for less than two years.

Olivia did not rise to withdraw with the ladies until her brother had given her a curt nod, and then she did so with only partial relief. There was no one among this group to whom she could speak with pleasure, even though the group contained two of her aunts, who would dearly love to bring her out this spring if only they were not too busy with their own affairs. A faint smile lifted the corners of Olivia's full mouth as she recalled their comments on the occasion of that discussion. It was not that she wished to spend several months in either of their houses, but Peter had proposed it, more to rid himself of her presence, she suspected, than to give her the pleasure of a season.

Her aunts had professed great affection for her, assured her that nothing would give them more joy than to see her welcomed into London society, and firmly denied that they were capable of such an endeavor. Aunt Davis was far too much the pinch-penny to ever give it serious consideration and Aunt Moore was far too indolent to contemplate such an enterprise without suffering palpitations.

Peter had made no further attempt to find a suitable chaperone for Olivia, so his sister assumed that she would spend the spring and summer at Stolenhurst as usual. The thought did not unduly upset her, but she would have welcomed a change of scene. Much as having her brother's friends in the house could distress her, there was little society in the neighborhood to engross her interest when she was there alone, especially during the London season.

Lady Elizabeth approached her, tugging her cousin along for support. "Are we to have the pleasure of seeing you perform in Peter's play this evening, Lady Olivia?" she asked archly.

"No, all of the necessary parts are filled, Lady Elizabeth."

The young lady toyed with the ringlets at the nape of her neck and remarked proudly, "Peter has promised that I shall be understudy for the female lead in *The Romp* which is to be performed later in the week. He knows that I am able to learn such speeches with the greatest ease and has promised to work with me during the next few days. One never knows when Mrs. Goodall's voice may give out, or she may come down with the flu."

Olivia regarded her with barely concealed astonishment. "You would wish to take such a role, Lady Elizabeth?"

"I would do what I could if the success of the play were in jeopardy," Lady Elizabeth replied stiffly. "Peter feels I would handle the role admirably."

Mrs. Dyer gave a snort of derisive mirth. "I cannot believe he is serious, Elizabeth. When has he seen you act? I remember your parts in our Christmas plays as children, and I would not say in all justice that you were an outstanding success." Her expressive face revealed her doubt, but at the same time she squeezed her cousin's arm in a conciliating gesture.

"Well, I have read some parts for Peter, cousin, and he was all admiration," Lady Elizabeth remarked, her eyes demurely cast down.

Olivia merely nodded encouragingly, but Mrs. Dyer let out a peal of laughter which attracted the attention of the men as they entered the room. Peter and Sir Noah joined the small group where they stood near the fire.

"Has Lady Olivia been entertaining you, Lila?" Sir Noah asked sardonically with an amused glance at his hostess.

"No, no, it is Elizabeth, Noah. She was telling us of her readings for Peter's theatricals," Mrs. Dyer explained as she moved to allow him to take a place beside her.

Peter flushed with annoyance, and sent a glare at his sister, though it rightly belonged to Lady Elizabeth, who was smiling beatifically at him. His tone was rallying when he proclaimed, "More's the pity you will not be able to judge for yourselves the talent Lady Elizabeth shows for comedy. I am convinced she would outshine us all."

Olivia took the opportunity to drift away from the group and approach her aunts. Her Aunt Davis, intent on her discussion with Aunt Moore, did not see her niece approach and was speaking unguardedly. "You may take my word for it that Lady Elizabeth will get him, and a good thing, too, for Olivia is far too young to manage a household of this size."

Indignation rose in her niece, since she had managed

the household with no help from her aunts for the past three years, but she gave no indication that she had heard the comment as she asked kindly, "Do you intend to join the theatre party, my dear aunts, or shall I have some card tables set out?"

Aunt Davis regarded her suspiciously but merely asked, "What do they perform this evening?"

"The Midnight Hour."

"Humph. Why can they never put on something acceptable? Such a charming theatre, and no expense spared on it or the scenery and costumes," she sniffed with a derogatory glance at her nephew, "and they never choose a play which is proper."

"I shall have the card tables set up in the Red Room, Aunt Davis. There will no doubt be a number of partners to be had." Olivia escaped from the two sour-faced matrons to undertake the task, and subsequently slipped off to her room, since she would not be needed during the evening.

She came upon Mr. Evans on the staircase, and smiled merrily at him. "I have escaped," she confided. "Do you go to attend the play?"

"Your brother has requested that I assist back-stage," he replied, his face blank of expression.

"He has no right to make any such request! Surely you do not mean to accede to him. There is no lack for servants to manage the dressing, make-up and scenery backstage."

Evans gave her a distorted smile and said solemnly "The Earl is currently paying for my services, Lady Olivia, and I would find it difficult to disoblige him."

"Well, I would not," she snapped. With an imperious finger she summoned a footman. "Please be so kind as to inform Lord Bolenham that I have need of Mr. Evans's attendance this evening and that he will not be at leisure to help at the theatricals."

Evans watched the tall figure until he entered the drawing room before he spoke. "I appreciate your concern for me, ma'am, but there is no need to irritate your brother. It is a small matter, after all."

Olivia shrugged. "If it is indeed a small matter to

29

you, you must please yourself," she said crossly. "Peter did it to annoy me, Mr. Evans, because I asked him to invite you to join the party at dinner. Where did you eat?"

"In my room. You must not think that I mind, ma'am, though I find it most generous of you to have made an effort on my behalf. I am well-acquainted with the awkwardnesses inherent in my position," he said softly.

Olivia studied him for a moment on the candlelit staircase. He had the manners and breeding of a gentleman; she could not be wrong in that. His curly black hair caught the light and his intent blue eyes returned her gaze steadily. "I have a mind to ask Miss Stewart to join me for tea in the old schoolroom, Mr. Evans. Perhaps you would care to join us?"

"Who is Miss Stewart?" he asked curiously.

"She was my governess and has stayed on to be my companion, though she spends most of her time hiding from my brothers when they are in residence," Olivia admitted ruefully. "She is an attractive woman of thirty, but as meek and self-effacing as one can find. My brothers terrify her with their loudness, to say nothing of their perpetual attempts to . . . well, never mind, it is not a serious thing with them. A mere joke because of her timidity, but she finds it difficult to accept it as such. Would you care to join us?"

"Nothing would give me more pleasure, Lady Olivia."

She explained where the schoolroom was located and appointed to meet him there in half an hour. Miss Stewart's room was located across the hall from the schoolroom—a spacious apartment, and her only complaint was that it was so far removed from Olivia's own suite, and Olivia might not hear her if she called for help. Although almost sure that her brothers meant no real harm in their mock attempts to seduce the governess, but rather to amuse themselves at her horror of their attentions, Olivia had made sure that the governess was provided with an ample lock to her door, one which had no duplicate key in the steward's room. Anything less would have meant an immediate departure from Stolenhurst, Olivia was sure, and she was fond of Miss Stewart in spite of the fact that the woman showed very little spirit and provided only mundane conversation for her younger charge.

When Olivia had identified herself and Miss Stewart had cautiously unlocked the door, the younger woman issued her invitation, prefacing it with the information that her brothers would be occupied in the theatre for the evening. Thus encouraged, Miss Stewart agreed to join Olivia and Mr. Evans, and they settled in the comfortable chairs at the south end of the schoolroom while a fire was laid for them. Evans appeared as the tea tray was borne in and wondered that he had never before met Miss Stewart, since he had been resident at Stolenhurst for two weeks now. If she did indeed hide from the Fullerton brothers, however, it would explain her absence, as they had been here for the whole of his stay.

The small party was most welcome to each of its guests after the various rigors they had undergone while Peter prepared for his coming of age festivities. Olivia had been too busy to spend much time with her companion, and Miss Stewart had stolidly refused to leave the schoolroom floor with Peter, Charles and Samuel in the house. Miss Stewart, even with her hair drawn severely back and dressed in the most inconspicuous manner, was obviously a fragile beauty, never cut out to be a governess in any household, much less her present situation. She was fascinated by Mr. Evans's description of his work of cataloguing the libraries of various country houses for his employer in London, and she became quite animated in her desire to learn more. Evans was enthusiastic in his efforts to satisfy her curiosity and to impress Olivia with his expertise on the subject. The clock on the mantelpiece of the schoolroom had not been wound in years, and the hours passed without the participants being aware of the time.

Sir Noah sat with Lila Dyer and Lady Elizabeth at the performance of *The Midnight Hour*. The little theatre, modeled on the old Opera House in the Haymarket, was rumored to have cost Peter sixty thousand pounds, and Noah had no doubt it was the handsomest and best-appointed small playhouse in existence, but he could not understand Peter's extravagant indulgence in such a venture. Adjoining the theatre there was a large foyer where refreshments were served to the guests between acts, and Lila and Lady Elizabeth, for all they had been there before, exclaimed at the innumerable manifestations of expense in the decorations and armorial bearings emblazoned on every side. Peter acted his role that evening with spirit and *élan*, and accepted the subsequent praise as his due. While Lady Elizabeth flattered Peter, Noah successfully urged on Lila the merits of retiring early for the night.

He appeared at her door, as he had on several previous occasions, and as they had arranged earlier in the evening, shortly after she climbed into bed. Having purloined champagne for the occasion, he grinned at her and carefully locked her door. Lila dimpled with pleasure as he lifted the champagne to show her his success and then drew from the pocket of his dressing gown two slightly smashed tarts, which he placed on the bedside stand with a gesture of rueful resignation.

"Actually," he admitted, "I would not be surprised if Peter would allow me to have a servant bring anything I wished, but it was more fun copping them."

Lila chuckled at his mischievous enthusiasm and patted the bed beside her. "You have a great future, Noah."

"I am only concerned with tonight," he asserted earnestly as he joined her on the bed. He surveyed the size of it with growing respect for Lady Olivia and muttered, "She was probably right in the first instance."

"I beg your pardon," Lila said, confused.

"It is nothing, my dear. Let me pour you a glass of champagne." He joyfully extricated two glasses from another pocket in his dressing gown and gallantly kept the chipped one for himself. "Nothing is too good for you, my dear."

Lifting her glass in a toast, Lila pronounced, "To an enjoyable evening."

"With a beautiful lady," he added, his eyes wandering appreciatively over her alluring figure, clad only in a nearly transparent negligee. He placed an arm about her shoulders and drew her closer to him.

It was at the moment of highest physical arousal for himself when Lila had just cried her delightful release, that it happened. Suddenly she gave an agonized groan and doubled up, much to his astonishment and horror. And then she began to retch while he held her slender shoulders and begged to know what he could do.

"It didn't work . . . yesterday," she gasped. "I thought it was not going to work." She gave a hysterical giggle and fainted.

Noah sat frozen for a moment, uncertain what to do. Then he sprang from the bed and hastily tied his dressing gown about him before dashing toward Olivia's room. It did not occur to him to go to Lila's cousin; his hostess would have all the resources of the house at her command. He pounded on her door and called to her but there was no answer. Finding the door unlocked, he pushed it open but discovered that the room was occupied only by an abigail soundly asleep in a chair by the windows. He shook the girl awake and demanded, "Where is Lady Olivia? I must find her immediately."

The girl's eyes opened with alarm and she stammered, "I . . . I . . . why?"

"It is an emergency. Where is she?"

"I suppose she must still be in the schoolroom," the girl answered sleepily, trying to bring herself to a semblance of understanding.

"Take me there," he ordered, impatiently holding the door open for her.

The abigail was new at Stolenhurst and had heard of all sorts of strange doings in the household, but the man's determination allowed for no hesitation. She led him directly to the schoolroom where Olivia, Miss Stewart and Mr. Evans were still engrossed in their conversation.

Three startled faces turned to Noah when he burst into the room. "I need your help at once, Lady Olivia." He hesitated before the curious faces and added, "Someone has taken sick."

Olivia rose instantly, and the other two with her. Noah exasperatedly shook his head at her companions and said, "She must come alone."

Miss Stewart, fearing the worst for her young charge, paled considerably and protested, "No, no, you must not go alone with him, my dear."

Evans could not feel much more comfortable about the command, aware as he had become when Noah swung around to them that Sir Noah had nothing on under the dressing gown. "Perhaps we can be of assistance, sir. It would not be fitting for Lady Olivia to go unaccompanied with you at this hour of the night."

Noah turned in desperation to Olivia, who was separated from her companions by some distance, and whispered fiercely, "It is Mrs. Dyer. You cannot bring the whole household with you."

Olivia nodded and turned to her companions. "There is no cause for concern, Miss Stewart. I shall be quite safe in Sir Noah's escort."

There were further protests, but Olivia ignored them and followed Noah from the room. The length of time it had taken him to find and extract her from her companions exacerbated his already frayed nerves and he very nearly allowed her to fall when she stumbled in her haste on the stairs. He caught her arm then and in his anxiety half-dragged, half-carried her to Lila's room.

Olivia hastened to the bed where the young woman lay unconscious, covered only by the bedclothes Noah had tucked about her. "Bring me some wet cloths," she ordered, and when he had turned to do her bidding she drew back the covers to see the poor woman's condition. She gasped in horror. "What did you do to her?" she cried faintly, shocked into speech.

Chapter Four

Noah turned from the basin where he was gathering cloths and gazed in stupefied dread at the blood on the bed. He shook his head to clear it and said, "Nothing. That is ... we ... I swear I did nothing which could have ... " He absently lifted the basin and returned hesitantly to the bedside and handed her a damp cloth, which she gently used to clean Lila's face. "I don't understand," he groaned. "She started to say something about it not working yesterday, and thinking that it would not work. I have no idea what she meant. There was no blood when I left her, I'm sure there wasn't. She had been sick, and then she fainted, so I came for you."

Olivia continued to sponge the woman's face and eventually her eyes, glazed with pain, flickered open. Lila's body shuddered and Olivia drew the covers over her once more as the older woman whispered triumphantly, "It worked. He said it would work but I could not believe it after yesterday." She closed her eyes again, a faint smile on her lips.

"Perhaps I should get her cousin," Noah suggested worriedly.

Lila's eyes opened momentarily and she murmured, "No, don't tell Elizabeth," before she once again drifted off to sleep or unconsciousness.

Olivia considered Lila's words for a moment and enlightenment came to her. "She has just lost a child, I think. Someone had given her something to make her miscarry, and at first she did not think it had worked. Should I send for Dr. Barker?"

"Yes, I think you should, but for God's sake, Lady Olivia, send someone who will be discreet." His handsome face was pale in the dim candlelight and a frown puckered the wide brow beneath his rumpled brown hair.

Without a word Olivia slipped from the room and down to the kitchens where she was sure to find the footman Peter insisted stay on duty during the night when there were guests in residence. She found with relief that it was Stafler and instructed that he go immediately for the doctor and bring him to Mrs. Dyer in the Green Bedchamber, where Olivia would be awaiting them. When she returned to Lila's room she found Sir Noah seated beside the bed holding the sick woman's hand, but Lila was not awake.

"I have sent for the doctor and I think it would be best if you were not here when he came, Sir Noah," she said gently.

"Yes, but it will be some time before he arrives." Noah rose to pull up a chair for her and paced about the room when she seated herself. "I didn't know about this, Lady Olivia, either that she was with child or that she had taken something to miscarry. I should not have brought you here had I known. We had some champagne and tarts and I thought perhaps they made her sick."

"You need not fear that I will spread any word of what has happened tonight," Olivia returned coldly.

He stopped his pacing and gazed directly at her from across the room. "I had no fear that you would, child. It is not that which distresses me but that you should be faced with such a situation at your age. I know you disapprove of me and your brothers for our way of life, and I would not purposely draw you into it." He came across to her and laid a brotherly hand comfortingly on her head. "I would not involve my sister in such a mess for the world, and I had no intention of doing so with you."

"And what of Mrs. Dyer? What of the mess she is in?"

Noah removed his hand from her head with a sigh. "I honestly cannot say, ma'am. Had she told me . . . I don't know." He shook his head uncertainly. "I will see she comes about, Lady Olivia, but you must remember that she is not a fledgling. She does not lack means as Mr. Dyer's widow, and she is old enough to choose her own way of life. You may not approve of her, but she does not ask your approval. It cannot have been pleasant to be married to that old mutton-head," he mused as he continued to wander about the room, "and there is no doubt that her parents forced her into the match, for he was rich and they were at low water at the time. Who can blame her for kicking over the traces now that he is gone? I certainly do not."

"You wouldn't," Olivia murmured.

He stopped by her, exasperated. "It is the curse of youth to see everything as black and white, Lady Olivia. I hope I shall be around when you discover that nothing is so absolute, that there is always a degree of right and wrong. Are you so sure of yourself that you can be judgmental?"

Olivia flushed under his intense scrutiny and regarded her folded hands. "I do not mean to be, Sir Noah, but I cannot but see the damage which comes from such wanton selfishness as is indulged in here at Stolenhurst. I do not claim to be disinterested and selfless, far from it. I would hope, though, that I would take responsibility for my actions. Peter is forever getting into scrapes and denying all blame, allowing someone else to extricate him. It is embarrassing and humiliating to me," she whispered.

"You take your role as a sister too much to heart, child. No one sees you as in any way to blame for your brothers' peccadillos."

Olivia's laugh was tinged with bitterness. "How can you say so? Even your own mother classes me with them, and she is not the only one. Have you ever been faced with an angry shopkeeper who declares that your brother has smashed his windows on one of his 'playful' night rides? Or a local squire who asserts that Peter has left a footman in a coffin at his front door in the middle of the night? Do you think Peter will deign to see these people?

37

Do you think I should deny his culpability? How am I to explain to them that it was just one of his thoughtless pranks, that he meant no real harm? The squire in his panic very nearly shot the footman. What would have come of that? But Peter does not care, nor would Charles or Samuel." Olivia felt tears stinging at her eyelids; she had never before given vent to her feelings in this way. "You say that you would not for the world involve your sister in such affairs. How do you know that she is not daily beseiged as I am with the consequences of your excesses?"

A twisted smile curved Noah's lips. "You forget my mother, Lady Olivia. Julianna has never, I am quite sure, been faced with any of the horrors you describe. I fear my mother may have in my youth, but it is many years since I learned discretion enough to handle my own affairs without her being involved."

There was the sound of arrival in the peaceful night outside and Noah strode to the window to flick back the green velvet draperies. "The doctor is here, and I will leave you to . . . handle my affairs," he said regretfully.

Olivia waited at the door of Lila's room for the doctor and dismissed the footman with her gratitude. Dr. Barker was an old and discreet friend, so she ushered him into the room saying, "I dislike disturbing you at night, sir, but I cannot be sure that Mrs. Dyer does not need some assistance. It would appear that she has miscarried . . . and that it was induced purposely." There was no use hampering him by withholding the facts, although they were difficult for her to give. "She has been awake only for a short time, when she mentioned that something had worked—presumably a drug or potion of some sort."

Dr. Barker nodded expressionlessly and proceeded to examine his patient. "There is no evidence of excessive hemorrhaging, Lady Olivia, but she should be watched throughout the night. She is sleeping now, which is the best possible restorative for her. I will leave something for you to administer in the event of further heavy bleeding, and some laudanum for the pain." He stayed with Olivia for a while issuing instructions and assuring her that Mrs. Dyer would not likely suffer any ill consequences after he left but that he would be more than ready to attend her at any time he might be called. "You should get some sleep, my dear. Have her maid stay with her."

Olivia nodded her understanding and walked with him to the front door before returning to the bedroom where she found Sir Noah awaiting her. After relaying the doctor's instructions, she set about the task of bathing Mrs. Dyer and changing her bed linen with Noah's help; she wished no servants to be involved in the night's happenings. There was nothing more to say to Noah, and she proceeded about her tasks silently, grateful that he did not speak to her.

"I think you will wish to sit with Mrs. Dyer, but you have only to come for me if you should need any assistance," she offered as she stood with her hand on the doorknob.

"You have already done more than I have any right to ask, Lady Olivia. I am sincerely grateful and apologize for the imposition on you." His troubled eyes rested on her downcast head and he pressed her hand before she slipped out the door.

Noah slumbered lightly in the chair by Lila's bed, aware of her movements and was wide awake when she spoke to him. "It is all right now, Noah. I hope I did not frighten you."

"You scared the devil out of me, Lila," he said softly. "How do you feel?"

"A bit nauseated, actually. Was Lady Olivia here?"

"Yes, and the doctor has been and gone. He thinks you will be all right but he left some medicine. Why did you not tell me, Lila?"

She made a helpless gesture. "I did not wish to have a child, Noah. I was told of an apothecary in London who could help me, but I was afraid his brew had not worked, such foul-tasting stuff. No doubt it was foolish of me to assume that since I did not have any children by Mr. Dyer that I was unable to do so. Honestly, it never occurred to me that it was he and not I who was to blame."

"I would have helped you to solve the problem if you had come to me."

"Would you?" She sighed and pushed her hair back from her eyes. "What could you have done, Noah? You do not wish to marry me, only to amuse yourself. I do not begrudge you that, how could I? And it would not be in keeping with my nature to sequester myself in the countryside for half a year, only to have the problems of finding someone to adopt the child. No, I saw only one solution and I acted on it. I will be more careful in future though, for this has not been pleasant." She gratefully accepted the glass of water with its few drops of laudanum which he offered her.

Noah sat silent, his eyes trained on her face but his mind abstracted. It was impossible for him to know if he would have offered to marry her. More likely he would have chosen one of the other solutions, perhaps not the one she had chosen; but that would merely have been for his own peace of mind and not hers. "Your cousin does not know of this?" he asked at length.

"No, and I do not wish her to. You do not think Lady Olivia will speak of it, do you?" she asked anxiously.

"Certainly not. I would not have brought her into it if I had understood what was happening, Lila, but she was very discreet throughout and assures me that the footman and doctor will be likewise. She did not allow any servants to be called but did what was necessary herself."

"She does not have an easy position at Stolenhurst, I imagine," Lila remarked. "It is unfortunate that her aunts are too selfish to take her away from here." Her voice had drifted into silence and she fell asleep a moment later.

When Olivia was summoned to her brother's library the next morning, she was surprised to learn that he had not joined the morning's hunt. She was even more surprised to find Sir Noah there with him. The solemnity about their faces alarmed her, and she turned immediately to Noah to ask anxiously, "She is all right, is she not? There were no further problems?"

"No, no, she is feeling fairly well this morning, Lady

40

Olivia, thanks to your assistance. It would seem there is gossip spreading through the house, though," Noah offered by way of beginning the discussion.

"I assure you I have spoken with no one," Olivia said stiffly.

Peter slapped a hand down on his desk. "The gossip is not about Mrs. Dyer, Olivia; it is about you. That silly new abigail of yours has been blathering in the servants' quarters about Noah coming to you in the dead of night with no more on than a dressing gown and that you did not return to your room for several hours."

"It will do no harm, Peter. Stafler was on duty last night, and surely he can set their minds at rest by informing them that it was necessary to call the doctor in the middle of the night."

"There is a very large house party in residence, Olivia," he snapped at her, "and every one of their servants has been spreading the tale to them. Having been up all night, no doubt Stafler sleeps during the day. Our aunts were beating on my door before I was out of bed this morning. Your reputation is damaged beyond repair," he said smugly.

"Ah, I understand now. You have sent for me to congratulate me."

"Mind your tongue, hoyden! No one will believe your prudish principles now, my girl, and there is nothing for it but for you to marry Noah."

Olivia stared in disbelief. "You have finally slipped your moorings, Peter. What do I care what your friends say of me? I would rather be shunned by that bunch of hypocrites than not!"

Noah interposed to say gravely, "It is not only these people, Lady Olivia. The tale will spread to London with them. I have assured your brother that I am prepared to marry you, since it was my thoughtlessness which compromised you." A muscle in his jaw twitched, but his eyes did not waver from hers.

"Well, I am not prepared to marry you, Sir Noah. I will not have *my* life ruined to save face with anyone."

"You will have to marry him," her brother roared, his face red with anger.

"And I tell you I will not. No one can force me to marry him, never think it!"

Noah rubbed his temples thoughtfully before speaking to the glaring brother and sister. "I do not think you understand the gravity of the situation, Lady Olivia. Not only did the abigail see me, but your companion and the library cataloguer as well."

"They are not likely to spread gossip throughout the household," was her stubborn reply.

"Miss Stewart has already informed me that she is leaving Stolenhurst today," Peter announced affectedly with a theatrical gesture of despair.

"Oh, for God's sake, Peter, we are not in one of your plays now. I will speak with Miss Stewart. It is no more than a misunderstanding which can be set right," she asserted, but she allowed Noah to draw up a chair for her and seated herself wearily in it.

"I tell you, Olivia," Peter rasped, "that once such a rumor is started there is never any ridding yourself of it. You cannot continue here among my guests without an announcement that you are to marry Noah."

"Nonsense! I will not be forced into a disagreeable marriage just to spare your blushes, Peter. I have blushed often enough for you, and you may do the same for me now. The whole situation is absurd, and the sooner you attempt to set matters to rights in a logical way, not in this havey-cavey fashion that serves to validate such ridiculous rumors, the sooner it will be over." Olivia rose, ignored her brother's blustering threats and left the room, closely followed by Sir Noah.

"Stay, Olivia," he said authoritatively when the door had closed behind them.

"I wish to hear no more on the subject, sir. I have done nothing wrong, and I will not act as though I had." Olivia's eyes sparkled with a mixture of anger and frustration.

"Nevertheless, your situation here will be very uncomfortable," he pointed out.

"It could not be less comfortable than being married to you."

"It would, though, you know. You could lead a very

pleasant life at Welling Towers, away from your brothers and all the annoyances you spoke of last night." His voice was persuasive, his eyes serious.

"What is it you want, Sir Noah? Are you afraid that your own reputation will suffer by these rumors of a liaison with a young, unmarried gentlewoman? I should really like to understand how you could agree to such a scheme."

"I have unavoidably damaged your reputation, child," he said stiffly, "and I wish only to do the honorable thing by you."

"I find that difficult to believe and totally unnecessary. Mrs. Dyer is a gentlewoman, and you were perfectly content to damage her reputation."

"There is no comparison between the two cases. You are an innocent child, and Mrs. Dyer is an experienced woman of the world." Noah drew his hand through his hair in exasperation. "No one thinks particularly ill of Lila for her . . . activities; but it would not be the same with you. At least promise me you will think on it, Olivia. The disdain you could meet with today might change your mind."

Olivia turned abruptly from him and disappeared up the staircase, as he watched her with a mixture of chagrin and doubt. Perhaps she *could* weather the storm that was bursting about her, but it did not seem fair that she should have to, piled as it was on her usual load of care. He would rather adopt her as a sister than as a wife, he thought ruefully, but the situation would not allow for that. What was worse was that the child was right; he did not wish it to be rumored that he had seduced her.

Chapter Five

Miss Stewart's door was locked as usual, and Olivia called to her as she tapped. The door was opened hesitantly and the companion looked past Olivia to make sure there was no one else in the hall before she bustled the younger woman into the room and relocked the door.

With the first amusement she had felt all day Olivia scolded, "There is no need to lock the door when I am with you, Miss Stewart. Peter tells me you are leaving Stolenhurst today." The room was scattered about with trunks and boxes into which growing mounds of belongings were being loaded even now. "I can but assume that this has something to do with last night."

Miss Stewart's face paled, and she seemed incapable of speech. Olivia took her hand and pressed it reassuringly. "You must not think that there was anything improper in my going with Sir Noah, my dear. One of our guests was most dreadfully sick, and I went to do what I could for her. The doctor was sent for and seemed satisfied with her condition. She is much better this morning."

"No, no!" the companion exclaimed pitifully. "I know you would do nothing wrong, Lady Olivia, but I must leave at once."

"You have had no word of troubles in your family, have you?"

"No. That is, I long to see them again. Yes, I feel I must see them," Miss Stewart hastened on.

Olivia regarded her perplexedly. "Then you intend to return to Stolenhurst?"

"No, no, never!" the companion cried with a shudder.

"Miss Stewart, my dear," Olivia said, taking the woman's hand and seating her on a chair before she knelt in front of her. "Please tell me what the problem is, why you are leaving. I do not understand."

Miss Stewart's flustered hands waved about in the air. "I cannot say. You will please indulge me, Lady Olivia. I would rather just leave with no more ado."

"But of course you shall if I cannot convince you to stay," Olivia said briskly. "I shall miss you, my dear. It is not that one of my brothers has been bothering you again?"

The pale face whitened further. "No, I promise you they have not. Do not question me further, I beg you."

Olivia shook her head drearily. "Of course not, ma'am. I will help you pack if you are intent on leaving." There remained nothing further to be said to the frightened woman, so Olivia spent the next hour carefully avoiding the subject while she assisted in gathering together all her companion's belongings, the trinkets and clothing accumulated over the last six years. When the trunk was full and the portmanteaus had been strapped, Olivia left her for a moment to order the carriage brought round. She took the opportunity to slip into her room and secure some money before returning to Miss Stewart.

It seemed incredible to Olivia that twenty minutes later she was waving a farewell to the woman who had been a constant resident in her home for so many years, and that she did not know why the companion was leaving. There was no doubt in Olivia's mind that Miss Stewart had said no more than the truth when she exonerated her of any improper conduct the previous evening, but that left her at more of a loss than ever to explain the departure.

No sooner had Olivia returned to the drawing room than her aunts descended upon her in a fury of disgust. They paid no attention to her explanations of the night's actual occurrences, but insisted that she no longer existed in their eyes. "Never," Aunt Davis proclaimed righteously, "has there been such a scandal in our family. I thank my lucky stars that this has opened my eyes before I took you into my own home to contaminate your cousins with your disgraceful behavior." Aunt Moore nodded an accompaniment to Aunt Davis' ravings, which lasted the better part of an hour, long before which time expired Olivia despaired of bringing them to an understanding of the truth and desisted in the attempt.

The rest of the day was a nightmare no less chilling. Olivia was ignored at meals and shunned by all in the reception rooms with the lone exceptions of Lila Dyer and Sir Noah. Even her own brothers would not speak to her, would not stand by her in this hideous mess. At times she could feel the tears pricking at her eyelids, and her chin quivered uncontrollably; but she refused to give in to the ostracism she faced. Lila Dyer, looking pale and seated most of the day in the drawing room, spent hours speaking with people in an attempt to furnish them with the truth, but they had rather believe the worst. Little gatherings would break off talking when Olivia approached, and would not open their circle to her. Eventually she escaped to the stables, only to see the reproach in the eyes of the staff there.

The despondence she had begun to feel did not lift under the influence of an exhilarating gallop across the meadows nor during a ride through her favorite part of the estate. The wind felt bitterly cold, the sky threatening with its snow-filled clouds, but she did not wish to return to the house where she would once again have to face those dreadful accusing stares. Finally she put her head down against the mare's neck and sobbed bitterly.

Noah found her in this condition and his heart ached for her. When he had wiped her tears, he said gently, "Let me take you home to my mother, Olivia. You need not marry me; but you will not suffer so there, and you can return to Stolenhurst when Peter has gone to London."

"I am afraid of your mother," she gulped.

Noah laughed with real amusement. "There is no

need to be, you know. I will explain the situation to her, and I assure you she will treat you well. Julianna would welcome a friend for she is often bored in the dead of winter when she cannot be outside so much." He studied Olivia's uncertain face carefully. "I could take you there in the morning; it is no more than a four hour journey even in this weather, if it does not snow too heavily. Olivia, you will only be needlessly hurt if you stay here while Peter's house party is in progress."

"And will you return to Stolenhurst?"

"I shall be guided by your wishes."

"Very well," she sighed, "I will go with you, Sir Noah, but just to spend a few days there. It is kind of you to offer after I have been so rude about refusing to marry you. I am sure that you feel the same undesirability as I do on the subject and would not misconstrue my words as being ungrateful for your attempt to save my reputation."

"Never," he responded with a grin. "And, Olivia, in view of the connection between our families, I must insist that you call me Noah."

She managed a tremulous smile as she nodded her acquiescence. Their ride back to the stables was silent, and when they entered the house, Olivia headed directly for her room. James Evans appeared on the stairs, and she turned her troubled, questioning glance on him. Would he cut her, too? But no, he offered a sad smile and stopped to speak with her. It was such a relief to be acquitted by someone other than the participants of the night's incident, that she was soon chatting away as though he were her best friend. When she paused for a moment, he apologized for keeping her and Miss Stewart up so late the previous evening.

"It was an enjoyable time," Olivia confessed, "but do you know that Miss Stewart left today? I could not understand her reason, but she does not intend to return."

"Most unfortunate. I fear you will sadly miss her company," Evans replied politely.

"Yes, I will miss her, but I am going away tomorrow myself for a few days."

His disappointment was patent, and it cheered her considerably. It would seem that *someone* cared for her whereabouts. She could not assign the same motives to Sir Noah, but she was willing to accept the visit to his home as the best solution he could presently find for the dilemma into which he had inadvertently hurled her. Her conversation with Evans was interrupted by her brother's approach; Evans quickly bowed and slipped away.

"Noah informs me that he has invited you to Welling Towers, Olivia," Peter announced. "I hope you will think better of your decision about marrying him while you are there." When Olivia said nothing, his anger mounted and he snapped, "You will disgrace the family if you do not." Still Olivia said nothing. "You do not plan to attend the masquerade ball this evening, I hope."

"No, Peter."

"I shall wish you a pleasant journey now as it is unlikely that I will be up when you leave." He turned away from her to return to Lady Elizabeth.

"And I shall wish you a happy birthday since I shall not be here," she replied softly and did not wait to see if he would make any reply but continued her journey to her room.

While Olivia stayed in her room packing, the masquerade ball for more than one hundred guests took place in the ballroom, and nearly every other room on the floor as well. Under her direction the main room had been decorated with festoons of hothouse flowers, and the ball did not begin until eleven. By the time supper was served at one, Olivia was fast asleep, but her name was on many lips over the champagne and lobster. Noah and Lila continued their endeavors to erase the stain from Olivia's reputation, but their efforts met with small success. Immediately after supper Lila, looking pale after the strains of the previous four and twenty hours, announced to her escort that she intended to retire.

"I will see you to your room," he offered, and they left unnoticed in the crowd. When they reached her door he stayed her a moment. "I am taking Lady Olivia to Welling Towers in the morning, Lila. I may be directly back or I may stay there for a few days."

Lila gave him a quizzing look. "Is there significance in this gesture, Noah?"

"I have offered to marry her to save her reputation, but she will have none of me," he admitted with a crooked grin. "Still, I cannot but think she will be better away from this house party, and I feel responsible for her predicament."

With a toss of her head Lila dismissed the gossip. "They will find something more interesting to talk of in a few days, Noah. I am wearied with trying to convince them of the truth of last night. It is a pity to see the child suffer, though, through no fault of her own." She narrowed her eyes thoughtfully. "Most of those resident here are well aware of your involvement with me and would not think two moments of this latest start if she were not the Earl's sister."

"Yes, and Peter is being a hypocrite about the whole thing. She does not have an easy life here, I fear; and I hope to convince her to stay for some time with Julianna. I have promised to go or stay as she pleases."

"It will be a boring party without you, Noah." Her eyes crinkled into slits of mirth at his expression.

He turned her toward the door as he reached to open it. "You will need some time to recover, my dear," he remarked with a wicked smile and a pat on her bottom. She stepped into the room but turned toward him again smiling encouragingly, and he drew her into his arms and kissed her thoroughly. "I will be in touch, Lila, if I do not return to the house party, and you know where to reach me if you should need me."

"You must feel no further responsibility for me, Noah," she said seriously, a hand resting lightly on his chest.

"It is not responsibility I feel for you," he mocked, "but lust, you brazen hussy." She giggled when he kissed her again. As he set her aside at last he said more sedately, "I do not seem to have done very well by you, Lila."

She touched the diamond necklace which encircled her throat, and smiled impudently at him. "I have nothing to complain of, Noah. I have had enough of conjugal fidelity for a lifetime, and I intend to enjoy myself now that I am a widow. So long as I enjoy you, I will see you. When it is over, we will go our separate ways with no regrets." She raised an eyebrow enquiringly and reminded him, "That is how we began, is it not, and how we plan to continue?"

Noah nodded, but a frown creased his brow. "You do not look to marry again?"

"Never," Lila retorted emphatically. "This freedom suits me perfectly. Why should I turn over my fortune to some man who will gamble it away? Or keep my bed for one man the rest of my life? I can be discreet enough to maintain my position without limiting my choice, Noah. Today I find you very attractive, but next month—who knows? It is the same with you; I doubt you would deny it."

"No, I do not deny it. Today I find you *very* attractive."

She slipped out of his renewed embrace and taunted, "You must leave now, sir, for I am exceedingly fatigued." Her tinkling laugh pursued him to the door as he obediently departed. "Good-night, Noah, and a pleasant journey."

Chapter Six

Since Noah had sent word to his home the previous day, Olivia found they were expected, though his tall, tight-lipped mother was not exactly welcoming. They sat down to a midday meal shortly after arriving, and Noah entertained his mother and sister with tales of the house party, omitting any mention of the events which had led to his bringing Olivia to Welling Towers. Julianna, two years Olivia's senior, was intrigued by her arrival and longed to get her alone to find out more. She had an opportunity directly after their meal was finished when Noah indicated that he wished to speak alone with his mother.

Julianna directed Olivia to a charming parlor on the first floor where they were seated on comfortable gray velvet love seats facing one another. The young ladies had met twice previously but only briefly, and they eyed each other circumspectly.

"I was so pleased to hear that Noah intended to bring you for a visit, Lady Olivia," Julianna began. "You do not mind leaving your brother's coming of age party?"

"No, I am relieved," Olivia admitted. "I suppose Sir Noah is telling your mother the circumstances which led to my visit, and you must be curious as well." She proceeded to explain as delicately as she was able the events surrounding Mrs. Dyer's sickness, and the subsequent misunderstanding in the household.

Julianna's eyes widened with concern and she murmured, "You poor dear. Why, I should die of embarrassment! How thoughtless of Noah to put you in such a situation!"

"It was unintentional and stemmed from his concern for Mrs. Dyer."

"Humph," Julianna snorted, then asked eagerly, "is she pretty—Mrs. Dyer?"

"Extremely. Have you never met her?"

"No, though I expect to when I am in London in the spring. She was in mourning last year when I was there; and though I may have seen her the year before, I did not know who she was." Julianna seemed to think better of her curiosity and changed the subject. "I understand your brother has built a theatre at Stolenhurst which is acknowledged to be the finest anywhere. Have you taken part in his productions?"

"When there was a need for me, and I have often coached the players in their speeches. Have you an interest in the theatre?" Olivia regarded her companion with some trepidation, for her experience with people bitten with the desire to act was not wholly felicitous.

Julianna considered the question for a moment. Her brown hair differed from her brother's by only a degree of lightness, but her eyes were hazel where his were brown. She was as surprisingly tall as her mother, though neither of them had attained Noah's lanky height. Julianna's eyebrows moved expressively when she spoke. "I have never acted, you know, but sometimes when I read a play I feel very involved in it. Do you not feel very dramatic when you read some moving speech of Shakespeare's?"

Olivia laughed. "Yes, but that is not the order of play Peter presents. His standard selection is *The Confederacy* or *The Romp*. A few months past I was Mrs. Sullen in *The Beaus' Stratagem,* and I found it very unnerving."

They had not noticed the door of the parlor open to admit Noah, who startled them now by announcing, "But she acted it extremely well, nonetheless." His eyes danced with amusement and Olivia knew he was remembering that Peter had brought him to her bedchamber to congratulate her on her performance. When she flushed and clenched her hands in her lap, he said apologetically, "I

52

know you do not enjoy such works, Olivia, and I will not tease you about it. Has Julianna managed to wrest from you all your secrets?"

His sister indignantly declared that Olivia had been more than willing to explain why she had arrived so unexpectedly at Welling Towers, an admission which only made Noah laugh and shake his head mournfully. "My mother hopes you will join her in the Winter Parlor, Olivia. I will take you there if you wish."

Olivia had a moment of misgiving, but automatically rose, since she really had no choice. Noah imperceptibly shook his head at his sister's questioning look, and she settled back in her chair, resigned. When they were in the hall Noah regarded Olivia curiously and asked, "Are you really afraid of my mother?"

"She reminds me of my grandmother with those piercing eyes and pursed lips. I feel she thoroughly disapproves of me, though I do not believe I have given her any reason. When Grandmama was alive I used to think that she could tell when I had gotten into mischief just by looking at me. Your mother is like that, too."

Noah nodded but replied, "It is a trick some people have, Olivia. If they make you feel guilty by appearing to know more than they do, you usually confess to it without their having to lift a finger. I admit it was disconcerting when I was young, and I was forever apologizing for some misdeed before ever Mother could have heard of it. You will find such people hold little power over you when you develop a confidence of your own." He could see that he had offended her by his reference to her youth and quickly continued, "I think you will like Mother when you get to know her. She is opinionated," he remarked dryly, "but seldom unfair. In this case I have received the brunt of her censure, as was only proper, and she understands that you were not at fault." He paused before the heavy oak door of the Winter Parlor. "Do not let her bully you, Olivia."

"You are not coming in with me?" she asked anxiously.

"No, she would only dismiss me, my dear. She wants to be private with you and assess your feelings. You have

53

only to be honest with her, as you were with your brother and me. I will be in the Small Library if you want me." He smiled his encouragement and opened the door for her.

The room into which he ushered her was of moderate size, its walls painted a warm toffee with dragged brush work, and its silk draperies of a slightly lighter shade framing windows overlooking the park. There were Chippendale mahogany bureau bookcases on either side of the fireplace, whose mantelpiece held some remarkably fine Bristol Delft. Between the windows was a handsome walnut bracket-timepiece above a folding mahogany spider-leg table. On a rosewood table with revolving top and fitted drawers lay an open book and an unfinished piece of embroidery. It was one of the most comfortable, quietly elegant rooms Olivia had ever seen.

Lady Lawrence was seated on a white velvet sofa under a Beechey painting of the king, and she beckoned Olivia to join her. "That will be all, Noah," she said, and he offered her a cheeky smile as he withdrew. She murmured, "Impudent fellow," but her tone was indulgent, and she turned her attention to Olivia.

"Sit here by me, Lady Olivia. I am distressed to hear what problems Noah has created for you." She did not look the least distressed to Olivia.

"He had no intention of harming me, ma'am. I feel sure it will all be forgotten soon enough." Olivia seated herself on the edge of the sofa and attempted to look at ease.

Lady Lawrence regarded her with pursed lips. "You are wrong, Lady Olivia. It is the sort of *on dit* which will be passed from person to person because it involves you, the sister of an Earl." She made no effort to conceal the distaste she felt for Peter. "Your brothers have earned a most unsavory reputation which will merely lend authenticity to such gossip. I presume Noah told me the truth when he said there was no foundation to it."

The older woman's accusing stare very nearly unnerved Olivia, who swallowed painfully before she spoke. "I am sure your son told you the truth. The only dealings we had that night were in aid of . . . a fellow guest who was sick."

"You need not be delicate with me, Lady Olivia. Noah has told me the *whole* story, I assure you, though it does him no credit. I am surprised that you did not succumb to the vapors under the circumstances," she said with a small nod of approval, just barely discernible by her companion. "However, you must not think that a damaged reputation is forgiven overnight. In this case, the aura of it may cling to you always. You would do better to accept my son's offer of the protection of his name." It was difficult for Lady Lawrence to say this, for although she truly felt it the proper course of action, she was not at all convinced that she wished her son to marry into the Fullerton family. She really knew very little of Olivia and was used to thinking of her as a part of the unwholesome household at Stolenhurst. "I think you have rejected the solution out of hand and should give it more thought."

Olivia studied the gray-haired matron for some moments before replying, "It would solve one problem merely to create others, ma'am. I am convinced you mean well, as it cannot be a match you would ordinarily approve, but I believe it would be a mistake." Suddenly Olivia smiled mischievously and asked, "Would you do so in my place?"

Her attack surprised the older woman, who frowned momentarily and then admitted with a suspicion of humor in her eyes, "No, I do not believe I would, my dear, except that I am inordinately fond of my son."

"Well, I am not," Olivia said, and then drew herself up abruptly. "That is, I have found Sir Noah most accommodating in the present instance, and I may have misjudged him previously; but he strikes me as too much of a piece with my brothers to appeal to me as a life-long partner." She realized that her honesty had not pleased his mother when Lady Lawrence stiffened.

"I assure you, young lady, that my son bears not the slightest resemblance to your ramshackle brothers. He has an affection for his family, manages his estates with the expertise of a much older man, is not in the least a spendthrift where money is concerned, and handles his affairs with women discreetly." The dowager glared uncompromisingly at Olivia.

"All that may be true," Olivia retorted, "but I hold him responsible for leading all three of my brothers into their excesses on the turf."

"Stuff! The Earl spent the Easter holidays from Eton five years ago at the Newmarket Spring Meeting with his brother Charles and won a thousand guineas. *That* was the start of his interest in the turf; I have heard him say so with my own ears. He did not even meet Noah until several years later." Lady Lawrence sat back with the satisfaction of having delivered a justified reproof.

Olivia bowed her head and muttered stubbornly, "As you say, Lady Lawrence. Nonetheless they are not discouraged in their pursuits by him."

Lady Lawrence leaned forward and tapped the younger woman's wrist with her fan. "Noah is not responsible for the conduct of your siblings. We are distantly connected with your family, but there is no question of my son standing in the stead of a guardian to any of your brothers."

"It is a matter of influence," Olivia declared stoutly.

"And how do you suppose Noah has influenced them to their extravagances when he has not indulged in them himself? Oh, I do not wish to puff him off as a model of upright behavior by any means. But he has not the strain of profligacy in him which each one of your brothers possesses, Lady Olivia. I am well aware at all times of how matters stand with his estates, and I assure you that Noah has never been so self-indulgent as to draw my disapproval—well, not since he came of age at any rate," she qualified.

Olivia was unable to make any rejoinder, but sat feeling miserable beside the older woman, aware of the justified criticism leveled at her brothers but much mortified by it. Lady Lawrence was not insensitive to Olivia's distress and softened toward the young woman. She patted her hand kindly and said, "You must not feel the weight of your brothers' indiscretions so much, Lady

Olivia. There is little you can do to change them, heaven knows, and you will only be hurt by trying."

"I cannot stop caring," Olivia murmured, her lips trembling.

"I am sure it is very proper of you, my dear, but hardly appreciated." Lady Lawrence sighed and gazed out the window. "You would do well to marry Noah."

"Thank you, no, ma'am. I do not wish to do so."

"Do you think to go back to Stolenhurst and continue as you were before? You cannot go to London."

"My aunts were not willing to have me in any case," Olivia admitted with a laugh, "and now they have disowned me."

"Stupid women. It distresses me to be connected with them."

"How are we connected, ma'am?" Olivia asked curiously.

"Your great-grandmother's younger sister married my grandfather's second wife's older brother," Lady Lawrence answered promptly.

"I should call that a very loose connection," Olivia grinned.

"Indeed. But you did not answer me, Lady Olivia. Do you intend to return to Stolenhurst as though nothing had happened?"

"Yes, when Peter and his friends have left. By then the servants will know the actual situation, and I will not feel uncomfortable with them. But my companion has left, and I do not think it had anything to do with my behavior." Olivia's forehead wrinkled in a perplexed frown as she once again considered the problem.

"I suggest you think on Noah's proposal. Now, run along. Julianna will be eager to press you for details of your conversation with me."

"Everyone seems to suspect Julianna of inordinate curiosity," Olivia laughed as she rose. "I found her very sympathetic."

"Just so," Lady Lawrence agreed with motherly pride, and waved Olivia from the room.

She hesitated in the hall, unsure whether she wished

to speak with Noah before returning to his sister. When a footman appeared she had him direct her to the Small Library where she tapped timidly at the door.

"Come in," he called and stood with a questioning expression by the satinwood library table. "Ah, she did not eat you, I see."

"Well, she is not so terrifying as I had thought," Olivia admitted as he seated her beside the table, "but I am afraid I displeased her somewhat."

"Because you would not marry me?" he asked quizzingly.

"No, because I told her I thought you responsible for leading my brothers into their excesses." His frown lowered the brows over his watchful brown eyes. "I have come to apologize to you for that. It has always seemed to me that *someone* else must be responsible for their conduct, that they were not so very corkbrained when they were younger. I suppose I lighted on you because of your mutual interest in horse racing. Lady Lawrence informed me that you did not meet them until they were already addicted to the track."

"I have done nothing to curb their enthusiasm, Olivia, but then I do not believe my offices would be of any use. Just as yours are not," he said gently.

"No, it is very frustrating. And they will only laugh at me now that they can pretend they think me guilty of improper behavior myself," she said sadly.

Noah realized only too well that they would do precisely that, and he once again experienced a real concern for the girl before him. It would do her good to be away from Stolenhurst and enjoy the country society about Welling Towers with his sister. "Do you wish me to stay here or return to Stolenhurst?"

"There is no need for you to stay," she said gallantly.

He tried to guess at her emotions, deserted by the one person she knew in a strange household. And yet she might feel uncomfortable in his presence as well. "As I am here, I shall attend to some household matters but I shall plan to leave again the day after tomorrow," he

58

temporized, and he did not miss the gratitude in her eyes.

"Whatever is agreeable to you," she replied as she headed for the door.

"Olivia." She turned inquiringly to him. "You may stay as long as you please, you know. After all, we are connected."

"Your mother explained the connection to me," she remarked blandly, "and it is exceedingly tenuous."

He smiled down at her. "Nevertheless, we are connected, and, as I said before, Julianna will welcome the company. I can have anything you need sent from Stolenhurst."

"I will think on it," she promised as she slipped out the door.

Noah reseated himself at the library table and absently picked up a letter opener, drawing it back and forth between his fingers as he thought about Olivia. She was really a very determined, proud young thing, but she had nowhere to go. Attractive, too, even enchanting when she confessed her problems as though they were surmountable. He shook his head, disheartened. Her situation was touching, she was personable, and probably quite capable of handling an ordinary household but not Stolenhurst. But, Lord, she was so young; two years younger than his own sister. He shrugged off the depression of spirits he was suffering from and hoped that his sister would be able to afford Olivia some pleasant hours.

Chapter Seven

Julianna was delighted to have a companion in her own home. The winter months had been gray and cold, and there was not as much visiting among the households of the neighborhood as occurred in better weather. But Olivia's visit provided an excuse for morning calls which could not be denied, and the next morning found all four of the residents at Welling Towers on an enjoyable round of calls which was to result in a stream of callers returning the compliment. Lady Lawrence arranged for a small dinner party for the young people to take place after Noah returned to Stolenhurst, since there was not time to plan it before he left. Olivia appreciated the time he spent with her and Julianna, making the morning calls and riding with them in the afternoon after she arrived, but she had only a twinge of regret when they saw him off the next morning.

Indoors the young women were often joined by Lady Lawrence in their pursuits of needlework, reading aloud and practice on the harpsichord, but she seldom accompanied them on their rides and drives about the estate. Julianna was fascinated by the accounts of life at Stolenhurst which she drew from Olivia, who had never felt so free in discussing her life there. Her brothers had rarely taken her on visits to London or the country estates of their friends, so most of her life had passed at Stolenhurst, for better or worse. Her friendships in the neighborhood were few, as the concerned parents of the young people were wont to view intercourse with those at Stolenhurst as highly dangerous to their offspring.

So it was that Olivia met Julianna's friends with a great deal of pleasure and was drawn into their circle. Any rumors of her conduct which might have filtered back from Stolenhurst had no chance of acceptance in Lady Lawrence's neighborhood. Lady Lawrence was respected, even revered, in her community, and the fact that she agreeably housed Olivia was refutation enough for her friends.

On the afternoon of the supper party Julianna watched with impatience the heavy snow falling. "I do not think it will deter the majority of our guests, but it's a nuisance. It could have snowed tomorrow," she chided.

"Yes, but then your guests could not boast of the obstacles they overcame to get here," Olivia laughed. She sat with some needlework near the blazing hearth with its steel grate and serpentine fender feeling the cozy warmth of the fire. "Are there guests coming whom I did not meet on our morning calls?"

"Only a few. Norissa's brother Alexander was not at home when we called and Caroline Pugh's youngest sister Lorraine. Mama says we may have some country dances later if we wish, and if our guests do not have to hurry home because of the weather. So you see, the snow really is a bother."

"Perhaps it will cease after a while," Olivia suggested hopefully, as she was even more intrigued with the idea of dancing than her friend, having only just reached the age where it was permitted her in company.

"Here are the Cutlers now," Julianna cried with a flush of excitement as the sounds of an arrival could be heard without. She drew away from the window and seated herself by the fire, saying, "I think you will find Alexander quite handsome, you know. Mama does not precisely approve of him, I fear, for he is a bit wild, but he is ever so much more exciting than the other young men hereabouts."

When Norissa and Alexander Cutler were shown into the room, Olivia had to agree that the tall blonde young man with his laughing blue eyes was indeed attractive. He wore his clothes with an elegance attained by few of the men she had met, and he had the faculty of making the people to whom he spoke believe they were especially important. But there was a particularity in the attention he paid to Julianna which Olivia realized was not unnoticed by either the recipient or her mother. Julianna blossomed under his regard and occasionally neglected her duties as hostess to remain within the radius of his charm. The situation made Olivia slightly uneasy, but she shouldered whichever of Julianna's burdens she was able so that Lady Lawrence would have nothing about which to complain. At the dinner table she found herself seated next to Alexander; Lady Lawrence had placed Julianna some distance away.

He bestowed a fascinated smile on her and remarked, "I understand you are Lord Bolenham's sister. I have often wished that Noah would introduce me to him when he stops here on his way to Newmarket."

"Perhaps he will some day. My brother is engaged for several matches at the Spring Meetings," Olivia responded.

"I *have* met your brothers Charles and Samuel in London—very good fellows," Alexander said enthusiastically as he speared a morsel of baked carp. "Had the most famous time with them one afternoon when we all dressed as postillions and took some carriages for a merry ride. Very nearly overturned one of them. Lord, you would not have believed the language the vicar used on *that* occasion." He laughed heartily as he placed the fish in his mouth.

Olivia could not share his enthusiasm for such a prank, since she had suffered the consequences of similar devilment for too many years. What she had to accept in her brothers she would not willingly condone in someone who was no relation of hers. Mr. Cutler was old enough, she thought, to be past being amused by childish high spirits which involved possible harm to other people, and Olivia was surprised that Julianna found him an admirable young man.

But such was obviously the case. When the dancing began, Julianna flushed cheerfully as Alexander asked her to stand up with him for the first set. The young men and women were of an equal number, due to Lady Lawrence's careful planning, so there was never a lack of partners for anyone. Olivia dismissed her concerns for Julianna during the dancing and thoroughly enjoyed the evening, which was not brought to an early close by any maturer discretion of its young members or any worsening of the weather. When the last of the guests had departed, Julianna urged Olivia to come to her bedroom for a chat about the evening.

"Was it not delightful?" Julianna asked, her eyes sparkling, when she had curled up in a chair by the fire.

"I have never had such a fine time," Olivia replied truthfully. "You have such charming neighbors, and they were so very kind to me."

"And did you think Alexander Cutler handsome?" Julianna asked anxiously.

"Very, but he told me of an adventure with two of my brothers which was not so pleasing to me," Olivia remarked cautiously.

Julianna frowned slightly. "Oh, you must not judge him on one action, Olivia. And certainly not if he was with your brothers," she giggled. "He is the most charming of all the men who were here, I think, and he is always so attentive to Mother. She is never softened by him, though, and it upsets me that you can so easily see that she does not hold him in high regard." Julianna tapped her fingers against the upholstered chair arm and gazed out into the black night thoughtfully.

"Does your brother like Mr. Cutler?"

"He has never said anything, exactly, but he is not one of Alexander's friends. Alexander has told me several times that he wishes Noah would accept an invitation to visit his home so that they might get to know each other better." Julianna colored slightly and did not meet Olivia's eyes.

"I had a chance to speak with his sister Norissa and the Pugh sisters during the evening," Olivia said in an effort to turn the conversation. "I understand they will all be going to London in the spring, except Lorraine, who confided to me that she was too young. She seemed a bit put out about it, for Mr. Brownley refused to admit that it was much jollier in the countryside in any case. Obviously he intends to make the trek to the metropolis himself."

"Loraine has been trying to attract Mr. Brownley's attention for the past two years. It was amusing when she was fifteen, but her mother has become annoyed recently and is forever urging more becoming behavior on her. Poor Lorraine." Julianna gave a sympathetic shrug, and appeared lost in her own thoughts.

"I will leave you now so that you may get some sleep. I am indebted to you and your mother for such an enjoyable evening." Olivia hugged her friend before making her way to her own room.

The room she had been given had walls hung with blue and white striped cotton and curtains to match. On the mantelshelf two glass chamber lights were lit and the fire in the hearth had made the room warm against the cold night outside. Olivia allowed the maid who had been sent to wait on her to remove her gown and then dismissed the girl so that she might sit at the dressing table for a moment and contemplate her evening at leisure. It had been a treat for her to be amongst guests unlike those so frequently at her brother's, but she had her doubts about Alexander Cutler, and it destroyed her peace that Julianna appeared to be attached to him. Olivia could not see that any good could come from such an affection and it sorrowed her that Julianna should be influenced by a loose-screw who found Charles' and Samuel's pranks amusing.

An image of James Evans occurred to her in her reverie, and she smiled. He was an attractive, pleasant young man with a serious pursuit in life, and he seemed very appealing after the unsteady, extravagant young men around whom she had grown up. With a sigh she climbed into bed and extinguished her candle.

The morning brought several callers, although the roads had received a liberal coating of snow. Mild sunlight sparkled off the snow-covered trees and bushes, and the visitors came into the hall stomping the snow from fur-lined boots. Since Alexander was one of the party, Julianna suggested that they wander about in the white world outdoors before coming in for hot chocolate. It would give her some time with him that was not under her mother's eyes, and she pushed the plan until the others agreed.

Olivia enjoyed the tramp through the snow, talking with Norissa Cutler and Caroline Pugh, while the other two Pugh sisters wandered ahead and Julianna and Alexander brought up the rear. Snatches of their conversation reached Olivia, but she made an attempt to ignore them; Julianna was deserving of what privacy she could arrange.

They crested a hill and were exclaiming at the view of the countryside for miles around glittering in the sunlight when a dog-cart whisked by on the lane below.

"It's Dr. Davenport," Caroline informed Olivia as she lifted her hand to wave. "He's the dearest old fellow! Mama calls him in at the least sore throat but he never grumbles about unnecessary visits."

Norissa joined her friend in waving to the doctor. "He must be out on a call. Perhaps Mrs. Pepperidge is about to deliver."

As the young ladies waved, they did not notice Alexander cup a ball of snow between his gloves, but they could not miss the result. The doctor and his beaver hat were accurately separated. Lorraine giggled, but the others froze with embarrassment. Only Alexander thought it a capital joke and acknowledged the waving of the doctor's angry fist with an elaborate, low bow.

"Oh, Alexander, you shouldn't have," Julianna protested, her brows drawn up with worry.

While the doctor reined in his pony and retrieved the hat, his face an angry red, Alexander waved aside Julianna's reproof. "Old Davenport is so stuffy it will do him good to have his dignity impaired a trifle."

Caroline and Norissa exchanged glances and quickly started to chatter about the weather, while Olivia remained mute between them as they headed back toward the Towers. Julianna and Alexander lagged behind them, and no one turned to include them in their conversation as they had done occasionally on the walk out.

Olivia could not assess whether the behavior had damaged Alexander in her friend's eyes, but it had confirmed her own opinion of him. He was not a lad of twelve to occupy himself with such mischief, but a man of two-and-twenty who should have a better grasp on what was seemly. Olivia determined to say nothing of the incident to her friend, however, for she had no wish to say "I told you so" to someone who had been so kind to her.

Two weeks passed during which Olivia found herself accompanying Lady Lawrence and Julianna to several dinner parties, an assembly and numerous morning calls as the weather became more favorable. Although she had given him no indication as to the length of her intended stay, Sir Noah had had additional clothing sent her with the wish that she would continue to enjoy herself with his sister.

"Famous!" Julianna exclaimed, as she examined the newly expanded wardrobe. "He has sent you enough to allow you to remain with me for months. Would you like some blue satin ribbon to trim this white gown? I have a length of it in my work table."

"It is sadly colorless, is it not? I have never worn it, though I should be grateful to my Aunt Davis for sending it to me. You do not suppose Sir Noah actually chose what to have sent to me, do you?" The thought brought a tingle of anger to her.

"No, certainly not. Noah would scarcely have sent such an uninteresting gown if he had sorted through your clothing. No doubt he had your abigail make a selection—if she is still there."

Olivia laughed. "It is hard to decide whether Peter would more likely forget to turn her off for all the trouble she caused, or keep her on as a lasting reminder of my 'disgrace.' "

"He probably has not given her another thought for any reason. I cannot imagine a brother being so careless of your feelings as not to stand by you in such a muddle, Olivia. We may disagree within our family, but we provide a united front to the world outside."

"You are fortunate, my dear. Such an attitude would never be assumed by my brothers, amongst themselves or with me. Perhaps it would have been otherwise if my parents had lived."

Julianna pressed her hand comfortingly as she rose to leave. "You must let us be your family, Olivia. We would not be so cavalier with your reputation and your happiness."

"Thank you. I treasure your friendship, Julianna, so generous and undemanding as it is, but I must return to Stolenhurst sometime soon. After all, it is my home."

Lady Lawrence came to her several days later while she was sewing, a letter clutched in one hand and a determined expression on her face. "I have heard from Noah this morning, Olivia. He is in London now and says that your brothers have gone there, too, but he hopes that you will stay on with Julianna."

"That is kind of him, ma'am, and I have derived no end of pleasure from my visit; but I should impose no longer."

"Nonsense, it is no imposition at all. Julianna would be biting her nails from boredom were you not with us, and I should have to find a thousand things to divert her attention from thinking of . . . No matter. And you have no companion at Stolenhurst, remember. It would not be wise to live there without one."

"I have no way of acquiring a companion, Lady Lawrence. It is hardly likely that any of my brothers would be willing to look into the matter for me." Olivia continued to sort the threads before her without meeting the older woman's eyes. She could not apologize for her brothers' neglect, but she admitted the fact of it with difficulty.

"I will write to make some enquiries for you, Olivia," Lady Lawrence offered. "There are a number of people in London who may have a recommendation to make. Perhaps even the vicar would have a suggestion. I do not think you should return to your home until the matter is well in hand. We are more than happy to have you here with us."

Julianna added her eager support to her mother's proposal and Olivia agreed to stay for a while longer to learn the results of Lady Lawrence's enquiries. Although Noah had indicated that he had no intention of returning to Welling Towers for several weeks, it was only four days after they received his letter that he arrived, laden with presents for his sister and mother, and even a book for Olivia. He was bombarded with questions by his family for some time, but eventually turned to his guest and said, "I should like a word with you, Olivia, in the Small Library." His countenance was surprisingly sober, and Olivia felt a shiver of apprehension as she nodded and followed him from the room, Julianna's curious eyes watching as they left.

Noah seated her in the chair beside the library table where she had sat at their previous interview, and more slowly took his own seat. He did not speak for a while but sat regarding her seriously. "I have rather a lot to tell you, but I am not sure precisely where I should begin."

"There is nothing wrong with my brothers?"

"They are much as usual," he replied dryly. "However, I learned two days ago that Peter has become engaged to Lady Elizabeth." He studied her impassive receipt of this news and continued. "There is no recent talk of your supposed impropriety at Stolenhurst, but it remains largely unrefuted, Olivia."

"I shall have to live with that." She raised her chin defiantly.

Noah made an impatient gesture with his hand. "You should not have to live with it. Mrs. Dyer and I have done what we can, but your brothers' reputations are a disadvantage, and we are seen only as apologists for you."

"I appreciate your efforts on my behalf, sir."

"There is worse, Olivia," he went on grimly. "It is necessary for me to be indelicate in order to explain it to you. While I was here last Peter made an approach to Mrs. Dyer, a very obvious and pointed approach. Unfortunately, Lady Elizabeth overheard the proposition to her cousin, and the two are now at disagreeable odds." He sighed and rubbed a hand over his forehead, brushing the brown locks awry. "In consequence of her jealousy, Lady Elizabeth purports to believe that you really did have a liaison with me. It is merely a means of discrediting her cousin's word, of course, but Lady Elizabeth is carrying it to vindictive lengths." He paused in an effort to find a kinder way of delivering the blow; but when he was unable, he proceeded bluntly, "Lady Elizabeth has declared that it would offend her sense of propriety to have you resident at Stolenhurst."

Chapter Eight

Olivia's hands clenched in her lap, but she made no sound. Her eyes momentarily beseeched him to say that it was not true, but she could easily believe it of Lady Elizabeth.

Noah regarded her sadly. "I spoke with Peter after hearing of Lady Elizabeth's pronouncement, and I could get no assurance from him that he would overrule her decision. In fact, if I may be blunt, Olivia, he told me that you were my problem now, and he had no intention of making any arrangement for you."

"It is really too bad of him!" she cried. "He must know very well that there is not a particle of truth in the whole sordid story. And you may be sure that Lady Elizabeth knows it also. She could not have been unaware of your ... connection with her cousin. How thoughtless and cruel of her to put me in such a position. And the hypocrisy of Peter! As if he has ever made any arrangement for me! I have been a thorn in his side, and he uses this excuse to pluck me out and toss me aside. God knows I did nothing more than lend assistance when it was needed. What did he expect me to do—lock myself in my room and ignore the emergency? Perhaps *he* would have done so," she muttered scathingly.

"There is no excuse for his behavior, so I shall make none. He is self-indulgent beyond bearing and exhibits no responsibility for himself or anyone else. I am sorry, Olivia; I would have spared you this news if I could, but you have every right, every need to know." As he watched the anger fade into a determined resignation in her eyes, he thought: she has had an unfortunate home all her life; now in essence she has no home at all.

He began to speak again, softly but firmly. "I am perfectly willing to take responsibility for you, Olivia, and the only question to be answered is what form the responsibility should take. Obviously you must stay at Welling Towers permanently. Your aunts have not relented in their disowning of you, since it is to their advantage not to." He gave a grimace of disgust. "You could stay here merely as my sister's friend, and I doubt that it would be unduly remarked in the neighborhood; but with Lady Elizabeth's attitude and the position she will achieve as your brother's wife, your prospects of marriage are limited. On the other hand, if you married me you would have a measure of freedom that you would not enjoy as a single lady, and the aspersions on your character would blow away in a reasonably short period of time."

Olivia still could not bring herself to look at him. "What kind of a marriage would we have?" she whispered.

For the first time he appeared reluctant to speak, and the only sound was the ticking of the long case clock by the door. But eventually he cleared his throat and said, "I cannot offer you a marriage devoid of wifely duties, Olivia. I have found myself haunted by the knowledge of Mrs. Dyer's abortion. I should like to have children, sons and daughters to grow up at Welling Towers and love it as Julianna and I have. And if you gave the matter thought, I do not believe you would particularly welcome a barren life yourself. But I would endeavor to allow you freedom from marital obligations to a large extent. I assure you I would be most discreet in any . . . outside activities, not as I have been while a bachelor. Our marriage should appear normal in all respects, and I would introduce you to London society after a period of time had blunted any gossip about you."

There was no response from his companion, whose face he could not read at all. "I would prefer, for the time being, that my mother and sister remain in the house, and

I am sure that you would welcome their company. If in the future you found it a strain to have your mother-in-law resident with you, she and Julianna could move to the Dower House." He attempted to lighten the tone of his monologue by suggesting, "Perhaps we might travel occasionally. I think you would enjoy that. Your allowance would be generous, and I would not deny you any reasonable expenditure on your clothing or your rooms."

Olivia saw her whole life stretching before her, dependent on her decision. At her age there was no possibility of setting up an establishment of her own—she had not the financial means nor the temerity to brave the censure of society. There were no relatives to come to her aid; she had only Sir Noah to provide for her. She could remain in his home as a guest, with the lingering stigma of the gossip about her. Years could go by without an offer of marriage to remove her from her dependence. Lady Elizabeth's vindictiveness would forestall her entering society in London, even if Lady Lawrence were willing to see her through a season there.

But if she married Sir Noah she would never have the opportunity to know love. She did not doubt that he would take care of her, would provide her with any material object she might desire. It had long been a dream of hers that one day she would escape Stolenhurst to a husband who loved her, a home she cared for, and children to love and raise in an atmosphere far different from that which she had endured. It was a silly fantasy perhaps, but an escape from her realities at Stolenhurst. More likely Peter would have forced her into a loveless marriage by some trickery, much as he was doing now. Sir Noah at least offered her the home and children she had projected, and she had come to think of him more kindly during this trial. Olivia lifted her head to look at him as he studied her carefully. She had intended to say that she must think on what he had said, but when she had moistened her lips she found herself declaring desperately, "You cannot wish to marry me."

"Why not?" he asked with a grin. "You are attractive, sensible, by rights above my touch, and a charming young lady. I have developed a sincere affection for you, Olivia, and wish to make you happy. Many marriages have much less to recommend them, my dear. I think we would deal well together." He quirked an eyebrow at her. "Your affections are not engaged by anyone, are they? If so, you must say, and I will see what can be done."

"No, no, I have met few young men of any worth," she replied with a fleeting thought of James Evans. She felt an admiration of Evans and was somewhat attracted to him, but there was no question of an attachment; she did not know him well enough and never would now.

"Well, I cannot claim any high standing in that regard, but I promise you I will do my utmost to prove an acceptable husband. Would you like some time to think about all we have discussed, Olivia?"

"Yes, if you please."

"There is not the least hurry. In either case you will remain here, unless you have any objections or any alternative to suggest."

Olivia shook her head, and he left his chair to come around to her. He took her hand and pressed it encouragingly. "You may discuss the matter with my mother and Julianna if you wish, but I would advise against it. It is your decision alone and only you can make the right choice for yourself. I would prefer that you marry me rather than merely join my household, if that is any inducement to you."

Since she had no wish to speak with Lady Lawrence or Julianna about the matter of marrying Noah, Olivia slipped out a side door, bundled in boots and a fur-trimmed blue mantle. The snow had melted, leaving the ground muddy, and there was a brisk cold wind; but she wandered about the grounds for several hours paying scant attention to the conditions around her. Most of her life she had felt lonely, with her parents and grandmother all gone before she reached the age of ten. Her brothers had shown her little affection and less interest; her governess had been a consolation but no real substitute for parents or friendships. The uncles who were guardians to her as well as to her brothers had shown even less concern for her well-being than for that of the males; and when Peter came of age, she had become his ward.

Olivia found herself at a charming Gothic summerhouse overlooking the coppice and brook to the east of the estate. There were elaborately carved benches placed about the small space and in seating herself she kicked against an old wooden case under one of them. Curiosity led her to pull the case out and examine its contents—a child's treasures, much as she herself might have collected years earlier. In a youthful hand "Noah Lawrence" was scrawled inside the lid of the box, and there were broken toys, crumpled messages, rusted keys, and a cardboard windmill. Olivia smiled at the collection and was about to replace it when she heard her name called. She responded automatically, and Noah soon arrived on horseback at the summerhouse.

He dismounted and joined her at the entrance, exclaiming, "Lord, child, you must be frozen! Jarette said you went out hours ago and had not returned." He studied her face and was relieved to note she had not been crying. There was a courage about her, faced as she was with such a tumult in her life, that he could but admire. Her face was pinched with the cold, but her eyes were calm.

"I have found something of yours," she said, ignoring his concern for her well-being.

"Here? What is it?"

Olivia beckoned him to follow her as she walked to the bench where the box still stood open, and watched him when he saw it. A slow smile spread across his face and his eyes sparkled playfully. "It is not where I usually kept it, but I remember trying to hide it from Julianna when she found its original location." He leaned over to pick up the rusted keys and made a vague motion toward the woods. "I had a strongbox buried there with my more valuable things. Do you suppose it's still there?"

"Shall we look?" Olivia asked, her interest aroused.

"Yes," he agreed with a smile. Then he shook his head. "No, I should get you to the house. You have been out far too long already."

74

"I'm not so very cold," she retorted stubbornly.

"Mother is expecting you for tea," he reminded her, and touched her rosy cheek with a gloved finger. "I promise to take you with me tomorrow when I explore for it. Will that do?"

A flash of anger appeared in Olivia's gray eyes. "I will not be treated like a child, Sir Noah. It is not necessary for you to bribe or placate me. I am eighteen and quite capable of passing up such a treat as digging up some stupid box of yours," she said sarcastically, barely saving herself from the disgrace of stomping her foot.

"So old as that!" he exclaimed, his eyes laughing. "A woman grown."

"Understand this," she retorted coldly. "There is no chance that I will marry you while you treat me in such a fashion. In one breath you speak of my begetting your children and in the next you call me 'child.' You cannot have it both ways, sir. If I am old enough to wed you and bear your children, I deserve the status of a woman in your eyes. I will accept nothing less."

The laughter in him died abruptly. It was cruel to undermine her precarious dignity so, and he spoke seriously. "I do not mean to offend you, Olivia. It is difficult for me to forget the youngster I met three years ago when she was all arms and legs, and not so very well coordinated. Do you remember that occasion, Olivia?"

His companion flushed and turned her head slightly aside. "I remember tripping over my own feet when I attempted to make you a curtsy," she managed to say.

"Yes, and landed in a cascade of skirts at my feet." There was no trace of amusement in his face. "You have been on your dignity with me ever since, determined either to prove yourself sophisticated or me a wretch. And I, well, I have felt protective toward you since then. Do not blame me for thinking of you as a child for these years, Olivia. It is merely the contrast of your innocence against all the distorted experience around you that makes you appear so. I mean it more as a compliment to your uncorrupted nature than a reference to your age. You are a reproach to those of us who have lived our lives selfishly."

They stood surveying each other solemnly for some moments. Olivia asked hesitantly, "If I marry you, you will not call me 'child' any longer? And you will treat me as an adult?"

"I promise." His intent brown eyes remained locked on hers.

She swallowed dryly and forced herself to speak. "Then I will marry you."

"Noah," he prompted.

"Noah," she repeated obediently.

"I will attempt to make you happy, Olivia. I would beg that you always be open with me so that I may never be in ignorance of your wishes and your needs."

"And you will teach me how to please you?" Olivia did not notice his startled look, which vanished when she continued. "I do not know you so very well, you know. Perhaps you do not like to talk at breakfast or be interrupted when you are doing your accounts. Peter would not allow anyone to drive his phaeton, and Charles would never ride with me if I asked him first. Samuel never takes chocolate in bed, but he does at the breakfast table. I suppose your mother and Julianna will advise me, but I hope you will be patient with me."

"May I teach you something now?" Noah asked, his eyes twinkling merrily.

"Y . . . Yes," she replied, dubious.

He took her hands and pressed them against his chest. "I want you to understand that I am an affectionate man," he said seriously, though a smile lurked at the corners of his mouth. "And if you wish to please me, now that we are betrothed, you will allow me to kiss you from time to time." At her skeptical look he went on gravely, "It is a very necessary preparation for marriage, Olivia. Such a small intimacy will accustom you to me, and you will feel more comfortable when we are . . . alone after our wedding." He felt the fingers he held tremble and knew it was not from the cold. Instead of further urging he went on matter-of-factly, "I had thought we might spend our honeymoon near Cheltenham, if you have no preference. I have a friend there who will be going to London next month, and he has offered me the use of his home at any time I may desire it. Would that please you?" He retained his grip on her hands.

A delighted smile warmed her eyes. "In the Cotswolds? I have longed to go there, S . . . Noah. You had intended we should marry so soon?"

"I think it would be wise for us to marry before your brother does. Lady Elizabeth will thereby be forestalled in her petty revenge. They do not intend to wed until June, but I would prefer that we set a date in mid-March. Tell me if you are not agreeable, Olivia."

She bit her lip nervously and shook her head. "I have no objection. Do you think I can go to Stolenhurst for a time, to organize my belongings? I would feel . . . wretched to have someone else gather them together for me."

"I will write Peter of our engagement and tell him that you intend to go there for a week or so. I think my mother should accompany you."

"Oh, that is not necessary. I would not have her displaced on my account," Olivia protested.

"She will be more than happy to do it for you, my dear. I doubt that any of your brothers will return there in the near future. Did you have any great longing to be married there?"

"I had assumed that I would be, of course, but I can see that it will not do." Her lips trembled in spite of her efforts to control them.

Noah increased his pressure on her hands against his chest. "I can arrange it so if you wish, Olivia."

"No, it is not necessary," she gulped against the lump in her throat. Darkness was coming on and a whirl of cold wind surged through the summerhouse and made her shiver.

Noah, quite unthinking, enfolded her in his arms and chastised himself, "I have kept you standing out in the cold after scolding you for being out so long. Come, let's get you home. I didn't think to bring an extra horse, unfortunately." He released her except for a grip on one hand. "Could you ride Emperor without a sidesaddle?"

"I suppose I could, but I will walk, thank you," she replied firmly, very aware that he held her hand.

He nodded and headed toward the house with her, the horse calmly plodding along behind them. When Olivia suggested that there was no need for him to walk, he merely grinned and retorted, "It would be most ungentlemanly for me to ride, my dear." Their ambitious pace left little inclination for conversation, and they were silent until Noah had left Emperor with a groom at the stables.

"Do you wish to be the one to break the news?" he asked quizzingly.

"I am sure you should be the one to tell your mother, but *I* should like to tell Julianna."

As they approached the door he released her hand and tilted her face up to his, a question in his eyes. She felt frozen with indecision, alarmed but curious. A shy, barely perceptible nod was the only sign she gave, but he acknowledged it by bending to touch her lips gently with his. It was the most fleeting of kisses, over almost before it was begun, and she felt a mixture of relief and disappointment. Noah very nearly kissed her again, he was so intrigued by her puzzled expression, but instead he hurried her into the house and ordered her to warm herself at a fire.

Tea was long since over, and she chose to obey his command in her own room where she would be undisturbed. She held her hands to the blaze and considered with some agitation that he had held her hand the whole way to the house, and that he had kissed her. Olivia searched her memory for any other time that she might have been kissed, but she could not clearly remember her parents, and her grandmother had not been particularly affectionate.

A tap at the door was followed by the arrival of Julianna, who had been concerned at her friend's lengthy absence from the house. "Shall I have a warm bath brought for you?" she asked anxiously at sight of Olivia huddled by the fire.

"No, I am beginning to thaw now. I did not mean to miss tea. Lady Lawrence was not upset, was she?"

"Heavens no! You do not have to be with us every moment, Olivia. Noah told us that your eldest brother is to be married, and I imagine you wished time to think about how that would change things for you at Stolenhurst," she suggested, her eyes full of curiosity.

"Oh, Julianna, you are a pet. It is wonderful how you can sit there burning up with questions and ask none but with your eyes, all the while intimating that it is all my own business and you would not intrude for the world."

"It would be most unseemly for me to ply you with questions," Julianna retorted pertly. "I should not dream of asking if you like the Earl's fiancée. Or if you think you will get along with her. To say nothing of never questioning you on whether you think it a suitable match for your brother, and whether it will settle him." She gave an exaggerated sniff deploring such behavior. "It would be indeed improper if I were to wonder how you will feel about Stolenhurst having a new mistress, for I know you have assumed that role for several years. You would never hear *me* putting such impertinent questions to you, of that you may be sure." Her giggle and twinkling eyes mocked her own propensity for ferreting out what information she could on anything that interested her.

Olivia shook her head sternly. "No, no, I am sure you would not. But, Julianna, I would rather discuss another matter, fascinating as the subject of my brother's betrothal is." Her friend's disappointed countenance provoked her into a laugh. "Your brother and I are going to be married, my dear. I should think that of more immediate concern to you."

Julianna gave a squeal of delight and hugged Olivia ecstatically. "Oh, that is famous! Does Mama know? When was it decided? Is the wedding to be soon? Are you to be married at Stolenhurst? Will you have a honeymoon?"

The answering of her questions took a considerable time, and Olivia was rushed in dressing for dinner. She chose the most becoming gown she could find and presented herself slightly breathless in the Drawing Room.

Chapter Nine

Noah, his sister and his mother were already there, and he came forward to take Olivia's hand. With a solemn formality that was somehow not in the least awkward he led her to his mother, who rose and kissed her cheek. "I am extremely pleased to hear this news, Olivia, and welcome you into our family. I feel sure you will not regret your decision." The piercing eyes were indeed softened by approbation, and Olivia instinctively curtsied. Julianna again began to proclaim her own excitement on the occasion, only to be interrupted by the announcement of dinner.

Noah had ordered that champagne be served with the meal, and with his first glass he silently toasted her, seated to his right. "I will want Mother to see that you have a proper wardrobe of brideclothes."

When Olivia demurred, saying that she had everything she needed at Stolenhurst, Julianna waved aside such a paltry reason for not enjoying a spree of buying. "Nothing will do but to have all new gowns, my dear. We shall have a glorious time in Norwich for Mama prefers it to Cambridge. Our dressmaker is every bit as fashionable as one you would find in London. Do you not suppose, Mama, that Olivia would appear to advantage in that cherry-red velvet we saw at the linen-drapers? It would make into the smartest evening cloak."

"I have no doubt it would be very becoming," Lady Lawrence agreed.

"And there was a gold satin with the most intriguing design, almost Indian. Olivia, you must have it! Oh, dear, you do not think it will be sold do you, Mama?"

"I would doubt it, at that price," her mother returned dryly.

Noah was watching Olivia's bemused face, which now became alarmed. With a grin he reassured her. "Mother thinks any material that costs more than five shillings the yard is exorbitant, my dear."

"Not for a satin, Noah! But Julianna *will* fall in love with the most mundane muslins at five and sixpence the yard. You need not fear that we will find Olivia just what is proper."

"Proper!" Julianna protested. "No, Mama, for Noah's bride it must be the very first style of elegance."

"And so it shall." Lady Lawrence turned to Olivia and surveyed the raven-black hair and creamy skin. "There are very few colors which will not become you, I think. Shall we make a start the day after tomorrow?"

Olivia glanced nervously at Noah, but he was beaming his approval. There had never been any reason (nor excuse, as she would have phrased it) for Olivia to purchase more than a few items at a time for herself, and the thought of a spectacular new wardrobe was exciting, if a trifle alarming. "I should enjoy it of all things, ma'am."

"Then it is settled," Noah declared cheerfully as he summoned a footman to refill Olivia's glass. "Can she be outfitted properly by mid-March, Mother?"

"Certainly, if we put our minds to it. If you would not mind, Olivia, I should like to have a look at what you have here before we begin, and you may tell me what remains at Stolenhurst. We can fill in and extend your wardrobe without the necessity of duplicating."

Olivia smiled gratefully. "Yes, I cannot like to be wasteful. Many of my clothes are useful yet."

"Useful!" Julianna snorted. "Just once you should have something really outrageous. I can see you now presiding over your first ball in a gown of white lace over shimmering satin, with a crimson ribband in your hair. We shall have any number of balls and routs when you are married. Have I shown you the ballroom? We seldom use it, you know, but all that is at an end! Noah will wish to show you off to everyone. The ballroom will be so crowded that there will be gentlemen standing on the galleries surveying the company through quizzing glasses and murmuring, 'Really, the most enchanting hostess, Lady Olivia,' in those dreadful bored voices they use for their praise. And Noah will lead you in the minuet, because it is so very graceful, and people will exclaim, 'What a handsome couple!' "

Embarrassed by such extravagant plans, Olivia blinked and surreptitiously scrutinized Noah's countenance. She could detect no hesitation, and though he laughed at his sister's exuberance, he did not discourage her. In fact he had begun to tease Julianna. "And where shall you be during all these festivities, my girl? Surely not hiding away in some corner?"

"Never. I shall be dancing with all the handsomest and richest men in the room, so that everyone will be jealous of me, except Olivia, of course."

Lady Lawrence regarded her daughter with fond exasperation. "By the time we return from London I dare say you will be more than exhausted by all the entertainments, Julianna. I must take Olivia on a thorough tour of the house, though, so that she may know how to *find* this ballroom you paint so exquisitely. I have no doubt it is in need of a thorough cleaning."

The more champagne she drank, the more Olivia found all this talk exhilarating. She felt Noah's eyes warm on her and basked in the glow of such a welcome into his family. The upset of being denied her old home faded into the background. "I could be in charge of seeing the ballroom cleaned. We have just done it at Stolenhurst."

Noah laughed. "Ever practical! You will have to take her in hand, Mother."

"I intend to do so right now, Noah," Lady Lawrence assured him as she rose to lead the ladies from the room. "We will leave you to your wine."

"Not on such a special occasion! We shall all withdraw, and have more champagne in the Drawing Room."

After Lady Lawrence had proposed a toast to the

newly engaged couple, Julianna declared, "I shall accompany Olivia and Noah on the harpsichord. Have you ever heard Noah sing, Olivia? He has the most impressive voice."

Although Noah protested that it was not so, laughing at his sister's high spirits, he did indeed join his voice with Olivia's. It seemed the sweetest music she had ever heard, and all the sweeter for her own brothers never being willing to join her. Julianna, her head in the clouds, continued at the harpsichord, humming as she played and frequently missing notes altogether, but superbly unconcerned by her mistakes. When Olivia wandered over to inspect the available music, with a thought to the next choice, Noah regarded the two unsteady young ladies with amusement.

"I think we had best call it a day, Mother."

"High time," she said, as she coaxed her daughter from the stool. With an arm about Julianna's waist, she led her from the room.

Intent on the sheets of music, Olivia was oblivious to their departure, and she found herself slightly swaying in the middle of the room with Noah shaking his head doubtfully at her.

"Have I done something wrong?" she asked anxiously, peering owlishly about the room as though the answer might come to her.

"No, my dear, but you and Julianna are both a trifle disguised. My mother will see to her."

"And you will see to me?"

"Yes, I will see to you, young lady," he replied firmly as he took her hand and drew her toward the door.

"I think I am perfectly capable of seeing to myself," she announced stiffly as she stumbled and he caught her.

"Do you? I think not. I should not have been so liberal with the champagne."

"I have had champagne before," she declared firmly as she made a great effort to put one foot before the other on their progress down the hall.

"I do not doubt it, but perhaps not in such quantity."

Olivia nodded her head sagely. "That would explain why I do not feel *completely* in control of my feet. Is it much further to my room?"

Noah laughed delightedly. "No, my poppet, only a few more steps."

When they reached her room he opened the door and rang for a maid. "You are like to have a fuzzy head tomorrow, Olivia, but I want you to remember this." He enfolded her in his arms and kissed her once, but with a deal more intent than earlier in the day. As he released her, she blinked up at him and said gravely, "I shall remember," before wandering to the bed where she flopped down heavily and curled into a ball before falling fast asleep.

Olivia's head felt more than fuzzy the next morning; it ached abominably. There seemed little use in rising early, so she closed her eyes again and awoke late in the morning. When she rose she became aware for the first time that she was wearing her chemise rather than her usual night dress. Despite her attempts to recall how this circumstance could have arisen, her only memory was of being kissed by her prospective husband. She dressed herself rapidly and descended to the breakfast parlor, which was deserted, though dishes of food remained on the sideboard.

A servant brought hot tea and toast in response to her ring, and she had just begun to consume her repast when Noah peered around the door. "Ah, there you are. I had begun to think you meant to sleep through the day," he remarked cheerfully.

Olivia flushed painfully at sight of him, and put a hand to her aching brow. "I . . . I had too much to drink last night," she stammered. "I apologize, sir. It will not happen again."

He smiled sympathetically. "Your head hurts, does it? Julianna is not even up yet." Noah became aware of her embarrassment and cocked his head questioningly. "Why do you blush so, Olivia? Surely not because I kissed you last night."

Olivia studied her plate intently. "Is . . . that all?

You did not . . . When I awoke this morning I was not . . . in my night clothes."

Noah took a seat beside her and placed a hand over hers where it rested on the table. "Goose! Do you not remember my ringing for the maid? No, I imagine you don't. When Marie came I instructed her to do what she could, but I warned her that she would not likely be able to awake you." He frowned at her downturned face. "It disturbs me that you could think I would take advantage of your condition, Olivia."

"It was just that the last thing I could remember was that you kissed me. You did not ask me if you might," she defended herself feebly.

"I thought we were agreed that I might . . . now and then. I should not like to have to ask you each time, my dear."

"Of course not," she replied with an unsuccessful attempt to appear sophisticated. "I did not mean to offend you, S . . . Noah. It is just that not being able to remember what happened last night has put me in some confusion. I have no doubt of your behaving properly toward me, or that I would behave correctly even in my cups," she proclaimed with a defiant tilt to her chin.

"Enchanting," he murmured as he rose to leave the room. "Would you like to ride with me this morning? It would help to clear your head."

"Very well," she replied, almost crossly.

Noah had not forgotten, bribe or not, his promise to take Olivia to dig up his strongbox in the woods. He mounted her on one of his own mares and took a shovel with him, but Olivia maintained an aloofness from his project which was in marked contrast to her enthusiasm of the previous day. The rusted keys were retrieved from the summerhouse before they galloped across the meadow to a heavily forested area where Noah explained to her his system for remembering the location of the box. "I would always enter on this path and count the trees on my left. Five trees forward, four to the left and then six to the right. Being fifteen was my goal when I was twelve," he laughed, "and the trees added up to that." When they had followed these instructions, they found themselves in a small clearing where the sun penetrated to the undergrowth. There was a sprinkling of crocuses coming into bloom not far from the spot under an ancient oak Noah indicated as his hiding place. In spite of herself Olivia could not prevent the anticipation which arose in her at the sound of the shovel striking the shallowly buried strongbox.

Noah removed his gloves and wiped the dirt off the box with his hands before offering the keys to Olivia to open the treasure chest. She was touched by the gesture but shook her head. With a shrug he bent and inserted the rusted key, scraping it about until it served its purpose. Noah lifted the lid to reveal the contents, surprisingly intact for the years they had rested in the damp forest. There was a small cache of guineas and a broken watch and chain which he explained his father had given him. A collection of toy soldiers occupied the largest part of the box, a remarkable assortment of intricately detailed figures, which Noah gazed on with a reminiscent smile and remarked, "Julianna could not resist them when she was playing with her dolls, and it upset me to see them casually pushed about her dollhouse as servants." He laughed at the memory. "Shall we put them away somewhere safe and save them for our son, Olivia?"

His casual acceptance of their betrothed state and future life as parents inexplicably startled her, and she nodded mutely. What to her seemed the most important, if necessary, decision of a lifetime was entered into by him with the seeming ease of deciding to purchase a new carriage or race horse. There was a comfort in his decisiveness and apparent lack of doubts, but there was also something bleak and distressing to her about this businesslike, unemotional progress toward the altar. He handed her one of the soldiers to examine while he unearthed the last treasure, a pad of foolscap on which he had scrawled the intimate thoughts of his youth. He pocketed this last almost guiltily; he had no intention of exposing his long-forgotten thoughts, very real at the time, to the woman at his side.

"We'll take the strongbox back to the house and

have it cleaned up," he said as she returned the soldier to him. When the treasure trove had been locked once again, he led her out of the forest, the box under one arm, the shovel gripped in his other hand. "I think we will leave the other box in the summerhouse, so that some day we will be surprised when one of the children comes home to tell us of finding it," he suggested with a smile. "And we will remember that it was the day you found it that we were betrothed."

This romantic flight of fancy might have pleased her if it had not been offered so . . . glibly. Olivia could not meet his light-hearted, quizzing gaze but murmured her agreement as he assisted her to mount. The euphoria of the previous evening had given way to the discouraging thought that, welcoming and fond of her as Lady Lawrence and Julianna were, she might have been *any* young lady so far as Noah was concerned. He had accustomed himself to the idea of marriage, and if it had been Jennifer Pugh whom he had inadvertently compromised he would be quite as satisfied to be marrying her as Olivia.

Alone with Julianna in her friend's bedroom, she tried to voice her thoughts. "Noah has a most . . . equable temperament, has he not?"

"Why, I suppose so. That is not to say that I have never seen him angry or annoyed, for I most certainly have." Julianna tossed her hair back with a vigorous shake of her head. "Sometimes he is very stern with me."

"Perhaps that is not precisely what I meant. He . . . he seems altogether at ease with the idea of marrying me."

Julianna regarded her with astonishment. "Well, of course he does, goose. Who would not?"

"But it is out of necessity, my dear. He would not be marrying me now if he had not unwittingly compromised me, and yet he does not act at all resentful or restive. He might as easily have been forced to marry someone entirely different."

"I should hope he did not embroil himself in such fiascos every day, Olivia! One would think to hear you talk that he had a whole string of mistresses, each one bent on some disaster which would lead to a young girl's ruined reputation."

"That is not at all what I meant, Julianna, and you know it," her friend protested. "It is just that I would expect him to be less . . . agreeable about the whole matter." When Julianna frowned with a lack of understanding, Olivia made one last attempt to share her burden. "I should think Noah would wish to *choose* his bride, rather than have one thrust on him."

"He's never shown the least inclination to marry at all, Olivia. You must realize that he is six-and-twenty and, as far as I know, has never offered for anyone, or contemplated doing so. He is very fortunate that out of his carelessness he should have reaped such a reward as you. Do you fear that he will not make a good husband? You need have no worry there, I promise you. He is very proud of his family and never treats us with anything but the greatest respect and devotion. You are too used to your own brothers, Olivia, and Noah is not like them. He is very protective and generous with Mama and me, and he will be with you."

Finding it impossible to express any more clearly the uneasiness she felt about Noah's behavior, Olivia gave up the attempt. After all, she could expect no more than he offered, and might have received a great deal less. Another man finding himself in the same position might have grudged her his name, which Noah certainly did not. It was silly to cavil at his good-natured acceptance of the situation; she was lucky indeed to have such an accommodating bridegroom. Thrusting aside the nagging doubt that there should have been more, she smiled at Julianna and said, "You are right, my dear. I suppose it is precisely because he is so different from my brothers that I find it difficult to believe my good fortune."

Julianna gave a tinkling laugh. "Doing it too strong, Olivia. Noah is the lucky one, and you make sure he knows it."

Chapter Ten

During the next few days Lady Lawrence and Julianna accompanied Olivia into Norwich for shopping expeditions and fittings, and into closer towns and villages for those items which could be purchased in the neighborhood. Noah escorted the three of them on a round of morning calls to acquaint their friends with the impending marriage. The news was excitedly received by everyone except Lorraine Pugh, who was currently despairing of Mr. Brownley, and had taken it into her head that Sir Noah might be a worthy object for her attentions. In the general excitement, however, her tragic pose was barely noticed.

On their return from one of these expeditions a week after their betrothal, Noah sorted through his mail and found the awaited reply to his letter to the Earl of Bolenham. "Your brother," he informed Olivia a while later, "writes briefly, giving his permission to our marriage, and allows that it would be proper for you to return to Stolenhurst for a short period to assemble your belongings."

"I dare say he did not think to send his best wishes."

"No." Noah's lips twitched slightly. "On the other hand, he did not offer me his condolences, either."

"You surprise me, sir. But you must not let that bother you, for I am sure he would condole with you, except that he is so relieved to be rid of me."

Despite such easy interchanges, Olivia was building

up a store of resentment against her fiancé. They rode daily, and he took the opportunity to teach her about his estate and to instruct her gently in her role as chatelaine. Although these lessons were conducted with finesse, Olivia chafed under them. It was not as though she were some country girl being elevated to an unfamiliar station. She was an Earl's daughter, an Earl's sister, and as such had, in spite of her youth, been in the position of mistress of an estate far larger than Noah's. One afternoon when Noah spoke of his obligations to the neighborhood as the local squire, Olivia felt her indignation rise to bursting point.

"I am not unfamiliar with such obligations, Noah," she snapped. "I have been in a position to carry them out in *my* neighborhood for several years. And I assure you that the demands made on an Earl are no less than on a baronet!"

"O-ho, so you are fretting at marrying beneath yourself after all," he returned.

"I will not be patronized," she declared angrily, reining in her horse.

"I had no intention of patronizing you, Olivia," he protested. "My own observation of your brother's nature did not lead me to believe that he would deal with his neighborhood in a very generous manner—except for making lavish expenditures which were seldom paid."

"If Peter was unwilling to meet his duties, I was not," she said through clenched teeth. "When necessary I used my own pocket money to relieve the suffering of some distress-ridden family. I am sick to death of your kindly delivered lessons on how to conduct myself as your wife, and I will not hear another word on the subject!"

Noah's jaw tightened grimly but he merely said, "As you wish, of course. It was not my intent to overburden you with your responsibilities."

His willful distortion of her complaint roused Olivia to a temper she had never displayed before. With a resounding crack she slapped him and urged her horse to a gallop, leaving him staring after her in astonishment. She did not draw in until she reached the stables, where she leaped from the horse and stomped out of the stable yard to the house without a backward glance. To avoid Julianna, she hastened up the back stairs and slipped into her room unobserved. It was some time before the angry flush left her cheeks, and much longer before the scene could be forced to the back of her mind. She fumed about her room, agitatedly picking up and fingering objects which did not belong to her and which she had to control herself from sending flying through the windows.

When a tap came at her door she pressed her lips together and did not respond. The maid Marie called to her that Sir Noah wished to see her in the Small Library. Olivia would never have contemplated making a scene in front of a servant and responded that she would comply with the summons. She did not, however, present herself to Noah for half an hour, the stubbornness of her anger still with her.

Noah coldly invited her into his sanctum and seated her beside the library table. Some redness remained on his face, and it offered her a grim satisfaction that did not amount to smugness but a nervous self-justification for her action. He did not seat himself but paced about the room slapping his gloves against his legs as though he wished he could do something else with them.

"The one thing I will not tolerate in a woman, in my wife," he corrected himself, "is such displays of temper. It is excessively ill-bred," he said scathingly.

"I consider it ill-bred to treat a social equal as an inferior," she retorted hotly, "and the one thing I will not tolerate in a husband is being condescended to."

He swung around and glared at her. She returned his stare with blazing eyes and was the first one to speak. "You forget sometimes, I think, that I had no hand in the present turn of events. It was not I who called for help when my mistress lay ill with an abortion I was responsible for. It was not my own reputation which made it possible for all those people to believe what they did of me—but my brothers' and yours. I may regret, but I have no control over, the fact that my brother should cast me out of my home, basically penniless and with nowhere to go. You *say* you are willing to accept the responsibility for me, that you would prefer me to marry you than to have me simply another dependent in your household.

"What is it to you, who have had so many, if you take me to wife and to bed? One woman is as good as the next to you, and probably you would not have planned to marry an earl's daughter. It is really not such a bad bargain for you, sir, since you appear insensitive to any thought of devotion between married couples. Do not think I dwell on marrying beneath me; it is of no consequence to me. But do not act as though I should hang on your words of proper conduct becoming your wife. I have known how to be a *baronet's* wife since I was ten!"

Noah's color had risen alarmingly and he gave a roar of indignation, but Olivia was not finished. "Do not think I would taunt you with such a paltry matter, sir, if you had not irritated me beyond enduring with your condescension these last weeks. Oh, you have been ever so kind, so considerate as to teach poor little Olivia how to disport herself as your wife. Have I given you reason to believe that I am so ill-suited to the job? I asked only to know of those personal things which are annoyances or delights to you which I might observe to your greater comfort and satisfaction. To *purposely* distort my meaning when we were riding was beyond anything. I would rather beg to Peter on my hands and knees than marry you under such terms!"

"Am I to understand, Lady Olivia," he asked stiffly, "that you are terminating our engagement?"

"Oh, I don't know!" she exclaimed exasperatedly. "You will not marry me if I display any temper, and I will not marry you if you condescend to me. If these are matters which cannot be mutually satisfied, then we should not marry."

"What would you do?" he asked coldly.

"There, you are doing it again! How do I know what I would do? I am not mistress of my own life, but it does not give you the right of any natural superiority. I am a woman, you know, one of that sex which may be shuttled about at the pleasure of yours. I can apply to Peter; he will be more than willing to establish me with some

92

crotchety old relation in the depths of Cornwall, no doubt, if I break my engagement. He would be relieved to have me out of sight, and out of mind. And when he forgets to send enough money to keep me, which I estimate would happen within the first three months, no doubt I shall take a job in some linen-draper's shop!"

The absurdity, and truth, of the picture she painted touched Noah with its essential pathos. It was true that the protective role he had taken toward her had led him inevitably to presumptuousness, perhaps even to the condescension of which she spoke. Her physical slap had wounded his pride no less than her sharp tongue-lashing on their relative social positions. He did not wish his hurt to overthrow his common sense, and he fought to regain control of himself and the situation.

Olivia remained in her chair, spent with her emotional outburst, her head in her hands. While he attempted to organize his thoughts and marshall his speech into an acceptable comment on her diatribe, she spoke brokenly through her fingers. "I am sorry that I slapped you, Noah, and that I have so lost my temper as to say unforgivable things to you. Please believe that I am grateful to you for all you have done and do not think hardly of me. I do not wish to impose on you, and you must no longer consider me your responsibility. For good or ill I am Peter's responsibility until I come of age, and I assure you that I am quite capable of making him bear that responsibility long enough to establish me elsewhere."

Her heartbroken speech finally mobilized Noah and he moved to stand beside her chair, his hand stroking her hair. "Do not be distraught, Olivia. We will work out a solution which will be mutually satisfactory. Perhaps I have been . . . condescending as you say. I was not aware of it, but I can see how it might appear so to you. Truly, my only thought was to make you feel comfortable here, for you must become mistress of the house with my mother still in residence, and that can be no easy chore."

This aspect of the situation had never occurred to Olivia and it only made her feel the more wretched. Noah watched her hands clench spasmodically in her lap, and he crouched beside her to take them in his. When she lifted her eyes to meet his, he said gently, "Let us acknowledge that we have both shown some temper today, and that we have both said things best left unsaid. I have no wish to terminate our engagement, Olivia, so the decision is yours. Do not base it on what has passed in this room today, though. I realize that to a woman of your birth and spirit I may seem overbearing sometimes; I doubt it is a matter which I can change. Only know that it is not a reflection on you personally, but rather a pride in Welling Towers and my family which has been instilled in me from my earliest days."

Olivia attempted to speak, to thank him for his understanding, but her lips trembled so that she was not able to do so. He put his arms about her and held her to him until the involuntary shivers which beset her were finished and she became calmer once more. Against his shoulder she whispered, "You can forgive me for what I have said?"

His hand stroked her hair and he replied ruefully, "So long as these resentments do not reflect your feelings when you are your ordinary, sensible self, Olivia." He held her at arm's length and studied the sad gray eyes. "If it is a source of pain to you that your birth is better than mine, well, then it would not be advisable to continue our plans. I cannot believe it is so, however; and you would have to be very convincing to persuade me," he said with a grin.

A wan smile rewarded his attempt at lightness and she moistened her lips. "I do not regard it, Noah, the difference in birth. The resentment I feel at my own dispossessed position is real, but unavoidable, and too much discussed already. I do not wish to break our engagement," she concluded over the lump in her throat.

"I'm glad," he said sincerely as he placed a chaste kiss on her cheek. "May I remind you that I wish you to be open with me? If you had spoken earlier of your irritation at my manner we might have spared ourselves this painful explosion," he offered gently.

"It would be difficult to tell you such a thing," she admitted seriously, "but I shall try to remember in future."

"Am I so unapproachable?" he asked, surprised. "My mother and Julianna seem to have no hesitation in discussing my shortcomings with me."

"My position is not the same as theirs."

"Olivia, your position in this household will soon be the most important one, in spite of the fact that you are most recently come. There will be no one to whom I owe more attention, more consideration. I do not fear that you will abuse the position at their expense, but I pray you will use it as you should to your own advantage. You are a little afraid of marriage, aren't you?" he asked suddenly.

"Yes, a little, but I dare say I will become used to it."

"I feel sure you will," he replied, his eyes dancing.

Chapter Eleven

Olivia was accompanied by Lady Lawrence and Julianna on her trip to Stolenhurst. She did not look forward to her own visit, but she was pleased on her arrival to be greeted most warmly by the staff. They made a great fuss over her, and she realized they were ashamed of their behavior before her departure.

Her days were spent in arranging for the dispatch of her belongings, and in rides with Julianna about the estate. Lady Lawrence accompanied them on some farewell calls Olivia wished to make, more out of duty than affection. They stayed a week and Olivia bid good-bye to her childhood home with less regret than she would have imagined possible only two months previously. It seemed unlikely to her that she would visit it in future when Lady Elizabeth held sway.

While Olivia made her journey to Stolenhurst, Noah set off for London, where he kept lodgings for his frequent visits. On the morning after his arrival he sought an interview with Olivia's brother Peter.

"Didn't expect to see you in town so soon, Noah. Tired of the chit already?" the Earl asked as they shook hands.

"No, Peter, I am not tired of her. I have come to settle the matter of her dowry with you." Noah took the chair to which his host casually waved him.

"Oh Lord, you cannot expect me to be interested in that. I shall give you my solicitor's direction, and you may arrange the details with him. I've spent a damn sight more time than I am willing to contemplate on my own approaching nuptials." His theatrical grimace hardened into a frown. "The good Lady Elizabeth is proving more trouble than she's worth, I'll wager. Her dear mother weeps copious tears at the mere mention of Elizabeth leaving her home, and her father is the hardest-nosed businessman I've ever met. Should have been in trade! He'd have made a fortune."

"And is Elizabeth still determined on her course of revenge against Lila?"

"She never swerves by an inch. Most stubborn woman I've ever met. And the upshot of it is that I never see the lovely Mrs. Dyer at all, since I must ever dance attendance on Elizabeth. I'll be glad when the wedding is over, and I can safely go my own way."

"I want you to remind Lady Elizabeth that her vindictiveness is damaging to my future wife, Peter. There are to be no more aspersions cast on Olivia's name."

"Damn it, Noah, I have no say in the matter. Olivia should have thought of her reputation before . . ."

Noah's brow was threatening. "Before what? You know perfectly well that there was nothing improper in our behavior that night. If Elizabeth must pick a quarrel with her cousin, let her do it over something unconnected with Olivia."

"There won't be any more talk after you are married, so what does it matter?"

"Sometimes I marvel at your lack of sensitivity, Peter. Your sister is not deserving of the gossip about her, and you have made no effort to stem it. More, you allow your own fiancée to damage Olivia's reputation. I won't have it." His cold eyes raked the Earl, who squirmed under his gaze.

"Very well, I shall see what I can do, but I doubt I will be very successful. Elizabeth is a termagant. I can't see what good it is going to do me to be rid of Olivia when I am saddling myself with such a wench," he declared incautiously.

Noah's jaw set firmly, and his eyes flashed fire. "There is no comparison between Elizabeth and Olivia,

Peter, and I will thank you to make none. Your sister has a courage and dignity far beyond her years. You have treated her shamefully, but she can still hold her head up."

"Oh, she would show you her best side, of course. Wait until she nags you about your spendthrift ways or the suffering shopkeepers in the village who have not been paid. Every lark becomes a monstrous crime in her eyes and she will wail about the poor squire whose pigsty you have destroyed. Pigsty be damned! No more than half a day's work to replace it, but she will march about the house for a week with those big gray eyes full of reproach. You're welcome to her, Noah!"

"I'm glad to have her, Peter," Noah retorted as he rose. When Peter handed him the slip of paper on which he had written the solicitor's direction, he sketched a bow and took his leave. Insufferable, pompous ass, he thought, with not a care for anyone but himself. For the first time he realized that he was indeed glad to be marrying Olivia. He might well have foolishly settled for some enticing maiden who possessed none of his fiancée's admirable qualities. She was young, yes, but she had a stature of her own. He need have no hesitation about her joining the Lawrence family.

Noah was rather surprised, when he repaired to the solicitor's office, to find that Olivia was well dowered by her mother and grandmother. The settlement which they drew took much less time than usual owing to Noah's determination to do generously by her. His provision of an allowance of considerable proportions caused the solicitor to raise his brows in protest. "Really, Sir Noah, it is not wise to allow so much money in a woman's hands. They rarely know what to do with it, and it leads to unfortunate excesses."

"In this case it will probably lead to assistance of the village school," Noah remarked dryly, "but I will bear your words in mind, and speak with Olivia about it."

The solicitor shrugged his disapproval but made no further protest. "The documents will be ready for you to sign in two days' time. Shall I have them sent round to you?"

"No, I shall come here if you will see that the Earl attends as well. As Olivia's guardian he must approve of the arrangements."

"He could not fail to do so, given such an advantageous settlement for his sister."

"Which he is unlikely to appreciate," Noah muttered with asperity before he departed.

When he had previously left London for Norfolk to break the news of Peter's engagement to Olivia, he had departed from Lila Dyer somewhat reluctantly, for he retained a measure of guilt associated with the occurrences at Stolenhurst. In addition, Lila was being harassed by her own cousin, and it made her position more precarious than at any former time. She had waved aside his concern and sped him on his way, undaunted by the spiteful nature of Lady Elizabeth's attack.

Noah in his role of betrothed man was very discreet in setting about seeing Lila on this occasion. There had been a brief reply to his letter advising her of his engagement, and she showed no reluctance to welcome him to her charming townhouse on Wimpole Street. Seated in a gold and white parlor in a gown of emerald green, she looked beautiful and it surprised him to realize that he had not really missed her while he had been away. But then, he had been rather busy.

"You look lovely, dear Lila, so I need not ask if you have been well." He smiled as he kissed the hand she offered him.

"Very well, Noah. I congratulate you on your engagement. It is unfortunate that Elizabeth should have made things so difficult for Lady Olivia because of me." She sighed and twisted a ring on her long, shapely hands. "You would have thought Elizabeth would have softened when Peter offered for her, but since she has not, I foresee a long division between us. I cannot forgive her her treatment of the child."

"Olivia would protest your considering her a child," Noah replied wryly. "She has called me to account several times on that score."

"I should think she will make you a good wife, Noah. There is an innate dignity about her which will

99

match well with your pride." She gave a mischievous grin. "You have not promised her fidelity, I take it."

"No," he replied seriously, "we have discussed ours as a convenient marriage. But I have promised discretion."

"Very fitting," she laughed, but she continued to twist the ring on her finger with an unusual absorption.

Noah became conscious of her nervous movement and leaned forward to take her hand. "Have you something to tell me, Lila? You need not hesitate."

She made a whimsical gesture. "You have been occupied for some weeks and I imagine you will be so for several months more at least. There is a viscount who . . . attracts me just now, and I have been . . . seeing him. I am much in demand, Noah, for the Monster has cleared the streets of their usual complement of women."

"Do not speak so of yourself, Lila, or I will think Elizabeth has some influence over you." He studied her face for a moment, and squeezed her hand reassuringly. "You were kind to see me to explain, my dear, and I wish you every happiness."

"You make it sound as though I were getting married," she replied crossly.

"Nonsense. You are determined on a life of happiness outside of marriage, and I have every expectation that you will manage it. I regret that our association must end; I have enjoyed it." He placed a fleeting kiss on her lips.

"I will miss you, Noah." And there was indeed a hint of moisture in her eyes as she watched him stride from the room.

Although a crisp wind whipped down Wimpole Street, Noah did not hasten as he headed for Bond Street. For a time he paused before a printseller's, and again at the hat-maker's, but he generally ignored the silk mercers and china sellers until he realized that it behooved him to return with a gift for Olivia. Now that he had decided on such a course, the only shops he passed were tea-dealers and razor-makers, but his progress was absent-minded at best, and he did not despair of a goldsmith or perfumer before he reached his lodgings in Bruton Street. What caught his eye, however, was a lady's workbox, in rosewood, decorated with engravings. One of the views bore such a resemblance to the lake at Welling Towers that he pushed open the shop door and entered.

The young assistant who came to serve him praised his choice, as he might have expected, but suggested that m'lady might prefer the spinning wheel instead. Noah regarded the toy dubiously; it would make a charming ornament to Olivia's sitting room, no doubt, but its essential uselessness would not recommend itself to her. The workbox, on the other hand, was not only charming, with its unusual design and standing on four tiny gilded feet, but it would see service. His hesitation prompted the assistant to claim knowingly that young ladies were more pleased with fripperies than everyday items.

Was Olivia so different from other young ladies that she would prefer a useful (though beautiful) item to a charming toy? Noah could not be sure, but his instincts drew him to the workbox. He lifted it to more closely examine the engravings, and when he saw that the oval one on the lid portrayed a dark-haired maiden in a forest, he had no further doubts. "I shall take this."

He tucked the wrapped parcel under his arm with a certain satisfaction and strolled the remaining distance to his lodgings, where he was informed that a Mr. Thomas awaited him in the drawing room. Lifting a quizzical brow he asked, "Someone I know, Robert?"

"I think not, sir, but he was most anxious to see you and hinted at some sort of official business, though his card shows no indication." The valet offered the card as he spoke.

There was no more than the name, but Noah agreed to speak with the visitor and shrugged himself out of his greatcoat with Robert's assistance. The man he found in the drawing room was unremarkable for any facial or physical characteristic, and Noah felt sure he had never seen him before. "Mr. Thomas? I am Noah Lawrence. How can I be of service to you?"

"Thank you for seeing me, sir. I have no wish to

intrude, but your name was suggested to me by William Potherby, and I had hoped that we might speak for a moment."

Noah waved the man to the chair he had risen from and seated himself opposite, negligently draping one leg over the other. "I have not seen William in some time. I believe he is now with the Foreign Office."

"That is true, and a very dedicated young man he is. There is some concern, as you would expect, over the developments in France this last half-year or so. Since the storming of the Bastille, the unsettled nature of affairs in France is of interest to our government. Mr. Potherby is aware of your longstanding friendship with the Comte de Mauppard, whom we believe to be active in the current state of affairs."

Noah nodded slowly. "Yes, Jacques has written expressing his wariness of the unrest resulting from what he calls 'The Great Fear.' "

"Fear, certainly such general fear, can lead men to acts of rashness which could disrupt the whole country, and have an effect on our own. The activity of the mob in Paris has already caused grave concern."

"Jacques hopes that the work of the National Assembly will alleviate some of the problems and achieve a stable social situation. Is it his views in which you are interested?"

"Not precisely," his visitor replied. "We are asking several men to visit France at this time in order to obtain as much information as possible on the nature of the disturbances and the attitudes of a wide range of people. It is essential that the government receive intelligence from the old and young, the rich and poor, the master and the servant. You have been recommended for a number of reasons. You have no tie with the government, but you have previously rendered it service—a matter in Italy, I believe. Also, you are young and personable. But it is your friendship with the Comte de Mauppard which is most essential."

"You want me to spy on him?" Noah asked incredulously.

"No, no, not at all. Your friend is in the thick of things and I doubt that he has any secrets to hide. It is his impressions and those of the people around him in which we are interested. How strong is the basis of this revolution, and in what direction is it heading? We would be interested as well in having you travel about the countryside to judge the concerns there. You must understand, Sir Noah, that there is unrest in our own country, and a proper understanding of the atmosphere in France would assist us in preventing any tragic consequences here. The information we wish is not secret, but it is diverse. We need interested and knowledgeable people to accumulate it for us. Would you be interested in assisting?"

"Yes," Noah said thoughtfully, "but you may be unaware that I am about to be married. I cannot leave England at this time, or for a while." For the first time he felt an annoyance at the imminence of wedlock. The stirring of his irritation at the implicit question of his independence made him offer, with a decided flourish, his services in the matter of a few months' time. "I will then be at liberty to be of service to my country," he concluded ironically.

To have to refuse such an adventure, and for such a reason, left him feeling edgy, and he lived recklessly in London for a few days, drinking, gambling and nearly being taken up by the watch. This last finally sobered him, and he met Peter at the solicitor's office in a fairly chastened frame of mind.

"From what Baker tells me, you have been too generous with Olivia, Noah. I understand the way to hold the upper hand with a wife is to keep a firm hand on her finances. A woman will be properly obedient when she is in need of the ready," the Earl laughed.

"Is that how you expect to go on with Lady Elizabeth?"

"I would, but her father is making it difficult. He expects me to make her an allowance the equal of her mother's. Well, I ask you, where is the comparison? Her mother has expenses that Elizabeth could not have for years. I think the old fellow would call the whole thing off, but Elizabeth will not let him. In the end we will make a compromise, undoubtedly, but I expect to get the better of him."

"I can think of nothing more depressing than having a wife pleading for money the livelong day," Noah returned dampingly. "Well, Peter, are you willing to agree to the settlement?"

"Oh, certainly. It's your funeral, my dear fellow."

When the documents had been signed and tied with a ribbon, Noah poked them into his coat pocket. "I hope you will attend the wedding, Peter."

"I don't intend to leave London until I go to Newmarket in April. No need for two trips."

"It's your sister's wedding, and I think she would appreciate your being there."

"I shall be far too busy preparing for my own, Noah."

Noah could get no further with the Earl. Nor was his success with Olivia's other brothers, Charles and Samuel, much more encouraging. Samuel was sure that he had an engagement in Kent about that time, and Charles gave an assent so vague that Noah doubted his intent was to do more than fob him off. As a devoted brother himself, Noah was not able to understand their total lack of interest in their sister; but since they showed no more fondness for one another, save in any self-seeking venture, he decided not to waste his efforts.

The journey back to Norfolk was sobering, with Noah's reflections on his impending marriage less light-hearted than before. The disappointment of not being able to drop everything and leave for France rankled at the back of his mind. He eyed with chagrin the work box on the carriage seat beside him. Probably Olivia would have preferred the useless spinning wheel after all. There was something in the female mind which eluded that of the male, he decided. They would rather have one's regard proved by a waste of money on some trinket than on an everyday item which could be kept by them year after year as a perpetual reminder. Both attitudes seemed grossly sentimental to him right then, and he pulled his hat down over his eyes to nap until they reached the Towers.

His arrival followed only by an hour that of the women, and his mother and Julianna were only too pleased to leave him with Olivia so that they might be about their business. It was an effort for him to be solicitous of Olivia on this occasion, though he was aware that her final parting at Stolenhurst might have upset her. "Were you able to arrange matters to your satisfaction, my dear?"

"Oh, yes, and it was not nearly so distressing as I had expected," she confided. "I have brought some of my childhood treasures to put in the schoolroom here. You had no problem with Peter?"

"No, he was bored by the arrangements but put no obstacles in the way." He thought to prepare her for a disappointment and took her hand gently. "It is unlikely that he or Samuel will attend the wedding, Olivia, though Charles may."

"I had expected no more," she replied sadly.

Thinking to cheer her, but now wholly convinced that the work box had been a mistake, he drew it forth from the cabinet where he had placed it on his arrival. "I found this in London, and I thought of you. That is, the engraving bears some resemblance. Perhaps you would have preferred something less ... mundane; but I believe it is a handsome little piece. Decorative, you know. There is no need to use it if you already have a serviceable work box. This scene," he remarked as he touched it with a finger, "reminded me of the lake."

"Yes, an uncanny resemblance." She studied the various engravings carefully and ran her fingers lovingly over the polished rosewood. "Thank you, Noah; it is beautiful." Her very real delight in the present was partially destroyed by the sudden realization that perhaps she should have brought him some little thing—a snuff box or a cane, anything—from her own journey. "Later I ... shall show you what I brought for the schoolroom, if you would be interested."

Disappointed by her reaction but determined to do

what he could to make up for his unfortunate choice, he said heartily, "Certainly, with the greatest pleasure. Another time I shall get you one of those toy spinning wheels."

"A spinning wheel? Whatever for?" Olivia regarded him with some confusion, and became aware that he was standing somewhat stiffly with that formality which comes from wounding someone's feelings. "Noah, I love the work box. Not only is it lovely in itself, but I have need of one. My own broke at the hinges just before I first left Stolenhurst to come here. I shall cherish it, I promise you."

"That's all right then," he murmured, his relief obvious. "It cannot be pleasant for you to have left Stolenhurst under these circumstances."

"Pooh, I scarcely regard it." She offered him a shy smile. "You must not be concerned for me."

But it was she who began to feel concerned for him over the next few days. He was more withdrawn than he had been at any other time during their engagement; and believing him, as she did, to have come back to Welling Towers from Mrs. Dyer's arms, so to speak, she did her utmost to accommodate herself to his moods. Olivia did not believe herself to be jealous of Mrs. Dyer, but she could have wished that Noah's life was as uncluttered of previous entanglements as was her own. She chided herself for such an unreasonable attitude, certainly not in keeping with her agreement to their practical marriage. Not even to herself would she acknowledge that it was the fact that he had stopped kissing her which upset her most. Olivia had come to depend on the affection, even such a small sign offered her, and she felt a sense of loss when it was withdrawn.

Chapter Twelve

With some embarrassment Olivia found herself promoting occasions when she and Noah might be alone. She assured herself that it was only proper for an engaged couple to spend a certain amount of time together, for there were matters to discuss about the wedding and their future life. Lady Lawrence and Julianna put no barrier in the way of such meetings, in fact encouraged them; but Noah remained polite and abstracted when he was with Olivia. One afternoon, a week before the wedding, they were riding through the village of Welling when Olivia reached out a hand to Noah's arm to attract his attention. He looked over, surprised, and said, "Is something the matter, Olivia?"

"I have no money left," she admitted, disconcerted.

Noah raised a quizzing eyebrow. "You have only to ask, my dear. I thought it was understood that I would meet any expenses inherent in preparing for the wedding. Mother said the bills were being sent to me."

"I tried at first to meet them myself," she confessed, "but there were too many. Your mother insisted that I have practically an entire wardrobe."

"That is just what I would wish."

Olivia drew a deep breath. "You don't understand, Noah. I need some pocket money."

"Very well," he agreed, puzzled. "Will five pounds suffice for now?"

"No, I need twenty."

"But, Olivia, if you wish to spend so much as twenty pounds you should have the bill sent to me. I do not consider it safe for a woman to wander about with twenty pounds in her reticule."

"I do not wish to have the bill sent to you," she returned stubbornly. "I wish to have the money."

Noah was surprised by her adamance. "Would you perhaps tell me why?"

"I would rather not."

"I can only surmise that you wish to buy something I would not approve of," he said with some ascerbity.

"That is not true. I would not be without a feather to fly with were it not for all those clothes I had to buy and have not the least need of. I came to Welling Towers with quite a satisfactory amount of money, since I had been able to save a bit from last quarter's allowance as well. Now it is all gone, and I need twenty pounds. You said you would not be ungenerous with me," she accused him.

"But I have offered to pay for your purchase," he protested.

"It is not the same. I do not wish to have the bill sent to you. That would be most . . . inappropriate. Please, Noah, may I have twenty pounds? I promise I will ask for no more until next quarter."

"It is not a matter of the amount." He dug into his pocket for his stocking purse. A perusal of its contents was unsatisfactory. "I have only twelve pounds and some shillings with me. Do you need the entire amount right now?"

"No, I can return to the village tomorrow," Olivia said placidly.

"Then I will give you the entire twenty pounds this evening," he remarked grudgingly as he stuffed the purse back into his pocket.

"Thank you, Noah. It is important to me."

"I can see that," he grumbled as they turned their horses toward home.

The evening passed and Noah did not provide her with the money. Olivia watched him reproachfully as he bid his mother and sister and her good-night, saying that he intended to read for a while. Allowing the others to progress toward their rooms, she hung back, her eyes intent on him. He had turned to kick the fire with a booted foot and only became aware of her presence when he headed for the Small Library.

"Did you wish to speak with me?" he asked innocently.

Olivia swallowed her chagrin and said sweetly, "You promised you would give me the twenty pounds this evening."

"So I did, but I have decided that I want payment for it," he responded with a slow grin. "Come here, Olivia."

She walked hesitantly toward him, her hands clenched nervously behind her. "What . . . what sort of payment?"

"Nothing so very difficult," he replied gently. "I have been remiss in my lessons on acquainting you with me, and I had thought to catch up a bit." Noah ran a finger about the oval of her face and touched her lips while she stood frozen, blinking seriously up at him. "You really are quite lovely," he murmured as he bent to kiss her. She accepted his kiss, as she had on other occasions, with a slight heightening of color but no other response. "Do you know that it is perfectly permissible for you to kiss me in return?" He regarded her with comically raised brows.

"I do not remember ever kissing anyone," she said shyly. "I am sure I would do it wrong."

"I doubt it. If you wish your twenty pounds you must make an effort for it."

"That is not fair. You promised me the money."

"And you shall have it, Olivia. Are you afraid to kiss me?"

"Yes."

"Then I will give you a choice, my dear. Is that not generous of me?" His eyes sparkled with amusement. "To earn your twenty you may kiss me or you may tell me for what purpose you wish the money."

Olivia regarded him stormily and then turned away to head for the door saying haughtily over her shoulder, "I will make my intended purchase on tick, Noah, and pay for it when I next receive my allowance."

He overtook her before she could leave the room and gripped her arm with a firm hand. "Oh, don't be so stuffy, Olivia. I was merely teasing you; I have your twenty pounds right here." He pulled out his purse, withdrew the money, and pressed it into her hand. "It is just that I am very curious about what you intend to purchase."

"You will know next week."

"Will I? And I will not disapprove?"

"Certainly not. Why should you think I would purchase something of which you would disapprove, Noah? You do not intend to keep a record of all my purchases, do you?" she asked crossly.

"No, my dear, but I consider it highly mysterious that such an expensive purchase is one whose bill you will not have sent to me."

"I do not wish for you to pay for it. This twenty pounds I can look on as my own, a reimbursement of monies I have spent on a wardrobe for you. Do not think I am ungrateful for my new clothes, Noah. They are lovely, but I would not have bought them were it not for your mother's insistence, and then I would have had the twenty pounds I needed."

Noah shook his head bemusedly at her rationalization. "If that is the way you see the matter, I am sure I owe you a great deal more than twenty pounds."

"Oh, no," she protested, aghast. "Perhaps it would be better to consider it an advance against my next allowance."

"For God's sake, Olivia, let us forget the matter," he said exasperatedly. "It is your money now. There is no need for an accounting of it now or in the future. I beg your pardon for making such a fuss over it."

Olivia was not proof against his disgruntled apology. She stood on tiptoe and placed a hesitant kiss on his lips. "Thank you, Noah." Before he could react to her gesture she had disappeared from the room, to leave him staring astonished at the closing door.

From the window of the Small Library Noah watched Olivia ride toward Welling the next morning after breakfast. He knew she was headed to make her purchase, and his curiosity was still high, but he shrugged and returned to the papers on the library table, intent on completing matters at the Towers before the wedding and honeymoon.

Olivia arrived at the shop shortly after Mr. Higgins put back the shutters. He had promised her that if she decided on the leather hassock he would have it delivered on the morning of her wedding, suitably tied with a red ribbon, as her bridegroom's wedding present. There had never been any question in her mind that it was precisely what Noah needed for the Small Library, but she was intent on paying for it herself. In spite of the trouble she had gone to for the twenty pounds, she felt it infinitely superior to having Noah receive a bill for his own present.

"This is a surprise, mind you," Olivia warned Mr. Higgins. "Please make no mention of it to anyone at the Towers."

His round face wreathed with a smile as he assured her that not a word would pass his lips. When he ushered her out of the shop, she found Julianna riding past, and she had a momentary suspicion that Noah had sent his sister to spy on her. Olivia was immediately ashamed of such a thought, for her friend was obviously bound for her usual music lesson and was delighted to have Olivia ride with her as far as Mrs. Trambor's cottage. Of course Julianna's natural curiosity prompted her to inquire Olivia's purpose at the shop, but she received only a vague reply which nonetheless drew no further comment from her.

On her return to the stables Olivia found Noah discussing the preparations for their honeymoon trip with the coachman while he waited to ride with her. He mounted Emperor and politely asked her in which direction she wished to proceed.

"To the lake, I think. I have not seen the swans in some time now." Olivia cast a glance at him from under her eyelashes. It was difficult to tell what kind of mood he was in.

"You have carried out your commission in the village?" he asked cheerfully.

"Yes, thank you. It took but a moment, and then I rode with Julianna to her music lesson."

"I have seen Alexander Cutler ride home with her from her lessons occasionally," he offered conversationally, his gaze intent on her.

"Yes, he does. No doubt they meet in the village."

"I think it far more likely he waits for her at Mrs. Trambor's gate," Noah replied dryly. When Olivia made no response he continued, "Yet he very seldom comes in to call, if I am not mistaken."

"No," she replied vaguely, "I have not seen him at the Towers in some time."

"Would you say, not since I have been in residence?"

"I could not say, Noah. If you have some interest in the matter, I suggest you discuss it with Julianna."

He accepted her rebuke with equanimity, but he was not ready to drop the subject. "I cannot like him, Olivia. He has no substance. I do not mean that he is not well-heeled, but that he is a frippery sort of fellow. Would you be willing to honor me with your opinion of him?" he asked coaxingly.

Olivia watched the swans glide gracefully about the lake before she responded. "He reminds me of my brothers."

"I doubt you could have issued a more blighting condemnation." He studied her for a while before he frowned and commented, "I do not like to speak with Julianna about him. He is fascinating to her and I cannot say anything without putting up her back. It would not do to force her into a rash decision. I am sure she knows that Mother and I would not be happy with a match in that direction and she is not of age. Have you talked with her about Alexander?"

"As little as possible. If she feels everyone is against her, she will have only him to turn to." Olivia met Noah's eyes only briefly, but there was complete understanding between them. "Perhaps she will meet someone interesting in London," she suggested, though she had no more hope of the possibility than either Noah or Lady Lawrence did.

"Perhaps. Shall we walk around the lake?" When she nodded, he dismounted to assist her from the mare, and tucked her hand under his arm. Cautiously, he said, "I would never ask you to bear tales about Julianna, Olivia, but if you should ever learn that she was contemplating any rash action, I hope you would not leave her to her fate. I have no wish to play the tyrant and in a year I will have to allow her what choice she makes, but for now I must follow the dictates of my conscience and protect her as I can." He stopped and turned to her. "Can you understand how I feel?"

"Certainly, and I would not abandon her to such a fate over any misguided scruples in connection with our friendship, Noah. I am very attached to Julianna and I wish to see her happy. It is impossible for me to think that her comfort lies in that direction, but when she is of age I hope you will not make her miserable with your disapproval if she is still determined on Alexander."

Noah reached down to pick up a pebble and skim it across the water, where it made ever-widening circles. "I will give her what support I can. There might come a time when she needs to know that her family is behind her."

Olivia nodded and they continued their walk in silence. The March sunlight glinted off the water and from the opposite bank they looked back on the horses and across the lawns to the house. "I am fond of Welling Towers," she remarked suddenly, almost to herself.

Noah smiled at her, his eyes full of pride. "It is a source of never-ending pleasure to me. The estate has been in my family for a dozen generations, and each one has succeeded in improving it. We will do our share." His enthusiasm was infectious and she turned sparkling eyes up to him. He caught her hand and drew her into a stand of trees where he kissed her and she tentatively responded. Pleased with her effort he hugged her affectionately and murmured, "I think we will suit very well, Olivia."

Chapter Thirteen

The morning of their wedding dawned sunny and crisp, and Olivia arose from her bed with nervous anticipation. She walked to the window to survey the early spring landscape with its promising patchwork of green and brown. A shiver passed over her frame and she had darted back to her bed when there was a tap on the door.

Marie entered at her summons, her face glowing with an excited smile, and set down a tray with chocolate and toast while she chatted. "You could not have a better day for your wedding, Lady Olivia. Such a bustle as there is in the kitchens. Miss Julianna is already astir and asking whether you are in need of her company. Lady Lawrence is as calm as ever, of course, and Sir Noah is with some friends in the breakfast parlor. Shall I send Miss Julianna to you?"

Olivia agreed that she would welcome her friend's presence and gave a sigh of relief when the maid left. Julianna was as full of the importance of the day as Marie had been, and every bit as talkative, but, recognizing Olivia's subdued aspect, she did not press her for responses to her rhetorical comments on the wedding and the glorious weather. The ceremony was to be early, followed by a lavish breakfast, and Julianna began the lengthy process of assisting Marie to dress her friend, before she slipped away to don her own bridesmaid's gown.

A profusion of black ringlets framed Olivia's face and escaped onto her shoulders from under the broad-brimmed, low-crowned chapeau of taffeta with straw lace. Her gown of white brocaded silk was trimmed with flounces, and its train fell from the modest neckline in back. Noah had sent a family heirloom—a stunning diamond necklace—which she wore about her throat.

Anxiously she studied her reflection in the dressing glass and allowed that, although Marie exaggerated, she did indeed appear presentable. Lady Lawrence arrived to escort her to the carriage, and bolster her flagging spirits. Julianna, dressed with quiet elegance, whispered her encouragement, and Olivia soon found herself seated in the carriage for the brief drive to the village church.

Noah appeared to advantage in a plum velvet coat with an embroidered waistcoat and cream-colored knee breeches. His warm smile made it possible for Olivia to steel herself to being the object of everyone's attention. Her brother Charles, tardily arrived but solemn for once in his life, gave her away with every sign of respectability.

Lady Lawrence, having assured herself that all was as it should be in the church, bestowed a benevolent smile on the couple and acknowledged to herself, not for the first time, that it was after all an excellent match and she was well pleased with her daughter-in-law. Watching them not as practically, but from her own romantic point of view, Julianna beamed with happiness. Here was the sister she had never had, and she loved her dearly. And her darling Olivia was the most fortunate of women to be marrying Noah, the kindest and best of brothers.

Very little of the impressively read service penetrated Olivia's consciousness; her hand shook when Noah placed the ring on her finger, and he pressed it sympathetically. Suddenly this man was her husband and there was no going back. There was nothing to go back to anyhow, she thought with a sigh, and then she smiled at him when he led her down the aisle to the carriage waiting outside the church. She could trust him to take care of her; perhaps even in time to care for her a little. But everything was moving so fast. Too soon they were toasted at the breakfast banquet; too soon she was changed into her traveling costume; too soon she was alone with Noah in the carriage bound for the Cotswolds.

"I have arranged for accommodation at the Blue Boar in Cambridge for the night," he told her. "If we make an early start in the morning, we may reach Buckingham tomorrow night and stay at the Swan and Castle. With any luck we will reach Roger's estate by the third night." She acknowledged this information with a nod, her head turned to gaze out the window. "Would you like me to read to you?"

Olivia was touched by the thoughtfulness of the gesture and turned to him. "That would be enjoyable, Noah. I find it difficult to read in a moving carriage."

His voice reading *The Exiles* was deep and soothing to her overwrought nerves, and when she fell asleep he marked the place and cradled her against him. She slept so soundly, undisturbed by changes of horses or the clamor of busy inn yards, that he was able to withdraw another book from the traveling bag and peruse it at his leisure. The last of the day's light was fading from the sky when she awakened to find his arm about her shoulder.

"I beg your pardon. I did not mean to sleep," she apologized as she attempted to sit upright once more.

He reluctantly removed his arm and assured her that he perfectly understood her exhaustion. "It is another hour before we reach the inn, Olivia, but there is food in the hamper if you wish."

It was more curiosity than hunger which caused her to lean over and lift the lid of the hamper. "There is enough here to feed a dozen people!" she exclaimed. "Shall I hand you something?"

Noah settled on a pork pie and, although she had not intended to eat anything, Olivia found she was ravenous and helped herself to a Queen cake, and then another, followed by an apple. Noah laughed and commented, "For a moment there I thought perhaps you were hungry."

When Olivia had swallowed the last bite she retorted, "I did not eat at the wedding breakfast as though I were not to see food for another week."

"I was fortifying myself for the demands of the day," he protested, his eyes full of humor. Even in the dim light he could see that her face paled, and he gently cupped her chin and lightly touched her lips with his. He was not surprised that there was no response; prudently he proceeded to regale her with stories of Cambridge, which was now but a short distance away.

The landlord himself led the way to their rooms at the inn, and Olivia noted with trepidation that although there were two of them, only one contained a bed; the other was a dressing and sitting room. Without attempting to consult his panic-stricken bride, Noah approved them and ordered a light meal sent up. Olivia wandered about the sitting room distractedly twitching at the curtains in an effort not to meet his eyes. Noah settled into a comfortable chair and watched her restless pacing for a few minutes before he spoke.

"Come and sit down, Olivia." When she had meekly obeyed, he asked if she had any interest in staying in Cambridge the next day to acquaint herself with the town and university.

"I . . . I really cannot say. Let it be as you wish."

He cocked his head teasingly at her. "But, my dear, I know Cambridge very well. It is you who have never been here before, and you alone can tell me if you wish to spend the day."

"No doubt it would upset our travel arrangements." She was relieved to light on this very logical reason, for she felt totally incapable of making even such a minor decision.

"There is no need to be rigid in our schedule, but perhaps we could stay here a while on our return if you decide you would like that."

"Yes, yes. That is very true."

Their meal arrived and, although she could not down more than a mouthful, she concentrated her whole attention on her plate and allowed her husband to carry the conversation with merely a murmur of agreement now and then. All too soon the dishes were removed and she found herself helplessly regarding her hands. Noah calmly retrieved *The Exiles* and read to her for an hour, but this time her agitation was too great to be soothed by his voice, and eventually he closed the book and rose. "I will send Marie to you," he said gently before he disappeared into the bedroom.

Marie found her mistress pale and silent, and did her utmost to cheer the young woman with anecdotes about the wedding that morning. Feeling that she had accomplished very little, she left Olivia seated in her nightdress and dressing gown in a chair by the fire, little warmed by the blaze. The door from the bedroom opened and Olivia heard Noah approach her and stand by the chair.

"I cannot do it," she whispered fiercely.

He drew a chair up beside hers and sat silent for a moment. "Tell me how you feel, Olivia." When she did not speak, he rose and extinguished the candles in the room, so that the only light was from the fire. Then he reseated himself and asked, "What is it you fear?"

"Everything."

A low laugh escaped him. "Surely it is not so bad as that," he protested.

"Yes, it is," she replied, her voice firmer. "Oh, Noah, it does not have to be tonight, does it?"

"No, it does not have to be tonight. I am not . . . repulsive to you, am I?" A note of hurt crept into his voice.

"Of course you are not! How can you ask such a question? I would not have agreed to marry you were that the case."

"Are you afraid of the pain?"

"*Is* there pain?" she asked, horrified.

He could have kicked himself for that misstep. "Well, yes, I understand the first time it is momentarily painful for a woman, Olivia. Do you feel embarrassed about the intimacy?"

"Yes."

"But we are husband and wife now, and there is no longer any impropriety."

"Pooh! There is a vast difference between impropriety and one's own feelings of modesty, Noah. How can you think that a few words spoken this morning would suddenly make me wish to dash into your arms?"

"I did not think it! It is very normal to have intimate relations on one's wedding night," he said stiffly, "and I assumed that we would be as other couples."

"Well, I cannot answer for all those other women, but it does not seem right to me to leap from a few kisses into bed." Her chin was raised stubbornly and she continued to contemplate the fire.

"Perhaps you would be so kind as to tell me what you consider the proper sequence of events, Olivia," he retorted. There was an embarrassed silence from his wife. He spoke more softly, "I understand what you are saying, my dear, and I shall endeavor to respect your . . . sensibilities. But you must do your part to promote our marital well-being. Are you prepared to take an active part in progressing toward intimacy?"

"I am not sure precisely what you mean, Noah," she said hesitantly. "You want me to kiss you?"

"Definitely that, but I will ask a great deal more of you." His voice was bland and his eyes in the dark were unreadable.

"You are frightening me. Tell me what you mean."

Noah rose to stand before her, an imperative hand stretched out to her. "In time I will show you, Olivia. If we are to progress slowly toward an ultimate mating, I see no reason why I should not teach you all I know about intimacy along the way. It will no doubt surprise you."

Olivia shivered and ignored the hand held out to her. "You are trying to intimidate me." The protest came feebly as she shrank back against the chair.

"Nonsense. I am offering you an opportunity most wives do not have, I assure you."

"I do not want such an opportunity, Noah," she pleaded.

"Of course you do," he replied stoutly. "Take my hand, Olivia."

Her eyes were enormous in the dark and gazed beseechingly at him. "If . . . you will not ask of me that I do more than . . . kiss you, I will come to bed with you now. I do not wish for you to teach me anything at all, please, Noah. We will have a marriage night just as other couples, I promise you."

A burst of laughter greeted this capitulation, and she stared at him with astonishment. "Oh, Olivia, you must not let me manipulate you so. I should not have frightened you, but I could not resist a bit of a fiddle. Have you so little trust in me? Do you think I would use you against your inclinations? Only let me guide you and you will not be afraid. I will not rush you, my poppet."

The indignation which had bloomed in her eyes gradually diminished to be replaced by a wan smile. "That was not kind of you, Noah. I did not mean to intimate that you would ill-treat me, only that I was frightened." She allowed herself to be pulled to her feet and enclosed in his arms. When his lips sought hers, she responded freely in an effort to show him that she did trust him.

Noah released her to replenish the fire before he drew her to the sofa, where he held her next to him. Olivia allowed herself to relax, bemused by the kisses he bestowed on her forehead, cheeks, nose, chin, and throat. The movement of his hands on her back was not so very alarming, but when he ran them down her arms, brushing lightly against her breasts, she tensed involuntarily. His mouth on hers became more insistent and his desire was a palpable thing, exciting and frightening her simultaneously. She drew back from his embrace, her gray eyes black in the dim light, and her face flushed. With a deft movement Noah shifted into the corner of the sofa and cradled her against him, saying, "You did not call my attention to my wedding present from you, Olivia. I very nearly did not see it before we left."

"I had completely forgotten it in the excitement. I'm glad you saw it."

"It was thoughtful of you, and one of the nicest gifts I have ever received," he assured her sincerely, his hands beginning to stroke her back once more.

"And I was overwhelmed by the necklace, but I would rather that your mother keep it as long as she lives," Olivia murmured.

"You must do as you wish on that score, my dear. She will not miss it, but I dare say you have jewels enough from your mother and grandmother."

"I do, you know, for there is a superfluity of them in

the family and only half are heirlooms." She was conscious that his hands were now tracing the line of her leg through the nightdress and dressing gown.

"Would I be mistaken in surmising that you found yourself short of funds to purchase that beautiful hassock?"

"Do you understand now, Noah? I could not have you pay for your own wedding gift."

"It is unfortunate that we quarrelled because of the money," he said dryly. "The gesture itself was enough, Olivia; I would not have minded paying the bill."

"Oh, I know you wouldn't, but it didn't seem right." His hands were caressing her thighs, and were it not that she could not concentrate on the discussion and the movement at one and the same time, she would have protested. "You are no longer angry with me about it, are you?"

"Was I angry with you? I cannot remember. You made me very curious, I recall, and I did not approve of your having so much money about your person." Her person he was now measuring with the span of his hands about her waist. "So tiny, and after all those Queen cakes," he murmured.

Olivia managed a strangled laugh, her alarm mounting rapidly. "I . . . I thought you needed such a hassock in the Small Library."

"And so I did. I am most grateful." Well, nothing ventured, nothing gained, he thought, as he moved his hands to touch the rapidly rising and falling breasts. Her breathing was irregular from her alarm and her hands flew to his in a fluttery gesture which might best have shooed chickens from a wheat field. Very calmly he turned to stroking her hair instead. "I have your real present in the bedroom, Olivia."

"You do? I thought the necklace was my present."

"No, that was but a family gift. There is a package on the bed for you."

"May I have it now?" she asked shyly, aware that his hands were once again running along her arms, brushing against her breasts.

"I cannot think you would like it, after all." There was a distinct note of disappointment in his voice.

Olivia frowned in confusion. "Well, of course I will like it."

"No, I am afraid not. I cannot imagine what possessed me to purchase it for you."

"You are teasing me. I am sure I would be pleased with any gift you gave me." The pressure against her breasts had increased, and with it the level of her agitation, but she did not wish her husband to think her ungrateful for his gift.

"I will return it and purchase you something more suitable," he declared with sudden determination. "Yes, that is the best solution. You will not mind waiting for your present, will you?"

"Noah, I fail to understand how you can have determined, without my even seeing it, that I will not like it," she protested, alarmed at wounding his feelings no less than by the continuing intimate touch.

"Shall I bring it to you? Would you like to see it at least?" His intent eyes were curiously eager, and she knew a moment's doubt; but his removal from the room would for a moment release her from this most upsetting contact.

"Yes, please let me open it."

Noah nodded briskly, removed her from his lap with a hurried kiss and strode from the room. Since he was gone only a moment she barely had time to touch her hair into place before he was handing her a box wrapped in silvery paper. The fire had burned down again and he went to renew it, which left Olivia to determine whether she was expected to await his return before opening the package. Her curiosity won out and she stripped the wrapping and removed the lid. There lay the fluffiest, most flimsy of nightdresses she had ever seen. She pushed it away from her with a gesture of despair and her hands rose to cover her burning cheeks.

"I knew you would not like it," he said sadly from behind her.

"I . . . It is quite beautiful, Noah." She swallowed painfully.

"Never mind, my dear," he said gently, his voice laden with wretchedness. "It was a stupid mistake on my part. I hope you will take no notice of it." He reached over her to retrieve the box. "I shall purchase an emerald pin for you. No, not jewelry. I shall find something you will like, I promise you."

Olivia could only think how hurt she would have been if he had told her that he did not want the leather hassock she had gotten him. Well, perhaps it did whisk through her mind, with a trifle of chagrin, that his gift might more properly have been given to a mistress than to his wife, but he had obviously purchased it for her because he looked forward to . . . She stayed his hand when he would have taken the box and whispered, "No, don't take it away. It is lovely."

"Do you think so?" he asked skeptically. "I chose the silver for your gray eyes and the black trim to match your hair. No, you are only being kind and would never have any desire to wear it," he said with renewed determination. "I shall return it. Please don't give it another thought."

Before she was aware what she was saying, Olivia firmly wrested the box from his slack grip and announced, "I shall put it on this very moment, Noah." She paused, horrified, and then purposefully stood, a grim resolution in her eyes. "I will only be a moment."

Chapter Fourteen

Olivia was gone a considerable time, and Noah spread the
coals so that there would be even less light in the room
before seating himself once more on the sofa. When a
quarter of an hour had passed and she did not return, he
gave a resigned shrug and started for the bedroom to
tell her that it was not necessary that she upset herself.
The door opened just before he reached it and he stepped
hurriedly back. Shivering with fear and embarrassment
more than the cold, Olivia entered the room with a
desperate wish to hunch her shoulders and bend over
double, but in actuality with a regal stature which froze
Noah. He kept his eyes on hers and said wonderingly,
"You . . . are stunning, Olivia. Come, you are cold. We
will sit by the fire." He shifted the sofa so that they
received the heat without too much of the light, and held
her lightly next to him. Because she was not able to meet
his eyes, she kept her head turned slightly, and he very
nearly betrayed his exquisite pleasure in seeing her alluring body by gasping.

Perhaps it was her youth, he marveled, that gave the
breasts such a pert tilt and the waist an amazing narrow-
ness. He had to call in all his reserves of will power not to
touch the firm thighs. "I should not have allowed you to
put it on," he apologized with unusual humility.

Olivia turned startled eyes to him. "Why not? I do
not please you?" Her voice cracked with emotion and she
felt like sobbing.

"Oh, dear God, never think that, my poppet! I have never seen a more beautiful body."

Her color heightened at this acknowledgement that he had studied her nearly naked form. "Then why should I not wear it?" she asked pitifully.

"Because I have maneuvered you into doing so, Olivia. Go and put on your dressing gown. Better still, go to bed. I will sleep in here tonight."

Exhausted by the emotional strains of the day and evening, Olivia put her head down and wept. Noah rocked her in his arms and whispered, "Forgive me, my little one. I should not have torn you about so. I told myself that I did it for your own good, but that is ridiculous. It was my pride I was protecting. Noah Lawrence was quite sure he could seduce his own wife on their wedding night. Do not cry, Olivia. We will take the necessary time to prepare you for such a step, only do not lose faith in me because of my strategies. I will be more frank with you in future, for I cannot bear to see you forced into such an upsetting position."

When her tears did not cease, and she seemed unable to speak or move, he lifted her and carried her into the bedroom where he placed her gently on the bed. He dipped a cloth in the basin of water and brought it to wipe her face tenderly. When her eyes opened, still moist with tears, he asked, "Can I get you something? A vinaigrette or a glass of water?" Silently she shook her head. Noah kissed her brow and stroked her black ringlets. "If you need anything, just call for me. I am a light sleeper." He rose wearily and pulled the covers over her, tucking them under her chin. "Forget all this nonsense and sleep well, Olivia."

Before he could leave she clutched at his hand and whispered, "I am being childish, aren't I, Noah? A grown woman would not be afraid, would she?"

"I doubt it has anything to do with age, Olivia, though it has a great deal to do with experience," he replied, his face serious as he crouched beside the bed. "I imagine a woman of most any age who has had as little contact with men—in the right context—as you have had would be afraid. It is difficult for me to understand your fear," he admitted, drawing a hand through his hair. "Men expect such experiences to be pleasurable. They have little modesty, perhaps rather the reverse." He gave a mirthless laugh and pressed her hand. "I had thought perhaps just being married would overcome a woman's natural shyness somewhat, but there is really no reason why it should."

"But someone older would go through with it all the same," she persisted.

Noah considered her statement for a moment. "Possibly. That would not necessarily make it the right thing to do. If you take such a step out of duty, hampered by fear, I imagine it is far more likely that those two burdens will remain with you. And I don't want that, Olivia. I *know* women can find it a pleasurable experience as well as men."

"Perhaps only certain women do."

"Don't fool yourself that 'bad' women enjoy it and 'good' ones don't, Olivia," he said shortly. "You are all given similar bodies, so the potential is there for each of you. If I deliberately swallowed food without tasting it, I would be denying myself a God-given sense to no purpose. To deny yourself the pleasure you can have during intimacy is no less absurd and unfair. That's enough talk, my dear. You should go to sleep."

Olivia's eyes indeed felt heavy with fatigue but she mumbled, "Do not sleep in the other room, Noah. Stay here with me, please."

"Very well, my dear." Noah discarded his dressing gown, climbed into the bed on the opposite side and drew the covers over him. Within minutes he could tell by her regular breathing that she was asleep and he disposed himself to do likewise, though he expected that it would be some time before he would accomplish that goal. The next thing he knew it was early morning with pale sunlight sifting through the chintz curtains. He turned to see Olivia huddled on the far side of the bed, not stirring.

Aware that she would be embarrassed to awaken in the sheer negligee with him to see her, he climbed out of bed and searched for her dressing gown, which he found carefully folded on a chair near the wardrobe. He quietly

127

placed it on the nightstand where she would see it first thing.

"Noah." He turned to see that her eyes were watching him, so he smiled and bid her good morning. "I hope you slept well, my dear. It is early, though, and there is no need for you to rise yet. I will be in the other room, and perhaps you will join me there later when you have dressed." A vague gesture toward the dressing gown concluded his remarks, and he bent down to place a fleeting kiss on her lips.

"Would you . . . stay here . . . with me for a while?" she asked hesitantly. "Unless you have something pressing to do, that is."

"Not a thing," he grinned as he sat down on the edge of the bed where she made room for him. "I would not even dare ring for Robert this early."

Olivia struggled to sit up in the bed and Noah hastily reached for her dressing gown, but she shook her head shyly. "It is chilly, though. Perhaps you could get a fire started."

It took him a moment to react to her suggestion, but then he jumped up abruptly and set about his task. Several minutes later there was a steady blaze and he glanced up to find that she was standing behind him warming herself. He drew two chairs in front of the fireplace, unable to think of anything to say. The gauze gown was completely transparent.

"Are you warm enough?" he asked after a while.

"Yes, the fire is toasty." Olivia sat curled up in the chair, but she made a valiant effort not to cover her breasts with her arms, as she longed to do. "There is no point in my going to this trouble for you, Noah, if you are going to stare at the fire."

He laughed and turned to her. "I did not wish to embarrass you, Olivia. Are you feeling so brave as to sit on my lap?"

"Almost," she retorted, her color heightened. After a moment she rose and gingerly joined him. He hugged her against him and started to kiss her. Olivia felt warm and comfortable in his embrace until his hands touched her breasts.

When she stiffened he asked casually, "Do you know why I touch your breasts, my dear?"

Surprised, she stammered, "I . . . suppose because you enjoy it."

A low chuckle rumbled through him. "Yes, I do, but mostly I touch you so that *you* can enjoy yourself. I cannot want you to be ashamed and embarrassed by your body. You should be proud of it, and familiar with it. I wonder why women are taught to ignore their bodies, except to attract men," he mused as he continued to fondle her. "There is something innately deceitful in that, don't you think? It is like luring a dog with a bone, and then not giving it to him, or giving him a stick instead. "You see," he confided, "men do not necessarily view a beautiful woman as a work of art, just as the dog does not view a bone in that light. Men tend to envision attractive women as partners in bed."

Olivia regarded him with fascination during this recital, never unaware of his hands, but distracted by the confidential manner in which he was delivering his lecture. "Are men then not interested in a woman's other qualities—her abilities as mistress of a home, or as a mother to their children, or as a companion with whom to have intelligent conversations?"

"Ah, there you have touched on an interesting point, Olivia. Certainly men are interested in those qualities, but if you wish for me to be frank with you I would have to say that the other thought comes first. It is usually discarded with old women and young girls, to be sure, and then one concentrates on other points of merit. But in the main the first thought will be of bed. You must not think too hardly on men for this aberation, Olivia. After all, there is the propagation of the species to be attended to," he philosophized.

"You are joking," she scolded him.

"No, certainly not," he protested. "Think about it a moment. Men are not lost to all sense of what is fitting, however. They are perfectly willing to bed women they would never contemplate taking to wife. That can be risky, as you may remember. No, what a man wants in a wife is another matter entirely, but it seldom stops short of wishing that she be desirable in bed. Now, let us consider the question of . . . No, that can wait for another time. I have promised to be more frank with you in our dealings, and I should like to point out to you that I have been talking to you in such a vein to calm your agitation, and to allow your body the freedom to respond, as it has."

"Yes," she whispered, "but how do you know?"

He explained to her, and continued, "I do not mean to embarrass you by speaking so, but only so that you will understand. The natural conclusion to such a state of arousal is mating; it is the object toward which the body aims. But," he went on in answer to her look of fright, "we shall not progress so far."

Although Olivia was relieved by his assurance, she found, paradoxically, that she was also just the least bit disappointed. When he kissed her she found herself responding in a wholly unprecedented manner, which appeared entirely satisfactory to him. His hands had continued to caress her, and her fear and longing were equal. Abruptly he stopped and murmured apologetically, "I cannot justify exciting you any further, Olivia, and frankly I cannot bear it. Put on your dressing gown and I will have breakfast sent up."

She gazed at him bewildered for a moment and then protested, "But what . . . will happen with my body?"

"In a few minutes it will relax, the excitement will fade. Don't be alarmed, little lady, it can be excited again," he teased as he lifted her from his lap.

Olivia flushed becomingly and murmured, "I certainly hope so," before drifting off to the stand where her dressing gown lay. Noah watched her wrap it about herself with a sigh; and when he could, he rose to ring for breakfast.

As they drove through the streets of Cambridge, Noah pointed out Trinity College and related a few amusing anecdotes, causing Olivia to comment, "You must have been happy here."

Startled, he glanced out the window. "I never thought about it much, but, yes, I suppose I was. My studies were not difficult, my friends were enjoyable and it was my first taste of real independence."

Once in the open countryside again, she was conscious of the two of them alone in the carriage and of his eyes on her. Nervously she folded her hands in her lap. "I like knowing where you spent your days at University."

"Why?"

"Because I want to know more about you. Really, you say very little about yourself."

"I am a private sort of person, Olivia." There was a subtle undertone to the statement, almost a stricture not to pry into his private life, and he saw her face cloud. Wishing to rid the air of any unnecessary restraint, he smiled and drew her to him. "On the other hand, I am an affectionate fellow, as I believe I have mentioned, and it has been at least an hour since I kissed you." He held her gently, kissing her lips and eyelids. "And I *think* you are very affectionate yourself."

Wonderingly she withdrew from his embrace. "I would not be at all surprised, Noah."

Chapter Fifteen

After dinner in their room at the Swan and Castle, Noah asked Olivia if she would like him to read to her a while and when she agreed he had her sit beside him so that he could put his arm around her shoulders. At first she listened to the story, but after a while she found herself studying his profile and wishing that he would stop.

He turned to regard her, a slight smile on his lips. "Would you like to change into your night clothes now?" When she nodded, he rose and set the book aside. "I will have Marie come to you."

Olivia allowed Marie to undress her and assist her into her nightdress and dressing gown, but when the maid had left she hurriedly changed into the silver and black negligee, covering it with the dressing gown once more, and seated herself by the fire to await Noah. He was not long in coming and extinguished the lights in the room before joining her near the fire.

"It has been another long day for you, Olivia. You must tell me if you wish to go to bed now."

"No, I . . . I would like to sit up with you for a while, Noah."

"Good."

"I have been thinking about some of the things you told me this morning."

"And?"

"Well, I wondered if what you said about men, and how they think of women, I wondered if maybe you thought that because it was true of you, and you merely assumed that other men felt the same way."

"I see. It is conceivable, but I would venture from the discussions I have had with men on the topic of women to believe that it is true of a vast number, and probably the majority of men."

"It does not bother you to feel that way?"

"No, how should it? It is not an obsessive thing, Olivia, but merely one of the first things to strike a man. We continue to play by the rules society has set down for us, so it can do no harm to think what we wish."

"Did you . . . think of me that way when we first met?"

He grinned. "Well, when we first met you fell into the class of young girls, my dear, and it took me a while to rid myself of that idea. Later, yes, I did. Perhaps I should explain that these are daydreams, fantasies, for the most part never acted on. But women dress attractively to gain a man's attention, and, like it or not, they get just that. I believe that is how our discussion of the matter started. Come and sit on my lap, Olivia. I was merely pointing out this morning that it is unjust for women to attract that attention, hold it through a period of time leading to marriage, and then expect that a man will not wish to act on it." She was seated on his lap and he proceeded to unfasten her dressing gown. When he saw that she was wearing the negligee he hugged her and said, "Thank you, my dear."

After he removed her dressing gown he set his aside as well, clad only in his nightshirt. "Do you think it is unfair that I should see your body and you cannot see mine?" he asked blandly.

"Oh, no," she murmured, horrified.

"I thought not," he said dryly. "Have you ever seen a man's naked body?"

"Never," she declared fervently. "I . . . I do not wish to, Noah."

He sighed. "I realize that, Olivia. Let it be for now." His stroking of her body had progressed slowly to her breasts. "When we return to Welling Towers I want you to consider redecorating your suite. Mother has retained it until now on my insistence, but she will have moved to a suite of rooms to the back of the house by the time we return. She showed you your rooms, did she not?"

"Yes, several weeks ago, but they are quite attractive now, Noah. There is really no need to refurbish them." The sensations she had felt that morning were again beginning to claim her and her words were slightly breathless.

"They are tasteful," he admitted, while he slipped the negligee over her arms and down to her waist, and she gave a shudder of apprehension, "but they are not in your style, I think." He touched her bare breasts for the first time unhampered by the gauzy fabric. "You do not mind, do you, Olivia?"

"N . . . no. I was only startled at first," she said softly. She watched numbly as he leaned to kiss each breast in turn, an urgent longing growing in her. "You do not think it would be wise to stop now?"

He straightened, surprised. "Are you not enjoying it, Olivia?"

"Very much," she admitted shyly.

"I see. You do not feel you wish to progress to the logical conclusion? You are still afraid of that?"

"Yes."

"Well, then we won't, but there is no need to stop now." He stroked her hair for a moment before again kissing her breasts. Then, with an almost casual movement, he lifted her and walked into the bedroom where he laid her on the bed and removed the negligee entirely. It was a moment before he extinguished the candle, and he noted her blush. His voice in the darkness was gentle. "It's only me, Olivia. Don't be embarrassed for your beautiful body." He climbed into the bed beside her and ran his hands loving over her breasts and down to her thighs. "You are a very dear person, with a special dignity of your own. Include your physical charms in that dignity, my treasure, for they are as much a part of you."

"My grandmother told me, just before she died, that I should take no thought to my body aside from my health; that I should concentrate on developing my mind."

"How old were you when she died?"

"Twelve."

Noah chuckled and touched her cheek tenderly. "Just beginning to develop into a woman, no doubt, with all the vigor of any healthy young animal. In a household full of young men and their friends, she probably thought to protect you. And the old have a way of forgetting how important our desires are to us when we are young. Did you like your grandmother?"

He had returned to caressing her and was giving such exquisite pleasure that for a moment she could not reply. "I . . . my grandmother? Well, I respected her, but I was a little afraid of her. Noah . . . oh . . . I . . . I am going to burst," she whispered fiercely.

"Yes, my dearest, it is like that."

"I'm not afraid anymore."

He searched the luminous eyes which beseeched him to release her, and brought her over the edge of pleasure, so that she was barely aware of the pain he caused on entering her. He held her for a long time afterwards, stroking her hair and kissing her eyelids. "You are a delight, Olivia."

They did not arrive at Frobess Grange until after darkness had fallen, but they were expected and Olivia was shown to a charming suite of rooms where she changed from her traveling outfit. The housekeeper had assured her that a meal would be served them shortly in the dining room and Marie assisted Olivia into one of her most becoming new gowns for the occasion.

Olivia made her way to the drawing room in the best of spirits only to find that Noah had not arrived there yet. She wandered to the harpsichord and sat down, to become immediately immersed in the madrigal she played. When the door opened she expected to see Noah enter, but it was the butler who announced, "Dinner may be served at any time, my lady."

"Please inform Sir Noah," she said evenly, though her confidence was shaken. Somehow it was awkward to be stranded alone in the drawing room when her husband should have been there with her. It was a small matter, she presently scolded herself; no doubt there was a reason for his delay.

The door opened again and Noah could be heard instructing the butler that they would dine directly. He strode over to her and took her hands in his. "Forgive me, my dear. There was a letter awaiting me which I felt should be answered immediately. You look charming. No doubt this is one of the gowns I reimbursed you for," he grinned.

Olivia had to make an effort to match his quizzing tone. "I thought you would prefer the hassock to an India print gown."

"You were right." He placed her hand on his arm to lead her to the dining room. "Roger instructed me that we are to treat his home as our own, so you must not hesitate to ask for anything you need. We will have him to Welling Towers sometime, with his sister and her husband. She is recently married and now lives in Suffolk; you have her rooms here. Roger is unmarried and assured me that the suite adjacent to the master suite is not currently fit for habitation. Never fear, though, Olivia. I will find your rooms." His eyes danced wickedly in the candlelight and he raised his glass in salute.

Olivia felt her cheeks color, hard as she tried to avoid it. There was no reason to be shy with him now when she had felt so relaxed that morning, she told herself, but she could not meet his eyes. "Whom did she marry, Noah?" she asked as she concentrated on cutting a bite of sturgeon.

"Lord Coweather. His seat is near Stowmarket, so they are not so very far from the Towers, but I never knew Margaret very well. She is Julianna's age, I believe, and rather a quiet woman. Coweather is a bit stiff-laced for a young man, but highly intelligent and active in the House. Roger simply kept bringing men here to visit until his sister met someone she liked, since she refused to go to London for the season. They seem remarkably well suited . . . as we are, my poppet."

Again Olivia felt unaccountably shaken by his attitude. Just as his remarks on their children had chilled her when they were first engaged, so his glib portrayal of their marital suitability disturbed her. Surely he did not give such incredible weight to their experience in bed that morning. Much as she had enjoyed it, and looked forward to further intimacy, Olivia felt that she had a great deal more to offer him than her body. And she wanted a great deal more from him than his.

"Are you feeling poorly, Olivia?" he asked with concern when she sat mute across the table for some time.

Startled, she raised her head and forced a smile. "I am fine; I was merely thinking."

"Shall you tell me your thoughts?" he coaxed with an engaging smile.

"Oh, no, they were not such as to interest you. This is a remarkably fine veal dish, is it not?"

Puzzled by her evasion, he agreed politely and allowed her to question him on his favorite dishes, and tell him of her brother Peter's accomplishments as a chef. He was distracted by her queries on the table kept by the Prince at Brighton, and was soon regaling her with escapades he had witnessed there.

When they had finished their meal she rose to leave him, but he protested that on their honeymoon surely he must be permitted to take his claret with her in the drawing room. "And perhaps you will play for me," he suggested hopefully.

Olivia was more than happy to have his company and to oblige him on the harpsichord. He soon joined her by the instrument and sang with her while turning the music. "I remember the first night we sang together," she remarked with a lamentable sigh.

"So do I. You and Julianna both drank more than you should have . . . and you thought the next morning that I had put you to bed." He lifted her hand to kiss it. "Shall I do so now?"

"I . . . it is early yet, Noah. I have been intrigued by how bright the moon is tonight. Could we walk in the gardens?"

"Certainly, if you would like that." He was determined to humor her, though it discouraged him that she was not as eager as he to repeat their morning's experience. With reluctance he rang for their outdoor wraps.

The evening was warm for spring; the moonlight bathed the yew hedges and rows of ghostly gray herbs with enough light to make walking amongst them a simple matter, and Olivia welcomed the exercise after being shut in a carriage for several days on end. She revelled in the sweet smells of new growth which filled the evening air.

"It's glorious simply to be outside again!" she exclaimed. "Not that your carriage is not the most luxurious I have ridden in, Noah, but all carriages are stuffy, don't you think?"

"Undoubtedly. Do you not wish to stay in the gardens?" He caught at her hand as she slipped on the stone stairs leading down to the lawn.

"No, I want to walk until my feet protest, until it is very late and the servants despair of our ever ringing for tea, until it is morning and I can gallop up those hills." She waved a hand at the black lumps against the lighter sky.

"I see you've been hiding from me the fact that you're daft, Olivia," he laughed, catching her enthusiasm. "We shall walk until your feet hurt or until I break my neck in the dark."

"I used to creep out of Stolenhurst on nights such as this. Of course, I knew every inch of the estate, so there was no harm likely to come to me. I doubt anyone even realized that I did so, except our coachman, and only he because I would often find him strolling around the grounds as well. He smoked an ancient pipe and told me how things were when he was but a stableboy at Stolenhurst."

"I don't believe I've met him."

"Peter turned him off," she replied bitterly. "It was not so hard on him as it might have been, for Lord Bouthy took him on immediately."

"Why did Peter turn him off?"

"My brothers took the carriage out one night for one of their . . . rampages and brought it back heavily damaged, with one of the horses so injured that he had to be destroyed. Crowther protested their treatment of the animals, which was not wise of him but certainly understandable in the circumstances. Peter lost his temper and turned him off without a reference, but Lord Bouthy did not let that deter him."

"When did this happen?"

"Perhaps half a year ago," she said sadly.

"And so you lost one of your friends. Why did your companion leave?" he asked curiously.

Olivia wrinkled her brow perplexedly. "She would not tell me, Noah, though she denied it had anything to do with the way my brothers plagued her. Nor did she believe tales of any misconduct on my part. I really cannot understand it."

"I hope you will write to her and offer any assistance she may need, Olivia. I doubt your brother would have thought to provide her with a reference."

"Thank you, Noah. I had planned to speak with you about it." Olivia turned to him gratefully. "It is thoughtful of you to concern yourself."

"I trust you will always rely on me in such matters of concern to you, Olivia." He pulled her into his arms and kissed her warmly. "Shall we put the servants out of suspense and go back to ring for tea?"

Olivia emerged from his embrace smiling. "I would be perfectly content to skip tea this once, Noah."

"Excellent." His eyes sparkled in the moonlight. "I find I have no desire for tea myself."

Chapter Sixteen

"Is it . . . usual for husbands and wives to . . . go to bed so often as we do?" Olivia curiously asked her husband several weeks later when they lay together in the mammoth four-poster at Frobess Grange.

"Does it matter?" he murmured, on the edge of sleep.

"No, of course not," she sighed.

Noah tentatively opened his eyes to survey her enquiring face. "I do not suppose it is, Olivia. That is, not once thay have been married for a while. I thought you were as interested as I." There was a questioning note in his voice, and his eyes were serious.

"Well, I am," she admitted reluctantly, "but it seems so incredibly self-indulgent."

"We are on our honeymoon; we are supposed to be self-indulgent," he laughed and rumpled her hair. "I doubt we will have such a luxury of time when we return to the Towers. Now we have nothing to do but amuse ourselves exactly as we see fit."

Olivia nodded and allowed him to fall asleep, his arm about her waist. There was certainly truth in what he said—both that they had the time to indulge themselves now, and that they would not have so much time when they returned to Welling Towers. It seemed ridiculous to worry, when he was with her constantly, about their return home. He had proved to be the affectionate man he had told her he was. She had found herself completely immersed in their physical intimacies, but she had a gnawing doubt that such a situation could continue.

Olivia had become dependent upon his attention, his affection; in fact, she thought with almost a sob, she had come to love him. And it would not do to love him, for although he exhibited a fondness, and a physical desire, for her, she could not feel that he returned a similar regard. There was still that measure of reserve about him which alarmed her. Much as he spoke, a casual wide-ranging conversation, he seldom spoke of himself or how he felt about things. He rarely told her the sort of stories she wanted to share with him of her childhood, her hopes and her fears. His topics were impersonal, almost always light-hearted and amusing. And although he appeared fascinated by her own revelations, which was consoling; it was disturbing to offer him everything she was, her innermost self, and have him offer her only what she could see before her. It was impossible for her *not* to give him what she could, she thought despairingly; it was the nature of her love.

Still, there was plenty of time for her to be alone with him and to get to know him better. When they returned home his mother and sister would have left for London for several months. Perhaps when he saw her, as his wife, in the setting where he had been raised, he would be more forthcoming. When they rode about the estate and visited tenants, when she had the ordering of the domestic affairs for his comfort, perhaps then he would put more value on her than he did now. She would seem more a wife than a . . . mistress then, a partner in more than bed. With this comforting thought Olivia fell asleep.

For Noah the honeymoon was pure delight; it was their return to Welling Towers that he viewed with apprehension. He became more withdrawn the closer they came to his home, Olivia more talkative. There had seemed no appropriate time to tell her that he expected a letter, possibly calling him away, when they reached the Towers. He listened to her enthusiastic plans and felt a moment's hesitation. It was unfair to leave her alone, completely alone, when they were so newly wed. His mother and sister would not likely return for more than two months. But if he had to leave, it would be an urgent project, and for his country, he reminded himself grimly. This marriage had been a necessity and should not distract him from his duty, no matter how felicitous his honeymoon had proved.

Immediately upon their return to Welling Towers Olivia was taken to her new suite by the housekeeper and found no sign of Lady Lawrence's recent occupation of the rooms. Rather they were obviously hers now with her own belongings carefully placed about on dressing table and bedside stand. The interconnecting door to the master suite, which had not been used in years, was now opened to her summons and Noah entered.

"They have put spring flowers here for me." She gestured to the daffodils and polyanthuses. Then, without looking at him, she continued, "Noah, I have never seen your rooms, and I wonder if you would be interested in showing them to me."

Noah tucked the letter he had brought with him into a pocket and took hold of her hand. "Of course I would, my poppet. My dressing room leads directly into your room, but my *bedroom* is just beyond." He explained the origin of several items of furniture, including the graciously carved half-tester bed with its burgundy velvet curtains and white counterpane, before showing her into the sitting room with its shelves of books and comfortable leather chairs. She was surprised when he asked her to sit down.

He remained standing, rather nervously fingering the letter which he had withdrawn from his pocket. "You may remember that I spoke of an urgent letter I received the day we arrived at Frobess Grange, Olivia." When she nodded, he arranged his face in solemn lines to indicate the seriousness of the matter to her and to hide his own misgivings. "I am in receipt of another letter today indicating that the business is most pressing, and that I should post to London directly."

Olivia could not easily mask the distress she felt at the shattering of her plans. With a supreme effort, she said calmly, "I see. Do you expect to be gone long, Noah?"

"It is hard to say, my dear; but yes, I cannot think it will be a short stay away from home." The expression in her eyes was not anger, and it was more than disappointment. Noah knew that his wife was hurt by his abrupt announcement and he hastily strode to her side to place a protective hand on her shoulder. "I truly do not wish to leave you, Olivia, and I would not if it could be avoided. If only Mother and Julianna were not in London. Could you write to your former companion and ask her to stay with you until they return?"

"Yes, I will try that," she replied with forced cheerfulness. "You must not give a thought to me, Noah, for I shall be quite comfortable here. I have a great deal to learn and I shall spend the time acquainting myself with my duties here."

"I don't want you spending all your time working. There are several neighbors you can visit—though many will have gone to town, of course. The weather is likely to hold good, and you will enjoy your rides, I know. And the library should provide you with whatever reading material you may require."

"I am perfectly accustomed to entertaining myself."

Although she had not meant it as a rebuke, Noah felt sensitive enough about his desertion that he took it as one. "You need not remind me that you were left alone at Stolenhurst frequently, Olivia. I am well aware of it and regret that I should be forced to go away so soon."

"I accept that your mission is important; you need not apologize. I cannot remember uttering a word of censure."

"I would take you to London, but I think there is not enough time passed as yet to make you feel comfortable there."

"I do not wish to go to London in any case, Noah."

"Mother and Julianna would provide companionship for you."

"I'm sure that is true but I have indicated that I do not wish to go, and you have said that you do not think I

143

should, so what is the point in discussing it?" Olivia shifted in her seat, aware that she had not exerted the proper control over her tone, which had sounded distressingly edgy.

Noah eyed her warily and spoke thoughtlessly out of his own agitation. "I hope you are not going to give a display of temper, Olivia."

Cheeks bright with anger, she rose from her chair and said coldly, "Certainly not, my dear sir. If you will excuse me, I should like to dress for dinner." She did not wait for his reply but glided out of the sitting room, through the bedroom and dressing room, where she closed the door with a decided snap. Noah watched her departure with a mixture of self-righteous anger and self-pitying chagrin. He made no attempt to follow her but threw himself into the chair Olivia had just vacated and silently cursed the circumstances which made it necessary for him to leave. That they had had their first quarrel since they were wed, and only once they returned to their home, filled him with foreboding.

A conspicuously silent meal followed their disagreement, and Noah allowed Olivia to withdraw while he sat on in the dining room. When he joined her later, she was seated at the harpsichord, fingering a haunting country tune. "I plan to leave early in the morning."

She nodded and continued to play.

"I should retire now if I am to be on the road in good time."

Again she nodded, though her fingers hesitated on the keys.

"There is no need for you to do likewise, of course," he announced with some asperity. "I am sure you would rather continue your playing."

Olivia lifted afflicted eyes to his and dropped her hands into her lap. "Would you like for me to come to bed now, Noah?"

"There is no need." He walked over to the bench where she sat and placed a chaste kiss on her cheek. "I doubt you will be up when I leave, so I will bid you good-night and farewell."

With bowed head Olivia whispered, "God-speed, Noah."

He turned on his heel and strode from the room, leaving her to stare vacantly into space. For some time she argued that the disagreement was his fault and he should apologize. After a while, however, she considered the possibility that she had not been entirely blameless. Still later it did not seem to matter which of them was at fault, for she could not bear the thought of his leaving her when they had spoken hasty words to one another. It could well be a long time before she saw him again, and she did not wish him to harbor a grudge against her which might turn him sour on their marriage.

Olivia rose and went to the desk where she drew forth paper, ink and pen. The wording of the note must be careful so as not to indicate that she felt him in error, and yet not so abject an apology on her part as to make him believe that he could twist her about his thumb. She crumpled two sheets before the message struck her as having the proper wording, and at the last she jotted a request that he awaken her in the morning so that she might have breakfast with him.

Unwilling to entrust the note to a servant, she bore it to his room herself with every intent of hastily slipping it under the door. She could hear no sound within and a sudden panic seized her that he would miss the note and never know that she had tried to make amends. Cautiously she turned the knob and stepped into the darkened room. He would leave his purse on the nightstand as he had at Frobess Grange, and if she put the note there he could not fail to see it.

Her eyes grew accustomed to the dark after a minute and she walked purposefully to the nightstand and quickly propped the note against the silver candlestick. As she turned to go her wrist was caught in a firm grip and she gasped in surprise.

"What have you put there, Olivia?" he asked softly.

"I . . . I wished to apologize, Noah, and to ask that you wake me in the morning so that I might take breakfast with you."

He pulled her down to sit on the edge of the bed. "It is I who should beg your pardon, my dear. I have been lying awake listening for you to come to your room that I might do so."

Olivia spoke over the lump in her throat. "I could not bear for you to leave when we were at outs, Noah. If I offended you, I did not mean to."

"Hush, dearest. Let us forget the matter." His fingers traced the line of her jaw and neck, touched the breasts under the satin gown. "Would you stay here with me tonight?"

"Of course, Noah. Let me send Marie to bed."

She returned shortly in the negligee and dressing gown which he had purchased for her in Gloucester. Her need of him had never been greater, and she clung to him when they were spent and whispered, "I will miss you, Noah."

"And I you. Rest assured I will be away no longer than necessary. If any problems should arise that you cannot handle with the help of the staff, you have only to contact Mother."

Puzzled, she asked, "Will you not be in London then?"

"Only for a short while, I imagine. My business will carry me out of town for the most part."

"I see. Yes, I will contact your mother should any emergency arise. Will you write to me, Noah?"

"When I can, my dear, but it will not always be possible," he said, trying not to sound evasive.

"Of course."

In the morning she attempted to present a cheerful front to him, but in his abstraction she was not sure if he really noticed. Noah had determined the previous evening, when he knew by her regular breathing that she was asleep, that he must put aside his doubts and concentrate on quickly and efficiently performing the task before him. There was no changing his mind now, and Olivia would be perfectly content at Welling Towers. Had she not told him that she was fond of the place? He thrust from him the disheartening knowledge that she would have no companion, and urged once again that she invite Miss Stewart to visit.

Olivia forced herself to regard his attitude as solicitous and not callous. She watched with a sinking heart from the drawing room window while the carriage pulled away. Assuredly there was much which could be done to occupy her time at Welling Towers, but that was all she would be doing—occupying her time—until he returned. There would not even be his letters to look forward to, she feared, for he had sounded discouragingly vague about any correspondence. With a sigh, she picked up the tambour frame and set a stitch.

Mr. Thomas welcomed Noah to a quiet corner of the Star and Garter the evening of his arrival in town. "I appreciate your coming so soon, Sir Noah. As I mentioned in my letters, it is no longer simply a question of sounding the views of the populace in France. We have a serious and urgent problem! The dispatches I mentioned have undoubtedly fallen into the wrong hands, though quite by accident. We would not consider sending you, a recently married man, except for your friendship with the Comte de Mauppard. I wrote to him as you suggested, and he instigated some enquiries which were more effective than those we had launched ourselves. As propaganda against the English in aid of renewed violence, the dispatches would be superbly useful; but as a method of blackmail, they are a lucrative venture."

Mr. Thomas frowned thoughtfully. "If I am not mistaken, they intend to use them for both. You see, we have already paid a price for them in a cloak-and-dagger exchange which yielded us only copies of the documents. The originals are still in the same hands as before."

"What sort of information did they contain?" Noah asked curiously.

"They cover a number of points, all of which could be damaging if used cleverly. The emigration of various noble families is discussed with offers of assistance from highly placed Englishmen. Our own government's views on the state of affairs in France might," the bland-faced man suggested, "be misconstrued as an active proposal for English interference in their domestic matters. Also, there was some reference to English sympathizers with the more radical elements."

"And you think I have some means of ferreting out the dispatches?"

"Frankly, I don't know. The Comte de Mauppard has been of great assistance to us in this matter, but he cannot align himself with English interests. Because of your friendship, you may be able to pursue the matter further. At any time the dispatches could be made public knowledge. In such an inflammable environment it would not take much to promote an irreparable breach between the two countries." He gave a helpless shrug. "There may be nothing you can do, Sir Noah, but we hate to make no effort at all. War between England and France is too common, and it may be inevitable if the progress of this revolution is drastic. We ask only, if you find yourself in a position to assist, that you visit your friend and learn what you can."

"I feel sure I can be spared for a while."

"Excellent. There is some need for secrecy. It is not generally known that the dispatches have gone astray, and we would prefer to keep the matter as close as possible. You may not be able to avoid meeting acquaintances in France; perhaps you could hint at some business negotiations there."

"If I have to. The journey may be short enough that I will not have to account for my whereabouts. In London it will be assumed that I am at Welling Towers with my wife."

When Noah left the Star and Garter he headed for his lodgings with a cetain buoyancy of spirits. Five years previously he had undertaken a discreet mission for the government which had led him to Italy, and he remembered with amusement the tangle of adventures, both political and amorous, which had beset him. By the time he reached his destination, however, his responsibility to his young bride weighed on him. The inability to explain his journey to France to either Olivia or his mother was exasperating. Certainly his mother would not be convinced by tales of business interests there, so it was better that she should not know of his plans. Optimistically, Noah allowed that the whole venture need only occupy a matter of weeks.

Chapter Seventeen

"Dear Miss Stewart, I am so glad you could come to stay with me. And you are wearing your hair differently. You look enchanting." Olivia hugged her former companion to her as she stepped off the Cromer-bound coach in Thetford. "James Coachman will see to your luggage. It is but half an hour's drive to the Towers, and there is not the least hurry if you would care to stop for some refreshment here."

"Thank you, no, I would rather have the journey completed. I am not the best of travelers, I fear." Miss Stewart allowed herself to be led to the carriage by her eager young hostess, who studied her inconspicuously. The silver-blonde hair was no longer drawn back severely, but worn most flatteringly about her delicately-featured face; and there was an openness about her countenance which Olivia did not remember in her shy companion.

When they were seated on the comfortable squabs away from the noise of the inn yard, Olivia sighed. "I could not believe my good fortune when I received your letter saying you were free. I had visions of you in some ducal seat instructing pretty-behaved young ladies in their maps and French. Did Peter neglect to send you a letter of reference? You must think me the shabbiest shatterbrain for leaving you without. So much has happened since you left Stolenhurst. You must let me make it up to you."

"I had no intention of seeking another post as governess or companion," Miss Stewart replied quietly. "My father had gone to great expense for my education, and when he suffered some reverses years ago, he thought it would be fitting for me to be a governess if I must need earn a living. It was not a wise choice, and I fear I did not do well by you, Lady Olivia."

"You must call me Olivia. You and I shall have the run of the Towers with not a soul to condemn such familiarity," Olivia laughed. "And I have not a thing to complain of in your kind companionship. Imagine what a treat it was for me to have someone as young as yourself to be my instructress."

The carriage started with a jolt and Olivia began to point out the sights to her friend as they progressed—the Castle Hill with its earthworks and the various priory ruins. "Noah took Julianna and me exploring several times before the wedding and I had hoped to visit the Dominican Friary again when we returned from our wedding trip."

"It's a great pity that your husband should have to leave you so soon," Miss Stewart sympathized, "and that his mother and sister are in London."

"Indeed." Olivia could not manage to suppress the sigh which came, but she smiled with forced cheerfulness. "I am attempting to redecorate my suite before any of them return. Shall you find it amusing to assist me in the choice of materials and colors?"

"I confess that of all things I find such a task the most rewarding. My father has been a linen draper and an upholsterer for many years. As a child he taught me about fabrics, how they would wear, which were the most costly, and which faded easily in the sunlight. Not that it did me the least good, you understand, for he would never let me assist in his work. Still, I believe my knowledge may be of use to you."

There was a confidence and an ease about Miss Stewart's conversation which Olivia found puzzling, if vastly superior to her former shyness. Perhaps it had taken no more than a removal from Stolenhurst, with the unwelcome attentions of the Fullerton brothers, for the woman to blossom; but it was scarcely to be credited, since they had frequently been away from home. "I feel sure you will be the greatest help to me, dear Miss Stewart, and a most welcome companion. You did not, I suppose, see any of my family in London?"

"Oh, no, for we do not live in a fashionable part of town. I understand Lord Bolenham is to marry Lady Elizabeth Blake this summer."

"If he can bring himself to the sticking point," she murmured. "My mother-in-law writes that he becomes more irritable as his marriage approaches, and Noah wrote that the settlements were not complete yet due to the tug of war between Peter and Lady Elizabeth's father." Her one letter from Noah, a brief, affectionate scribbling really, she kept with her at all times and knew by heart. He had said he would be in town only a few days and not to expect to hear from him for some time. And Lady Lawrence had had no more to add; her subsequent letters indicated that she was annoyed with her son for leaving his bride alone so soon after their marriage, but Noah was not in London and his mother appeared to have no idea where he had gone. Olivia put aside from herself, as she had many times before, the vexing question of why it had been necessary for him to leave her and where he had gone.

* * *

Paris itself showed little outward change from Noah's visit of the preceding year, but his friend Mauppard had developed grave lines on his previously youthful countenance.

The Comte raised bushy black brows. "You have come about the dispatches? I would have thought being burned once was enough. Your government wasted several thousand pounds recovering forged documents."

"Yes, a shame. Have you any suggestions?"

Mauppard pursed his lips thoughtfully. "The conviction has grown in me that the man who holds them is well educated. His letter proposing the original exchange, though attempting to disguise the fact, was not entirely successful."

"Do you think they will be used as anti-English propaganda?"

"This is not a propitious time for France to declare war on England, my friend. But holding such documents could be a future security for, say, a radical group, who intimated that they have the means of proving English interference." His discussion was interrupted by the advent of his sister Françoise, a statuesque goddess with golden brown hair and intriguing blue eyes.

"Ah, Sir Noah, thank God you have come! Perhaps *you* can convince Jacques to go about a bit more. He is become very dull, you know, with his politics. No balls and parties, no dancing and singing, just talk, talk, talk. Shall the Church administer property? Is Mirabeau in the pay of the King? Can the Marquis de la Fayette organize a government?"

"Enough, Françoise," the comte said sharply. "What you hear, you do not repeat, else I shall send you into the country. Noah is my friend, and I have few secrets from him; but there are others whose discretion I cannot trust."

"There are those who do not trust *you*," she retorted. "Daily more people cut me on the street just for being your sister."

Her brother shrugged. "It is unavoidable. Those who will not see that the times are changed will not help themselves. You will have to accustom yourself to such slights."

"Never!" she declared hotly and stomped from the room.

Mauppard offered Noah an apologetic smile. "It is hard for her. May I get you a brandy? Tomorrow I will take you about with me to see what you can learn, but for tonight let us leave off such serious talk. Tell me about your bride."

*   *   *

The early May sunlight filtered through the draperies and made it impossible for Olivia to determine the color of the fabric which lay newly-unwrapped on the bureau. When she had swept back the draperies and studied the material, an edge of irritation crept into her voice. "It is *not* the color I ordered. I want my bedchamber to be like a breath of spring with bright yellows like daffodils. Have you ever seen such a sickly color? There is green in it, and it will not match anything else."

Miss Stewart examined the offending fabric and agreed. "Certainly it is not at all the color of the sample. Would you like me to return it, Olivia? I think perhaps you should have a rest, and I have several errands I might do in the village."

"I am perfectly well, I assure you, and will see to its return myself. How many days have I waited for it? Ten? And now I suppose I shall have to wait another two weeks for the right color. As if the damaged chaise longue were not enough! And that silly maid knocking over my embroidery threads so that they were a tangle. We will never finish the room before . . . Lady Lawrence returns."

"But, my dear, that is more than a month away. Don't fret. Long before then everything will be perfect, see if it isn't." Miss Stewart regarded her friend curiously. "It is not like you to let such little things upset you, Olivia. We have been indoors too much. Today we should take a long walk in the park."

Before Olivia could reply, there was a tap at the door and Marie entered to present the mail. Eagerly Olivia lifted the two letters One was from Lady Lawrence, the other was for Miss Stewart. She very nearly stamped her foot in her annoyance. Why did he not write? Where was he? It was *weeks* since his only letter, which was already coming apart at the creases, and she had been forced to leave it in the jewelry box so that it did not disintegrate altogether.

Miss Stewart's letter was from her "particular friend." No more information would she divulge on the writer, and Olivia felt all the curiosity Julianna could ever have exhibited. On each occasion when one of these letters arrived, Miss Stewart excused herself and went to her room to read it, only to return with a quiet glow of pleasure about her. And each day when one of these letters arrived, which happened several times a week, Olivia felt a stab of envy. There was no doubt in her mind that Miss Stewart's correspondent was a man and that he was the cause of her companion's blossoming.

"Won't you read your letter here today? Is your friend still traveling?"

Although Miss Stewart would have preferred to go off alone with her treasured letter, she agreed to remain, aware of Olivia's own disappointment and nervousness. Later she could reread it and cherish every word, but now she quickly broke the seal and scanned the lines for any information she could impart.

"My friend has been in Yorkshire, but must travel to Shropshire before returning to London." With a flush she skipped the tender (though proper) phrases he had written. "Everything is a burst of color in the East Riding and my friend has visited the Beverly Minster. But I must not keep you from Lady Lawrence's letter."

Aware that she was unlikely to learn anything further, Olivia opened her own missive and devoured the voluminous news her correspondent always sent. There was no mention of Noah.

"Is your mother-in-law well?"

"In excellent health, I should say, and as active as ever with her scathing pen. I am advised that Lady Elizabeth has taken to using rouge with disastrous effect and that Peter is the talk of town with his theatre parties and ridiculous clubs." She referred to the letter and read, " 'His latest club has such rules as that there may be no more members admitted into the room than it will hold; that every member with two ideas shall be obliged to give one to his neighbor; and that if any member has more sense than another he be kicked out of the club!' " She set the letter aside with a shrug. "I do wonder that people put up with Peter."

"I dare say he is generous with his friends."

"No doubt too generous." Olivia stared moodily at the fabric on the bureau. "If Peter received the wrong materials, he would not bother to return it; he would give it away. He would not bother to pay for it either, of course."

"If you would be interested in my staying an additional week or two, Olivia, I would find it possible."

Olivia brightened. "You know I would be delighted.

155

Then I may not be alone before Lady Lawrence and Julianna return."

"Shall we take a walk now?"

"Yes," her companion replied, pushing the fabric back into its wrapping. "And I shall write my mother-in-law when I return. I dare say there is no hurry in finishing the room." For God only knows when Noah will return, she thought, and when I shall be able to tell him that I am with child.

*　　*　　*

Day followed unsuccessful day with Noah searching in vain for a lead. Even Mauppard's contacts proved of no use. The beautiful but spoiled Françoise, tired of her brother's associates, continued to press for livelier entertainment. When she found Noah alone at breakfast one morning she immediately launched into an attack.

"One week from today is the ball of the Franchauds, Sir Noah. Surely you must wish to attend such a grand occasion! And Jacques must come, too. They are laughing at him—and at me! Me! I tell you I have been the most sought after lady in society, and they dare to laugh at me." She tossed the golden brown hair and her eyes flashed with spite. "I will show them, but you must convince Jacques to attend the ball."

Annoyed with her conceit and vindictiveness, Noah was nonetheless unwilling to thwart her plans. The gathering would provide a new opportunity for his discreet enquiries. "I will speak with Jacques."

There was an air of frantic indulgence at the ball, an intensity and self-consciousness which amounted to an almost hysterical pursuit of pleasure. Françoise, magnificent in a rose-colored, hand-painted silk gown which fell from her bosom in clinging lines and exhibited an alarming amount of décolletage, was, as she had predicted, soon surrounded by an admiring circle. To his amusement, Noah found himself being used by her to bring to heel a handsome, older nobleman, the Vicomte de Preslin.

On being solicited by him for her hand in one of the long, formal sets of dances, Françoise fluttered her fan demurely. "I should love to, Vicomte, but Sir Noah is so persistently at my side that I hardly dare desert him. These Englishmen are fiercely intense in their devotion, you know, and have little regard for our conventions."

The vicomte, a man well into his forties, with a cold, proud face, surveyed Noah with contemptuous eyes. "The English have little regard for *any* conventions, if you will excuse my saying so, Sir Noah. Tradition was, I believe, a French word long before it was adapted by your country, and incorrectly at that. It is *traditional* in France for a young lady to accept a dance with whom she pleases, unhampered by the thought of causing anyone distress."

Piqued, but formally polite, Noah protested, "I had no intention of deterring her, I assure you." He watched as they joined the dance, Françoise glowing with triumph, the vicomte gravely attentive to her loose-tongued chatter. No need to let the incident discompose him, he decided, with an attempt to shrug off the irritation he felt with both of them, but he was immediately accosted by someone who caused an equal amount of concern. An aged friend of his mother's who was returning from Italy to England by way of Paris approached him.

"I understand you are recently married, Sir Noah," she remarked, her eyes brightly inquisitive.

Noah smiled disarmingly and replied, "Indeed, Mrs. Beaglett. Lady Olivia and I were wed in March at Welling Towers and regretted that you were out of the country and unable to attend."

"I missed a number of interesting occurrences this winter," the old lady said sadly. "No doubt I shall find your mother and your bride in London next week when I return there."

"My mother, yes, but Lady Olivia is at Welling Towers. She wished to stay there while I was away on business."

"Business brings you to Paris, Sir Noah?"

"Yes, a small matter. I doubt I shall be here long." Although he managed to turn the subject, Noah was grateful when Françoise appeared at his elbow to insist that he meet one of her cousins. He turned to Mrs.

Beaglett apologetically. "If you will excuse me, ma'am. I trust you will have a safe and pleasant journey to London."

It was the devil of a nuisance, for now he would be forced to write his mother to forestall her inevitable astonishment on being informed of his presence in France. He would have to write to Olivia, too, he thought, with a measure of apprehension, and she was not likely to understand how he could have wandered so far from his home without advising her. It was all very well that he knew his mission was necessary; there was no way of indicating that to Olivia. Annoyance at the untenability of his position, and his lack of success, swept over him, and it unfortunately crept into his note when he wrote to his wife.

Chapter Eighteen

Time hung heavily on Olivia's hands. The decoration of her suite was complete, and she had turned to other areas of the house for inspiration. While they watched the removal of a chair which she particularly loathed, Miss Stewart asked hesitantly, "You do not fear that your mother-in-law will object to any of the changes?"

Olivia grinned. "Not Lady Lawrence. She will be graciously approving when first she sees them and in time will actually come to like them, I think. Noah probably will not notice particularly, and Julianna will confide to me that she has longed to be rid of that chair for years. Besides," she continued with a slight lift of her chin, "I am now in charge of the domestic matters here."

"Yes, of course." Miss Stewart bent to her sewing and did not meet her friend's eyes.

"Oh, you know it is not like that! I am . . . restless." Olivia had intended to say bored, but thought it unkind to speak so when she had Miss Stewart's companionship. "You have been the greatest help to me in making these changes, and I would be foolish beyond permission not to take advantage of your expertise while you are here."

Miss Stewart laughed. "You cannot bamboozle me, Olivia. Your taste is excellent and I have had very little to do with the outcome. I would caution you, though, on the expense you are incurring."

"Noah said I was to redecorate my suite."

"Yes, but he had no thought of your replacing a

chair here, and a sofa there, with new draperies for the Summer Parlor." Miss Stewart studied Olivia's set face skeptically. "Had it occurred to you that it is boredom and . . . restlessness which often lead your brothers to their extravagances? It begins so simply with no real intent of harm. One day there is nothing to do and you notice that the paint is scratched on the phaeton. Well, there is nothing for it but to buy a new one.

"At least one whole day can be whiled away inspecting the various coaches for sale, or, better yet, having one built to your own specifications. Now that will occupy you for even longer, and who cares for the extra expense? No, the standard seats will not do, and the wood for the splinter bar should be stronger. Ah, yes, and you will have the very latest springs and the harness should be specially ornamented perhaps. Now, if you were to go over to Norwich you might find a better designed side lamp. Pretty soon you are making special orders to the wheelwright, the smith, the painter, the liner, and the trimmer, in addition to the lamp and harness makers. And then, with a brand new phaeton, it seems only right to look for a more perfectly matched pair of bays or chestnuts!"

"Oh, stop, stop," Olivia giggled. "I see what you are saying, and of course you are perfectly right. We shall find more things to do that are not an unnecessary expense. But *not*, I think, a visit to the Pugh grandmother or Mrs. Trambor. Even Lorraine Pugh's company pales on one after a visit or two. She seems so young and flighty, don't you think?"

"She will grow out of it in time, I dare say," Miss Stewart replied unconvincingly.

"Perhaps." Olivia lost interest in the subject and said sadly, "I should so like to hear from Noah. It is vexing not to be able to write to him, for I have some news to impart." She unconsciously touched her belly and Miss Stewart pretended not to notice.

"Well, his business is no doubt very pressing," Miss Stewart consoled her. She kept her eyes fixed on her stitching as she said, "You find married life agreeable, I expect, even though he is not here."

"I don't feel married at all when he isn't here," Olivia muttered with asperity. "I might as well be at Stolenhurst."

"Now, Olivia, you cannot mean that! Here you are truly the mistress of your own home."

Olivia gazed out over the park and around to the lake. "Yes, and I do love it here. Shall we take a hamper down to the lake and toss bread to the swans?"

In an attempt to heed her companion's advice, Olivia sought other outlets for her disquiet than the luxury of replacing serviceable pieces about the house. She made her letters to Lady Lawrence longer with descriptions of her activities, the status of the housekeeper's boil and news of the village. But each time she wrote she was reminded that she was unable to write to her husband, and she had no wish to tell Lady Lawrence her special news by post. In fact, she had no wish to tell her mother-in-law at all until she had told Noah.

Strolling into the stables one day she was reminded of Miss Stewart's treatise on phaeton building. She had long had a desire to learn to drive one, but her brothers would not accommodate her wish. Before the wedding Julianna had frequently let her tool the gig along the lanes when they were returning from the village, but she had never had two horses in hand. The phaeton at the Towers was of the high-perch type with its seat hung over the four-foot front wheels. When Olivia surveyed it she was alarmed by the height of the driving seat.

"T'aint so bad as it looks, m'lady," the coachman assured her with a grin. "Have a mind to try your hand at it, do you?"

"I've never had two in hand, James. Do you think you could teach me?"

"I reckon so. More than once I've seen you handle the gig, and you've a nice touch. If I was to harness up that sweet-tempered pair Sir Noah bought last summer, I doubt you'd have the least problem."

Olivia's eyes sparkled with real enthusiasm. "Then I shall do it right now . . . if you can spare the time."

"Not much happening here these days, m'lady." He regarded her acknowledging nod sympathetically. "Won't be long now before I go to London for Lady Lawrence and Miss Julianna." He was careful to make no mention of Sir Noah, though he was as curious as the rest of the staff as to what could have taken that gentleman away from his bride.

While she waited for him to harness the horses to the phaeton, Olivia perched on the top of the fence. June. It was already June with the bees humming in the clover and the sun burning down on the bright green grass. And where was Noah that he could not write? He was not in London. His mother's letters made no mention of him, though her disapproval was so patent that it reeked from between every line. Lady Lawrence was apparently also displeased that Julianna was seeing more of Alexander Cutler than she could approve, but Julianna's postscripts and occasional notes were full of him, and the delightful balls she attended where the ladies sighed over "her" Alexander.

Olivia absently brushed a fly from her forehead and watched the harnessing of the horses without attention. What possible excuse could Noah have for being away so long? Everything would be all right if he would only write. She allowed the coachman to hand her up onto the seat, her fear of the height forgotten. Noah would be surprised and pleased to learn that she had interested herself in driving . . . when he could be told of it.

For several days she applied herself assiduously to her new lessons, thinking them one small way in which she might gain her husband's interest when he returned. On her first excursion through the village she very nearly ran down the parish beadle, and she could see no reason for James' inordinate amusement at the incident.

"But m'lady, his expression! Then, too, him almost coming to blows with the inn signpost on the green when he backed into it to get out of your way."

"Well, I suppose it was funny," she conceded with a lurking smile, "but it is no recommendation for my driving."

"Don't you worry none, ma'am. You're doing right well, all considered. Why, I remember the first time Sir Noah had two in hand as a lad. Very nearly ran over a post he did, and with his father all red in the face from exasperation. And do you know what the lad said? All cross he was and says he, 'It is no place for a post, Father. Could we not have it removed?' Couldn't 'ave been more'n five or six at the time, I dare say."

"He hasn't changed," Olivia muttered, and returned her attention to her driving.

Hot, and slightly disheveled from her lesson, she entered the house for the first time with no thought of a letter from her husband, so intent was she on seeking the coolness of the interior. Miss Stewart, beaming angelically, hastened to her in the hall and murmured, "There is a letter for you, my dear."

Thrusting her gloves and hat on the table before the servant could reach her, she said breathlessly, "From Noah?"

"The housekeeper said it is surely his writing. The tray is in the Summer Parlor." Miss Stewart watched indulgently while her former charge, oblivious to any eyes on her, rushed down the hall with less than her usual grace. She would leave Olivia alone for a while to savor her letter in peace.

The new blue draperies in the Summer Parlor were drawn against the heat of the day, but Olivia immediately recognized the French origination of the letter and froze. What the devil was he doing in France? Nervously she broke the seal and perused the contents of the concise message—he was well, in France on business, and could not tell when he would be returning to Welling Towers. He offered her no return direction and only vague assurances of his affection.

After an absence of close to two months he has nothing to say to me, she thought bitterly, as she tossed the letter from her and angrily pulled at the bell cord. Frolicking about in Paris, no doubt, and proving that one need not be tied down by marriage. When the servant appeared, Olivia ordered lemonade for two and sent an invitation for Miss Stewart to join her. By the time her companion appeared, she had schooled her face to a semblance of calm, but her distress continued to seethe in her mind.

163

"How delightful that you have heard from Sir Noah," her companion said with a gentle smile.

"Yes, he has journeyed to France on business and assures me that he is well," Olivia replied, forcing a smile to her lips. "It is uncertain when he will return, however. Did you hear from your friend today?"

Miss Stewart colored slightly and nodded. "Yes, I had an interesting letter with many descriptions of the countryside in Shropshire. I have never traveled that way myself but my correspondent made it all come alive for me in the telling. No doubt Sir Noah has done much the same for you with descriptions of France."

"It was a hurried letter."

In spite of Olivia's brave attempt to conceal her disappointment, Miss Stewart had known her too long and too well to be under any illusions. The long awaited letter had not lived up to expectation, and her heart ached for Olivia. Perhaps, after all, she would not return to London when her traveling friend did, but stay with her former charge until Lady Lawrence was expected home.

She was about to give this assurance when Olivia said abruptly, "I did not notice the other letter," and proceeded to break the seal while the lemonade was set out for them. Her eyes brightened as she read. "Lady Lawrence has set a date for their return and it is but two weeks from today. She says that Lady Elizabeth and her cousin had a wordy confrontation at Lady Hopkinton's ball." Somehow it was comforting to Olivia to know that Mrs. Dyer was in London, since Noah was not. Only recently had she begun to feel violently jealous of Mrs. Dyer, thinking that somehow, somewhere, Noah must be with her, if he made no effort to return to his wife.

For a brief time Olivia had revelled in the knowledge that Noah had enjoyed himself in bed with her, that she had been able to please him. But soon the suspicion had worked its way into her mind that any willing woman would have provided similar pleasure to him, and certainly Mrs. Dyer was a willing woman. The knowledge threatened to crush her at times, and it was scant solace that Mrs. Dyer was in London. There were no doubt many willing women, in England and in France, who could please her husband. And so she sometimes lay awake and ached for his body next to hers in the black stretches of the night, wondering where he was, and with whom.

* * *

After Noah sent the letter to Olivia, he would gladly have called it back. How could he have been so heartless as to have taken his vexation out on her? There was no use in his staying on in Paris, given his notable lack of success. He had done what he could. Now he could surely return home in good conscience. The decision was taken on the moment, and he was more pleased than depressed as he sought out his host.

Mauppard was in his cabinet frowning over a letter and he gestured Noah to his side. "See what you can make of this, my friend. It concerns your dispatches."

The note, from an associate of Mauppard's, was cautious. " 'When you had me witness the exchange of documents, I saw nothing familiar in the peasant who transacted it. However, when walking in the Rue Basse du Rempart yesterday, a gentleman preceding me into a banking establishment bore some resemblance to the fellow, and I enquired his identity. He was Armand Dupin, secretary to the Vicomte de Preslin. I can be no more definitive than this.' "

"Preslin having the dispatches would not be at odds with what we know," Mauppard mused as he carefully destroyed the note. "His disdain of the English is well-known, and it would give him pleasure to embarrass your country. But if he has them, they could hardly be in more dangerous hands. He will know precisely how best to use them to his own advantage."

"Your sister shows a marked interest in him."

"She's in love with his fortune and he is content to glean any information he can from her careless chatter," Mauppard replied cynically. "If he has the dispatches, it will not be easy to retrieve them. He's not a man I would care to cross."

165

"No." Noah recalled the cold, proud face, the biting tongue, the hard eyes. "Still, it is the only lead we've had. Tell me about him."

Nothing he learned gave Noah the least desire to become further acquainted with the vicomte but he felt it his duty to pursue the matter. Françoise was in a position to provide the means, and Noah found her in the salon surrounded by large bouquets of flowers, fingering a card with unconcealed triumph.

"Ah, Sir Noah. Did I not tell you the ball would be delightful? I am inundated with flowers and bonbons this morning." She waved a languid hand about the room. "What did you think of the Vicomte de Preslin?"

"A striking-looking man, and very clever."

"Rich. He is very rich, Sir Noah. His is one of the first families of France, and he is not at all pleased with Jacques's politics." A smug gleam appeared in her eyes. "He cannot resist me, even with such a disadvantage as a brother intent on destroying the privileges of his own class."

"Where is Preslin's seat?"

"Near Moulins in Bourbonnais. A magnificent palace and everything in the first style of elegance."

"I am surprised he is in town when he could escape this heat and relax in such surroundings. By now London will be thinning of company. Bourbonnais. I hear there have been disturbances there."

"Bah. Nothing to speak of. We take no heed of these brigands. We would be in the country ourselves if it were not for Jacques' work at the Assembly," she said crossly.

"I am sure you will not lack for invitations to visit the country," Noah remarked with an all inclusive gesture about the flower-filled room. "Perhaps even to the vicomte's magnificent home. But no, I suppose he must be cautious in associating with you if he is set against your brother's politics."

"No such thing!" she flared. "If I were to give even the smallest hint that I wished to visit the palace, he would organize a house party on the instant."

"Oh, my dear," Noah retorted with twitching lips, "you exaggerate."

She regarded him with indignant blue eyes. "You have a very small concept of the power I hold over him, sir."

"Well," Noah laughed indulgently, "do not neglect to have me included in the invitation. I should like to see this remarkable palace."

And if Françoise was not able to convince the vicomte to organize a house party on the instant, later in the day she advised Noah with a self-congratulatory smirk that he would be welcome to join the party there in two weeks' time. The delay was a further oppression to Noah's impatience to be home, and he attempted to compose a letter to his wife but, being unable to offer any valid reason for prolonging his stay in France and hopeful that he need be there only a short time more, he at length decided not to write at all.

Chapter Nineteen

Lady Lawrence's last letter from London contained news of the preparations for Peter's wedding, to which all of the Lawrences had been invited at the last moment, and which Olivia's mother-in-law had no intention of attending, since Olivia would not be there. "I find it not the least elevating," she wrote with understandable vexation, "to be included in a guest list of five hundred odd, where the bride is widely known to have spent a thousand guineas on her gown and then changed her mind about it, and the groom makes mockery of the wedding service with his drinking companions each night." The letter ended with Lady Lawrence's expressions of relief that she would be returning to Welling Towers shortly now, as the town was hot and Julianna had found several young ladies willing to assist her in seeing Alexander Cutler on the sly. Olivia acknowledged her mother-in-law's exasperation at being unable to keep Julianna in check in town, but wondered if she would have any greater success at the Towers.

While Miss Stewart dabbed at her eyes in the inn yard, Olivia rallied her by declaring, "I hope those tears are not on my account, my dear Miss Stewart. In a few days Lady Lawrence and Julianna will be here and I am sure it will take my sister days to tell me all she's done in London. By that time perhaps Sir Noah will have completed his business and returned."

"I do hope so." Miss Stewart determinedly blew her nose and thrust her handkerchief in her reticule.

"And you will have many pleasant hours hearing of your correspondent's travels. You may even think of some tales of your own to relate, though I would be the first to admit that we have not led an especially exciting life while you have been here."

Miss Stewart smiled gently. "It is exactly what I could have wished, Olivia. Nothing pleases me more than the decorating we have done. I will be sure to send you some fabric samples from town for the extra cushions you found in the attics. I do hope the others will be pleased with the results."

"How could they help but be?" Olivia protested, laughing. "I shall miss you and hope you can return to visit when the whole family is here."

When the guard called the passengers to board, Miss Stewart was handed in and waved with forced gaiety from her window seat to Olivia, who stood rather forlornly by her carriage returning the gesture. Olivia's hand dropped to her side as the coach moved out of sight. She was tempted to remain in Thetford to buy a new shawl or a pair of boots but mindful of Miss Stewart's admonition on spending money out of boredom, she allowed herself to be handed into the carriage.

During her solitary ride back to the Towers she tried to lift her spirits with thoughts of her progress in driving the phaeton, of her charming new suite, of being reunited with Lady Lawrence and Julianna. But her mind would not obey her. Why should she have to be alone, she thought resentfully. Why did Noah not return? What did he expect from her? She had done all she could to make him happy and had intended to do more when they were at the Towers together. What had she done wrong to make him leave her for all this time, with his paltry excuses of business in Paris? They were never-ending, unanswerable questions, and she tired of the uselessness of asking them of herself. Wearily she climbed out of the carriage and entered the house.

*   *   *

Noah rode escort to the carriage which bore Françoise and a married cousin, acting as her chaperone, to the Vicomte de Preslin's palace near Moulins. Proud as he was of Welling Towers, Noah had to admit that it bore no comparison to the magnificence he observed as he rode through the triumphal arch. The towers of the palace were visible to the left, but immediately in view were the lake with its old stone bridge, miles of oak-studded parkland and an obelisk down an avenue of elms to the right.

Françoise took Noah's arm as they were ushered into the Great Hall. "Did I not tell you it was *extraordinaire?* The columns, the painted ceiling, the suits of armour, the ironwork on the balcony. There is nothing to match it in all of France, I promise you. And wait until you see the state rooms with their tapestries and frescoes. It is a fairy tale palace with no possible spot left ungilded. Ah, and here is our host."

The vicomte advanced with a formal smile of greeting which was perhaps the closest he came to being warm. Taking Françoise's hand, he raised it to his lips and murmured, *"Enchanté.* You do me honor to grace my home."

"I am delighted to be here again. You remember my cousin, Madame d'Astai, and Sir Noah Lawrence."

While Françoise chatted gayly with her host, Noah covertly studied the man. His noble brow was accentuated by the moderate wig he wore, and every feature was perfectly modeled, but there was a tightness about the mouth and a superciliousness in his gaze which suggested no possibility of compromise. It was only fancy, of course, but Noah thought it a rather ruthless face, denoting a man whose will one opposed at one's peril. As they were led along the vaulted corridors, Noah expressed his admiration of the building and a desire to see the whole.

The vicomte was all condescending politeness. "I shall have my secretary conduct you about the house if you wish, Sir Noah. He is as familiar with it as any member of the family could be."

Encouraged by Noah's enthusiastic interest, the secretary, Armand Dupin, led him not only over the principal apartments but the kitchen and stable courts as well. Although there was a great deal to admire in the chapel and the long library, the state rooms, drawing rooms, and saloons, Noah was most concerned with the location of the estate management area and the vicomte's private office.

"I find it convenient," Noah remarked, "to have my own office at Welling Towers located near my estate agent's."

"Yes, it simplifies matters a great deal. My own office is here directly beside that of the estate office, and the vicomte's is but a step around the corner in the West Wing. We pride ourselves on the efficiency of our organization here, Sir Noah."

"It is evident that you do. My own arrangements are not on so grand a scale, of course, but I can appreciate the measures you have taken to facilitate matters." As they passed into the West Wing and the secretary made no effort to open any of the doors, Noah mused, "I might be wise to establish more system to my work. My desk is perpetually a flood of papers and books. But there, I dare say even the vicomte is unable to keep a tidy desk."

M. Dupin was grossly offended. "A well-regulated mind cannot tolerate disorder about it," he said sternly and turned back to a heavy oak door they had passed. He carefully selected a key from the ring he held and unlocked it, standing so as to allow Noah a view of the room, but no entry. "You see, the vicomte has never a book or pen out of place."

Quickly Noah ran his eye over the room, with its enormous mahogany desk and matching cabinet, book shelves and chairs. True, it was orderly; it also presented rather the impression of a fortress. The desk and cabinet both had locks of startling size and apparent durability. "Remarkable. I am impressed and shall account it a lesson," he said ruefully as the secretary snapped the door closed behind him. Surely there was no way to get to the dispatches if they were harbored in *that* room.

* * *

The carriage which swept up to the portals of Welling Towers with Lady Lawrence and her daughter was loaded down with trunks and portmanteaux. Olivia had been watching for their arrival and hastened to greet them as they stepped down from the vehicle. Julianna, having sustained a lecture from her mother during the last hours of their journey, on the necessity of seeing less of Mr. Cutler now that they were returning home, was outwardly subdued but inwardly rebellious.

Olivia very nearly tripped over her skirts as she flew to her mother-in-law and hugged her. "It is so *good* to see you both. I can hardly wait to hear all you have to tell me about London." She turned to Julianna and cried, "What an enchanting carriage dress! You are blooming. I can see that all the balls and parties have agreed with you. Did you see the Prince of Wales? Is the Duchess of Devonshire as beautiful as they say? Did you meet Mr. Fox? You have hardly written a line, and now you must tell me all."

"I'm glad to see you, Olivia, but I am tired," Julianna murmured as she moved away. "Perhaps we shall talk later."

The hurt in Olivia's eyes did not escape Lady Lawrence, who immediately launched into an account of their journey, concluding, "I cannot tell you how delightful it is to be home and to see you, Olivia." She patted her daughter-in-law's arm as they walked across the hall.

"After you have rested and refreshed yourselves, we have a very elaborate tea planned for you. With all the things you like, Julianna," she urged hopefully.

"I dare say we did not miss one day in the whole time we were in London when we did not have a sumptuous tea at one house or another."

Olivia nodded, unable to speak. When they had disappeared up the stairs, with one last warm smile from Lady Lawrence, she settled in the drawing room with an open book, shaken by her sister-in-law's attitude. When the travelers joined her, she and Lady Lawrence talked while Julianna concentrated her attention on the cream puffs.

At length, Julianna asked, "Have you heard from Noah?"

"I had a note from him in Paris," Olivia admitted.

Julianna sniffed. "I don't think he would have told us he was there at all if he hadn't happened upon Mrs. Beaglett."

Although she thought her daughter was probably right, Lady Lawrence said reprovingly, "There is no need to be rude, Julianna. Your brother's affairs are his concern alone, and we need not trouble where they take him." She turned rather hesitantly to Olivia and continued, "I am glad that you heard from him. Did he make any mention of when he intended to return home?"

"He said he had no idea. You learned nothing further from Mrs.—Beaglett, was it?"

"Only that he was with a very attractive French woman," Julianna interposed before her mother could speak.

Lady Lawrence frowned at her daughter and restrained an impulse to shake her. Casually, she remarked, "Yes, Noah was with the Comte de Mauppard and his sister, and indicated that he did not expect to be in Paris long, but that must have been some weeks ago." She was unable to say anything further, lest her own annoyance at the situation show as clearly as her daughter's. With relief she acceded to Olivia's suggestion that they be shown the projects she had worked on during their absence. Her enthusiasm was greater than Olivia had expected, and thus rather suspect, but Julianna had little to say.

The last room to be inspected was Olivia's bedchamber, and after expressing her admiration, Lady Lawrence excused herself and left the two young ladies alone. Olivia could think of nothing to say, but stood staring at the toes of her white kid half boots.

Julianna grasped her hands. "Dearest Olivia, I do not know what has come over me! Mama harangued me for two hours before we arrived and has put me in the sullens. I beg you, pay no heed to me, my love. Your decorating is delightful, and I am sincerely pleased to be with you again." Her eyes were over-bright with unshed tears, and she averted her face from Olivia's gaze.

"I am sure no one would wonder at your nerves being on edge after such an exciting season and a wearying journey," Olivia returned gently.

"Well, you seem in such spirits, when it cannot have been much joy to be here alone for so long. I should like to strangle my brother," she said fiercely.

"I have not been alone most of the time, you know. Miss Stewart's company was most enjoyable."

"But you were wont to say that she was afraid of her own shadow."

"And so she was, but something has given her a new confidence. I think perhaps it is a beau, though she would never say. She received several letters, and planned the length of her stay accordingly."

"Aha," Julianna declared triumphantly. "She is doubtless engaged in a clandestine affair with a most unsuitable young man."

Olivia laughed. "I should not think so, for she intimated that she would see her 'correspondent' when she returned to her father's house."

"I shall persist in believing that their love is being thwarted," Julianna asserted with a lift of her chin, "and I have every sympathy for her."

"Did your mother thwart you in seeing Mr. Cutler in town?" Olivia asked with as much empathy as she could manage in her voice.

"She could not," her friend said stiffly. "Alexander is invited everywhere, Olivia, and we saw him continually at balls and routs. You would not believe how the other young ladies envied me his . . . attentions. There is no one else in London half so handsome or so gay; everyone said so."

"Did he frighten away all the other young men from you then?"

"Not at all! They were intrigued by his obvious partiality and buzzed round like bees." Juliana laughed awkwardly. "Mama was very pleased about that of course, and never hesitated to point out to me when Alexander was with another lady so that I might pay attention to some other man. But his devotion was not swayed, I assure you, even by the diamond of the season, Esther Draskin. She is quite beautiful, but Alexander assured me that she has not a thing to say for herself."

"Peter says that is often the case with the beauties and

the heiresses, but it never seemed to keep him from hanging about them. I hope he will make Lady Elizabeth a decent husband."

Julianna shook her head doubtfully. "He will probably pay not the least attention to her after their honeymoon. I think he already has his eye on a very charming lady married to an old codger who does not bother to accompany her to town." She stopped abruptly when she realized that the description was not far off from what might be applied to her brother. With a painful flush she rushed on, "I must see that my clothes are put away properly, Olivia. Tomorrow I will show you all the new things I have brought from town, but now I must see if I can unearth the lovely shawl I found for you. Please excuse me, my dear."

When Julianna returned to her room she found her mother seated formally in a straight-backed chair while the maid nervously unpacked a trunk under her watchful eye. The maid was dismissed on Juliana's arrival, and Lady Lawrence turned the full effect of her scowl on her daughter.

"It is difficult enough," Lady Lawrence said coldly, "to face Noah's wife under the circumstances without your assistance in adding hurtful details, Julianna."

"I know, Mama." Her daughter paced agitatedly about the room, avoiding her mother's eyes. "I have apologized to Olivia for my behavior, but I seem only to make matters worse."

The dowager wagged her head sadly, the anger diminishing while the frown remained. "I cannot excuse Noah's behavior in this matter, but you and I shall have to endeavor to do the best we can. Keep her occupied, Julianna, and make light of your brother's travels. It may be that he has a legitimate reason for being in France, though I cannot conceive what it would be." The older woman rose wearily and placed a hand on her daugher's arm. "You must not let our differences cause pain to your new sister."

Julianna bowed her head and said softly, "I would not do anything to hurt Olivia, believe me. In future I shall watch my tongue." Her mother nodded and left her alone. Before summoning the maid to continue her unpacking, Julianna drew a note from her reticule. She perused it carefully, bouyed up once more by Alexander's professions of devotion and his assurance that he would soon be in the countryside with her. The note was then carefully placed in her dressing table under a pair of gloves she seldom wore.

* * *

While Françoise concentrated her attention on the vicomte, Noah took to making secret excursions into the West Wing when he could detach himself from the house party. Having learned that there was no access to the vicomte's office from the exterior, it being a floor above ground level, he determined to check whether it was always locked. Noah was careful to avoid meeting anyone, as he had no business in that part of the house, but on one foray he found himself in the middle of a corridor with nowhere to hide when M. Dupin rounded the corner ahead of him and regarded Noah with frowning surprise.

Nonplussed for a moment, Noah quickly murmured, "Ah, just the man I was looking for."

"You should have sent for me, Sir Noah."

"No, no. There was not the least need to disturb you from your work. Though who can work on such a fine day . . ." Desperately he scoured his mind for a reasonable excuse for being found alone in the West Wing. "It is merely a matter of a case of wine which I have been offered in the village for a very reasonable price, but I am not familiar with it." He named the most rare vintage he could recall from his own cellars.

"You have found a case here?" the astonished secretary asked.

"So I am told. I have not seen it as yet. Do you think there is something strange about the business?"

"Be sure of it! There is not a bottle to be had, as I well know, having been on the lookout for the vicomte's own cellars for some time." M. Dupin attempted to hide his disdain for so gullible an Englishman, but he was not entirely successful.

"That settles the matter, of course. I thank you."

Noah gave a brief nod and strolled away in the opposite direction.

The close call and a lack of any means to enter the office, which might or might not contain the documents for which he searched, determined him to abandon his efforts. His wife—to say nothing of his mother and sister —would already be annoyed with him for his long absence. Of course, he could do precisely what he wanted, but he *wanted* to be with his wife again. He had not the least desire to hurt her. It was, in fact, his intention to pamper her. Already he had accumulated a number of gifts for her in his wanderings, and he was eager to see her reception of them. Shortly, a message (of his own devising) arrived summoning him to London.

Francoise pouted and his host politely regretted the necessity of his departure, but he bid them farewell at breakfast and retreated to his room to see his portmanteaux quickly packed. Although rumors of brigands in the neighborhood had been scornfully denied over the meal, even in his room in the South Wing he could hear a commotion growing which belied such overconfidence. At first his only thought was of the possible inconvenience this might cause to his leaving, and he rang for a footman to convey his belongings down to the stables where a hired carriage awaited him.

The servant arrived agog with happenings at the main gate. "A rabble with staves and rocks are trying to smash in the gate. Perhaps you should not leave just now, sir."

"There are surely other exits," Noah protested.

"Several, but there may be more of the brigands in the neighborhood."

"Well, be so good as to carry my portmanteaux down in readiness. I shall leave when I can."

"It should not be long, sir. The Vicomte de Preslin has rushed to attend to the matter."

Noah, suddenly offered one last opportunity, impatiently watched the man's exit. In such an emergency it was just possible that the vicomte's office door would have been left unlocked, had he been there at the time the information reached him. Noah headed directly for the West Wing.

The corridor was deserted and the door shut but Noah found that it opened when he turned the brass handle. Slipping quickly inside, he closed the door and looked about him. The cabinet and desk were closed and locked, he discovered when he tried them. If he had such papers, in which would he be most likely to store them? Deciding on the desk, he looked about for some article with which to work on the locks, but there was nothing. Confound the man for his tidy habits! From his pocket he withdrew his own keys, choosing the smallest as the most appropriate. But this was not an ordinary desk lock and the small key merely rattled in the hole. A somewhat larger key was a closer fit and he worked with it for some minutes before he heard a click, almost indiscernible against the sound of shots being fired outside.

A hurried search of the drawer disclosed nothing of interest to him. When he had begun to work on the lock of a second drawer, he heard footsteps in the hall and froze where he sat. The windows were his only means of escape, and the office was a floor above ground. He hastened to unlatch a window and contemplated the drop from the balcony as the footsteps came closer. His grip on his cane tightened as he strained to hear the sounds from the corridor over the noise from the main courtyard. The hurrying footsteps passed by.

Noah hesitated a moment before returning to the desk. An image of Preslin's cold eyes and harsh mouth rose in his mind and was pushed aside. He wiped the sweat from his forehead and palms, and set to work on the second drawer. After what seemed an eternity the lock clicked, and he slid open the drawer: the dispatches rested on a neat stack of the vicomte's personal papers. A quick scan assured him that they were the originals.

As he closed the drawer and slid the dispatches into his pocket, he heard more footsteps in the corridor and once again hastened to the window which he had left open. There was no mistaking the victomte's stentorian tones and those of the deferential M. Dupin. Noah gained the balcony and closed the window behind him. Any jump was preferable to being discovered in the vicomte's office in possession of the English dispatches. Without another thought, and grateful there was no one in sight, he leaped.

Chapter Twenty

Olivia endeavored to maintain a cheerful attitude with her mother-and sister-in-law; but the longer Noah stayed away from home, the more distressed and resentful she became. After the awkwardness of Lady Lawrence and Julianna's arrival home, Olivia felt no inclination to share her knowledge that she was with child. Dr. Davenport had confirmed her condition, and had been sworn to silence on the matter. She stubbornly adhered to her determination to apprise Noah of the information first if it were at all possible.

As she had promised, Julianna was more careful in future when speaking with her brother's wife, but Olivia found her preoccupied. One day as they strolled into Welling, Julianna announced, "Alexander is due home today."

"Oh, have you heard from him?" Olivia was surprised that Lady Lawrence would allow the two to correspond.

The other girl started guiltily and rearranged the cover of her basket. Mrs. Trambor, her music teacher, had been kind enough to allow Julianna to receive Alexander's letters through her, but Julianna had no wish to cause any trouble for the good woman. "When we left London, he suggested this date for his arrival," she answered carefully. "He wished to stay for your brother's wedding."

"I see." Olivia attempted to work some enthusiasm into her voice. "We shall look forward to having him call at the Towers and tell us all about the wedding."

"He may not call right away."

But Alexander had no hesitation in doing so. He was perfectly willing to beard Lady Lawrence in her den, and would have done it more often (despite her barely civil behavior), if Julianna had not pleaded with him to moderate his visits. "No one," he whispered to her as Lady Lawrence poured their tea across the room, "could object to my calling on you when we have not seen each other for weeks, and I am but returned to the country."

Olivia, a witness to Lady Lawrence's frown, sought to draw the couple into general conversation. "Mr. Cutler, I would be especially interested to hear of my brother's wedding ceremony. I understand you attended it."

"It was more a performance than a ceremony, Lady Olivia," he laughed. "Never saw such elegant trappings—red carpets all over the place, so many flowers that half the ladies sneezed through the entire service, and Lord Bolenham declaiming his lines as though he were in the latest drama at Drury Lane. The train of Lady Elizabeth's gown was so studded with diamonds that I expected all the rolled-up gentry to follow after her on their knees so that they might recover any stone that came loose."

"And were my brothers Charles and Samuel there?"

"Oh, yes, *everyone* was there. Well, not Mrs. Dyer, of course. She and Lady Elizabeth are still at odds, but it seems to have no effect on the lovely Lila. I understand she is already ensconced at Herstwood for the summer, as Lord and Lady Edmonston are connections of hers, and they left town some weeks ago."

Lady Lawrence chose to change the subject. "And your parents, Mr. Cutler? Are they well? Did your sister enjoy the season?"

"My esteemed parents are in high gig, Lady Lawrence, as the result of this season may be that my sister is married off. They have every expectation that Mr. Topptor will come up to scratch. Norissa is coyly uncertain about it, herself, but the gentleman has been invited to our home, and accepted with gratifying alacrity, according to my mother."

Glancing nervously at her mother, who was not likely to take this careless description of the romance with approbation, Julianna suggested that she, Olivia and Alexander might walk in the garden. Her mother made no objection, and Olivia found herself a not particularly welcome third. She would not have accompanied them at all, of course, except that she knew Lady Lawrence expected it of her, so she fell behind the couple to gather flowers and closed her ears to their whispered conversation.

As the days passed, however, Olivia was convinced that somehow the two managed more privacy than Lady Lawrence would have approved. Although Julianna was frequently in Olivia's company, Olivia was sure that she contrived to see Alexander without her mother's knowledge. Lady Lawrence stoically accepted that she could not completely control her daughter even at Welling Towers, but her continual efforts to do the best she could caused a tense atmosphere to pervade the house.

* * *

Noah's leap took him onto a grassy mound which rose just beyond the flower border alongside the house. As he touched ground he heard an ominous crunch in his right ankle, which, due to the unevenness of the ground, had taken most of his weight. He cast a hasty glance back up at the balcony, but there was no one there, and he tentatively put his weight on the injured leg. A searing pain nearly took his breath away but with the aid of his cane he managed to begin the painful walk to the stables, constantly glancing behind himself to see whether the vicomte had come out on the balcony. It would not do to allow the stable staff to observe his pain or his awkward walk, so he compressed his lips and forced himself to walk as naturally as he was able.

Although the hired carriage was waiting, the staff advised against his leaving with brigands in the neighborhood. The thought of being forced to remain, with the certainty of the missing dispatches being discovered in a relatively short time, made Noah's blood run cold, but he calmly turned to the coachman with a questioning look.

"Never listen to the wailings of such chicken-hearted fellows," he said disgustedly, spitting into the dust beside the coach. "We've a blunderbuss on the box and a pistol inside; no one will bother us."

Relieved, Noah climbed cautiously in and slumped against the aging upholstery. His leg throbbed with pain, and after the carriage was beyond the gates he rested it gingerly on the seat opposite. The rocking and jarring of the drive was an agony, but the need to put as much distance as possible between himself and the Vicomte forced him to grit his teeth and settle back to bear the pain. Only once, after crossing a high-sided stone bridge, did they catch any view of the threatening mob, but a rock accurately pitched at the window sent a shower of glass shards hurtling through the carriage. One splinter lodged deep in Noah's shoulder, and as soon as the carriage had proceeded beyond the range of the group, he ordered a stop so that he could probe the wound and remove the imbedded glass. The flow of blood which resulted drenched his coat and waistcoat, and he was forced to accept the coachman's help to bind it properly.

"Can't travel like that," his assistant remarked judiciously. "Best put up at an inn."

"Off the main road," Noah insisted. "Somewhere we won't be found."

Although the coachman regarded him with a puzzled frown, he did as he was bid. At an inn at Yzeure, Noah's wound was cleaned and dusted with basilicum powder, his damaged ankle tightly bound and he was put to bed. The loss of blood, the pain and the frustration combined to make Noah a less-than-agreeable guest, but a rosy-cheeked maid eyed him with frank approval each time she brought or removed his tray. He was allowed an alluring view of her bosom whenever she bent over him to pump up his pillows or wipe his feverish brow. As he recovered his strength the girl offered herself in exchange for his taking her to Paris. Tempted by her light-hearted attitude and attractive person, Noah yet felt a strange reluctance and teasingly put off her advances.

When the wound had healed sufficiently that it was not likely to reopen during his drive, and he was able to move about somewhat with the assistance of his cane, he announced to the maid his intention of leaving the next day and sought her assistance in having all ready. During the night he was slightly awakened, well after midnight, by the movement of someone climbing into his bed. A soft, naked body snuggled against him and he automatically encased it with his arms mumbling, "Olivia." The girl's titter of laughter brought him fully awake and he regarded her with amusement. "Persistent little thing, aren't you?"

She dimpled prettily. *"Mais oui, monsieur.* Do you not . . . desire me?"

Noah could not deny his desire, but he gave her a gentle push, saying, "Run along now. I cannot take you to Paris with me."

The girl pouted ludicrously, her face crestfallen, but she made no effort to climb from the bed. With an impatient gesture, Noah threw back the bedclothes and, grasping her about the waist, set her on her feet beside the bed. Her nightdress lay bunched on the upholstered chair by the moonlit window, and Noah gestured imperiously toward it. She walked hesitantly toward the chair and slowly retrieved her apparel, Noah's eyes on her the while. Standing so that the moonlight clearly revealed her form, she whispered, "You would not have to take me to Paris. I know that English gentlemen are generous."

With a groan, Noah shook his head determinedly. "Go to your bed, child, and stay there, if you please. I have a long distance to travel tomorrow."

A shrug of resignation was followed by the rapid donning of the nightdress and a small curtsy before she slipped from the room. Noah buried his head in the pillow and cursed himself for a fool. If he had not awakened with his wife's name on his lips . . .

*   *   *

184

July brought no improvement in the situation at Welling Towers. Julianna continued moody and evasive; Lady Lawrence maintained an undercurrent of annoyance with her daughter. They were both thoughtful of Olivia, but she could not be unaware of their antagonism toward each other over Alexander Cutler. As the summer wore away with no word from Noah, Olivia's spirits sank lower than ever. It was not until the last week of July, when she returned from a drive with Julianna, that she was finally presented with a letter.

Julianna regarded her anxiously as she broke the seal, but Lady Lawrence pointedly picked up her embroidery so that Olivia might have a chance to peruse the message in some privacy.

"Noah is in London now," his wife announced after a few minutes. "He must go to Herstwood for a few days before returning home, but assures us that we will see him in just over a week. He says that he looks forward to being with us again." And he tells me that he has missed me, Olivia concluded silently. She had expected to experience a great relief when she learned of Noah's return, but her hopes were now dashed. It had not escaped the attention of anyone in the room that Herstwood was Mrs. Dyer's present situation; and, though no one commented, Olivia was aware of Lady Lawrence's silent disapproval and of Julianna's agitation.

"I will barely have time to finish embroidering the cushions," Olivia remarked to offset the heavy silence. "Noah's room must be aired, of course, and his valet summoned from Attleborough."

Lady Lawrence joined willingly into Olivia's discussion of the provisions which must be set in motion before Noah returned, but Julianna abstractedly fingered her gown and said nothing. As soon as she possibly could without being reprimanded, she slipped from the room.

The warmth of the day precluded her wearing a cloak, and Julianna took care that she was not observed when she left through a side door. She was already late for her appointment with Alexander, and she did not wish to try his patience. It was not that he did not understand the difficulties of her escaping from her family, she told herself, but it was his natural eagerness to see her which caused him occasionally to be short with her if she were tardy.

Julianna wound her way swiftly past the hedgerows and copses, ever careful to remain out of sight of the house. She arrived at the summerhouse slightly breathless to find Alexander pacing the floor, occasionally pausing to flick a bit of dust from his boots or coat sleeve. He turned at her entrance to survey her with some irritation. "I was about to leave, Julianna, thinking that you had forgotten me."

"Oh, Alexander, you know I would not," she cried, hurt. "I could not leave sooner, as Olivia has received a letter from Noah."

His dark eyes showed a flash of interest before he asked dubiously, "Is he returning at last then?"

"Yes, in about a week." Julianna turned from him sadly. "I think we shall not be able to meet so easily when he is here."

Alexander pursed his lips thoughtfully and tapped his whip against his leg. Abruptly he grasped her hand and drew it to his lips. "It is time you decided, Julianna. You will never get your brother's approval, or your mother's."

She gave a nervous shake of her head. "They cannot prevent my marrying you once I come of age in January."

With an impatient gesture he muttered, "You wish to wait so long, my dear? I am not so complaisant, I fear. Half a year at the very least, and with doubtless no more joy from them at that time. We would do better to present them with an accomplished fact now; they will grow to accept it."

"It would disgrace my family for me to elope," she whispered piteously.

"Nonsense. They are very practical, and you refine too much on their reaction. Your brother dotes on you, and you are Lady Lawrence's pet, except insofar as I am concerned." He gave a mock bow and his mouth twisted awry.

"I know they will come to approve of you when they know you as I do," Julianna protested fiercely as she placed a consoling hand on his arm.

"Of course they will, but only once we are married will they come to know me. And it would be well for me to marry now, as I will come into a little property from my great aunt when I do so. I have already exceeded my present funds." There was a certain defiance in his tone as he spoke and a subtle threat. "I cannot wait until January for you, Julianna."

"But it is not so very long," she pleaded, pale-faced. "Perhaps I could lend you something from my allowance."

"Don't be absurd," he barked. "Such a pittance would accomplish nothing. We would be very comfortable on what I will have from my great aunt, and your own settlement." His eyes intently studied her frightened countenance.

"Noah could withhold my money until I am of age."

Alexander laughed with no amusement. "He would not, though. To what purpose would he leave you unprovided for when it is only a matter of months before you come of age?"

Julianna hesitated, uncertain. It was true that Noah was unlikely to be spiteful or mean, and Alexander truly cared for her, she was sure. Not that he would not wed another if he were forced to do so by his lack of means, she thought with panic. His father would give him no more money, as he had roused that gentleman's anger by continued solicitations. Julianna recalled the envy of so many young ladies in London who would have given an arm for Alexander's attention. Esther Draskin, for instance. Would the beauty agree to elope with him? Dismally Julianna admitted to herself that Esther probably would, were he to approach her. She could not bear the thought of Alexander wed to another. "Very well," she agreed. "I will go with you."

Alexander smiled triumphantly and kissed her warmly. "Excellent. We must leave before your brother returns, of course. I will make arrangements for Tuesday night, my love, and advise you where and when to meet me. Now do not be a gudgeon and tell anyone or let on what you are about, Julianna," he said sternly, holding her eyes with his. "We must be miles away before we are discovered, so that we cannot be caught up."

With a nervous nod she acquiesced and turned to go. "You do love me, don't you, Alexander?"

His mind was on other matters by now and it was a moment before her words penetrated and he responded stoutly, "Of course I do, Julianna. How can you even ask?"

"I wished to be sure," she murmured before, without meeting his eyes, she grasped her skirts in her hands and dashed out of the summerhouse. The elation of knowing that she would soon be his wife did not stop the tears which poured down her cheeks as she hurried back to the house.

Noah's journey had been anything but pleasant. The remaining pain from his ankle and shoulder permitted him to travel only moderate distances each day, and he endured the frustration of breakdowns in his hired carriage and adverse weather for the channel crossing. And then to be told he must travel to Herstwood to deliver the dispatches to Viscount Mortley! Noah could scarcely contain his impatience to see his wife again—to hold her in his arms and gaze into those trusting gray eyes, to make love with that beautiful, responsive body, to listen to her eager chatter. But what was he to tell her of his own absence? How could he possibly account for such a prolonged absence?

Viscount Mortley listened with interest to all Noah had to relate of the recovery of the missing property and the situation in France. "In spite of your injuries, you appear to have enjoyed yourself," he remarked laconically at the end of Noah's recital.

"I did rather," Noah admitted with a grin, "but I look forward to returning home." His countenance grew grave. "At times I fear for my friend Mauppard."

"With cause, I believe. Should you need assistance in the future to spirit him from France, I hope you will not hesitate to call on me. We owe him a debt of gratitude for his assistance."

Noah was unaware of Lila Dyer's presence at Herstwood until he met her at a ball that night, and he found himself chagrined rather than pleased. He wanted nothing to delay his speedy departure to his bride and, surprisingly, he found himself no longer attracted to her.

A slow smile spread over her lips as she divined his thoughts. "It is just as well, Noah, for I do not believe Viscount Mortley would approve."

His startled look amused her, and he replied ruefully, "I dare say he wouldn't, though I was not aware he was *your* viscount. You are looking well, Lila. Are you happy?"

"Yes, I should say so," she replied judiciously. "He is a trifle stuffy at times; on the other hand he is rather distinguished, don't you think?" Her eyes wandered over the crowd until they rested on the man of whom she spoke, who acknowledged her glance with a cordial nod.

"A most admirable man."

Chapter Twenty-One

As the preparations for Noah's arrival progressed at Welling Towers, Olivia became more concerned about her sister-in-law. It was perhaps natural that Noah's sister had mixed emotions about his return. On the one hand, she would obviously be happy to see him after such a long absence; on the other, his presence would no doubt forestall many of the secret meetings Olivia suspected she had with Alexander. But Julianna went about the house distractedly, her face looking rather pinched and her eyes often slightly reddened. Olivia thought perhaps her new sister had had a quarrel with her beau, but her tentative inquiries were softly rebuked.

Alexander had arranged for a carriage to be at the southwest gate of the estate at midnight and he cautioned Julianna to bring only a bandbox with her, as she would not be able to manage more. He did not offer to escort her in the dark from the house to the gate.

When the ladies parted for the night, Julianna hugged Olivia impulsively and murmured, "I could not wish for a better sister, and I am so glad for you that Noah will be home soon," before she disappeared in the direction of her room. Olivia lay awake for a while contemplating Julianna's plight. Perhaps if her devotion to Alexander had sustained such adversity it would be well for Olivia to champion her cause with Noah and Lady Lawrence. Not that she liked Alexander any better; but it would be bleak indeed to stand alone against the whole of one's family for the love of a man, and Olivia sympathized with her. If only Alexander were not such a feckless nodcock, it would be easier to assist Julianna, Olivia thought with a sigh. Restless now, she rose from her bed and wandered into Noah's suite of rooms with a candle.

Outside there was no moon and her candle gave little light in the room, but she placed it on the bedside stand and sat gingerly on the half-tester bed. It would not do to be found there, of course, but she felt sure the entire household was asleep, and it was comforting to sit and remember the one night they had spent together at their home. Olivia placed her hands on the growing area which she concealed as best she could from her fellow occupants in the house and smiled gently in the shadowy light. Noah would be pleased about that, at least.

When she rose to return to her room a movement out on the lawn drew her attention. Leaving the candle behind her, she walked to the window, but she was unable to distinguish the figure now disappearing into the woods. Perhaps it was a maid or footman bound for a secret assignation. Olivia returned to the stand and retrieved her candle, thinking that Lady Lawrence would certainly wish to look into such a matter, but knowing that she herself would do nothing whatsoever. Her sheets were cold by now and she shivered as she tucked the bedclothes about her.

As she started to drift off to sleep the realization came to her that the figure on the lawn might have been Julianna. But that was wild speculation and highly unlikely. Olivia lay for some time trying to rid her mind of such a preposterous notion, but it would not go away. Finally she rose from her bed, determined to just peek in at Julianna's door to make sure that she was fast asleep as she should be. Nothing less would allow her any peace, she thought with exasperation.

Wrapped in a warm dressing gown, Olivia glided noiselessly through the corridors to her friend's room. The door squeaked when she opened it, but there was no response from the bed. Without a candle she could not see well, but she did not find it necessary to walk all the way to the bed to see that it was unoccupied. Olivia stood motionless regarding the empty bed while she considered what was best to be done.

Lady Lawrence should be informed, of course, but she would be forced to send someone after her daughter, and the scandal would spread about the neighborhood. Olivia remembered her promise to Noah that she would not overlook such a contingency out of sympathy for Julianna, and she had no inclination to do so. From her youth it had been instilled in her that such an elopement was a disgrace, and she could see no excuse for Alexander. Julianna would come of age in just five months and had more than once told Olivia that she waited only for that time to wed her chosen young man. Why then should she elope now when there was such a short time left to wait?

There was no use in trying to understand the reasons behind her flight, Olivia decided impatiently as she softly closed the door and raced back to her room. I will bring her back myself, she thought grimly, and perhaps no one need ever know. Her dressing gown disposed of, she hastened to the wardrobe to choose a warm outfit before she realized that as a woman abroad that late at night she would be courting danger. Instead of abandoning her plan she turned to Noah's dressing room and awkwardly outfitted herself in stockings, breeches, a shirt, waistcoat, and riding coat.

Her black curls she tucked under a bicorne hat she found, but she wore her own boots for comfort. Ever aware that her mission was not without its peril but hopeful that she would be back to retrieve it before anyone entered her room in the morning, she scribbled a note explaining her absence. Then she hurried down to the side entrance through which she planned to leave, but decided at the last moment to carry one of Noah's duelling pistols which she had been shown some time before. Olivia had not the least idea how to operate such a weapon, but it made her feel safer to have it with her and she tucked it in the band of the breeches.

All was silent in the stables and it was her desire to disturb no one. The mare pricked her ears at Olivia's soft voice and stood patiently while her mistress awkwardly saddled her in the darkness. Everything was taking so long, Olivia thought desperately, and I cannot be sure in which direction they have headed. It seemed logical that they would go first to Ely, and the figure Olivia had seen on the lawn could only have been headed for the south-west gate.

Olivia led the eager mare out of the stable, then carefully closed the door and mounted. There was no activity anywhere about the house or stables and she urged the mare immediately onto the grass to deaden the sound of hoofbeats. Once through the southwest gate she gave the mare her head, confident in the animal's stamina and sure-footedness. No other travelers were about, and there was no indication of a carriage having recently been along the road, but Olivia had expected none. She touched the pistol to bolster her courage in the blackness of the night and whispered encouragement to her horse.

An hour later and almost half way to Ely the mare pricked her ears forward, and Olivia perceived a carriage traveling at a good clip in the distance. In spite of her exuberant start, the mare was beginning to flag; Olivia prayed silently that they had indeed reached the end of their journey. She rode alongside the carriage; but the blinds were drawn, and she was forced to call to the coachman. He was startled to hear a feminine voice and immediately drew the horses to a stand. Alexander's voice issued from the enclosed carriage demanding to know the reason for the halt, but he was enlightened soon enough when Olivia thrust open the door.

Julianna's face, poking out from under her bonnet, looked haggard in the dim light of the side lamp. "Dear Lord, Olivia, you should not have ridden after us!"

"You must come home with me, love. This is no way to start a married life. I will intercede for you with Noah, but you must not shame your family with such a helter-skelter flight," Olivia pressed gently.

"She is not going home!" Alexander roared. "She is going with me and you will kindly leave us, ma'am."

Olivia frowned at the young man. "If you wish to marry my sister-in-law, you must go about it in such a fashion as will not disgrace her, Mr. Cutler. She will be of age soon enough, and my husband and her mother will not stand in her way then, I assure you."

"I have no intention of waiting, Lady Olivia, and you cannot convince me otherwise. You would do well to return to Welling Towers without a word to anyone," he added coldly as he made an attempt to wrest the carriage door closed.

Julianna gave a cry of protest when she saw Olivia's arm struck by the door, but Alexander pushed her firmly back on the seat. "I would advise you to stand clear, ma'am," he ordered Olivia, "for I am about to instruct my coachman to proceed."

The pistol had appeared suddenly in Olivia's hand and she pointed it steadily at Alexander, who regarded her with astonishment. She spoke quietly but firmly. "You are going nowhere with Julianna tonight, Mr. Cutler. Get out of the carriage and instruct your coachman to climb down from the box."

"You would not use that weapon," he blurted uncertainly.

"Try me."

Alexander did as she ordered. Olivia next tied the mare to the rear of the carriage while she kept the pistol leveled at him. After a word of comfort to Julianna, she climbed on the box and urged the four horses to turn in the middle of the road.

"You do not intend to leave us here, surely?" Alexander shouted in protest.

"I do, you know. A good walk will perhaps clear your mind and convince you of the wisdom of keeping silent in this affair. If no word is whispered abroad of it by you or your coachman, I will undertake to keep Sir Noah from . . . acting hastily when he hears of it. If not . . . well, I cannot answer for the consequences."

Olivia left the young man spluttering in the road, his coachman's face a mask except for the twitching of his lips. Of necessity Olivia kept the horses to a sedate pace and after a few miles halted them so that she might check on her passenger. Julianna was huddled on the seat, her face wet with tears and her body shaken with sobs.

"Do not cry, my love," Olivia consoled her as she stroked the strands of hair from her friend's face. "He should not have induced you to do such a thing. Surely you knew that Noah would not oppose you once you came of age."

"Y . . . Yes, but Alexander . . . wished to be married now," Julianna gasped brokenly. "He comes into some . . . property on his marriage and he is short of funds."

"Not a very flattering reason for eloping," Olivia suggested gently.

"Oh, I know it was wrong! I have worried over it for days. But he would marry someone else if I would not go, because of his debts, you understand, not because he does not love me." The rain of tears came harder.

"I am sure Alexander is fond of you, Julianna, but I think you would be wise to accept that he was using you for his own purposes. And a man who would do such a thing would not make the right husband for you."

"And is Noah not using you?" Julianna asked bitterly.

"Your brother offered me the protection of his name when I was stranded, my dear," Olivia answered over the lump in her throat. "He used no deceit to entice me to marry him, nor was he in need of my money. I had no choice, but you do, love. Do you think that even if Noah had been in Alexander's circumstances he would have acted as Alexander did?"

Julianna turned her stricken face away from her friend's intent eyes. "No," she whispered painfully. "Noah could never do such a thing."

"I do not think he could either," Olivia said softly. "It was hard of him to leave me so soon after our marriage, but he had never promised me that he would be a faithful husband nor be forever at my beck and call. He promised me his protection and his financial and social support. You do not wish a marriage of convenience, Julianna, especially not one that is only convenient to your husband. Let us return to the Towers. You must be exhausted."

Olivia wrapped the rug about the young woman and returned to the box. The drive seemed to take longer

195

returning than it had coming, and Olivia had more time than she wished to consider her own marriage and Julianna's distress. She had not meant to be hard on her friend, but there was no use allowing Julianna to love an illusion when the means were at hand to show her the reality of the situation. In speaking with Julianna so openly Olivia had tried to put her own situation in perspective; and though it hurt to admit the truth, she found it somehow comforting as well. She would try in future to see her own marriage as one of convenience and not romanticize it on the basis of her honeymoon.

As they approached the southwest gate Olivia was faced with a decision as to what to do with the carriage and horses. To take them to the stables would arouse the men there; to leave them in the road would be unfair to the tired animals. When she drew them to a halt before the gates, Olivia sprang down and consulted Julianna. As the night was warm, they decided to unharness the horses and allow them to graze in the pasture. The carriage was left beside the gate, and the two young ladies led the mare to her stall.

There was no activity about the stables or the house, so Olivia and Julianna were able to return to their rooms unobserved. Olivia took her exhausted friend to her room and helped her undress for bed before she whispered comfortingly, "We will talk in the morning, love. There is no need for anyone to know about your adventure."

Olivia removed and hid the clothes she had borrowed from Noah's dressing room so that she could inspect them for dirt before putting them away. The note she had left she now tore and crumpled before climbing into bed exhausted, where she fell asleep immediately. Nothing further disturbed her sleep, but she found herself in some pain when she awoke late the next morning. She rang for toast and chocolate in bed, but did not feel like consuming them when they were brought. When Marie returned for the tray, she discovered Olivia white-faced and doubled over with pain.

"Shall I send for the doctor, m'lady?" she asked, frightened at the sight.

"Yes, I think it would be best." Olivia's reply was barely audible and the maid hastened from the room.

Lady Lawrence and Julianna were with her before she had time to consider what to say to them. The older woman's face contorted with concern and her daughter's eyes rounded with anxiety. Taking Olivia's hand, Lady Lawrence asked, "Where is the pain, my dear?"

"I fear it is the child," Olivia whispered, stricken.

"Is Dr. Davenport aware that you are with child?" Lady Lawrence asked bluntly.

"Yes, I have seen him."

"Why did you not tell us, Olivia?"

"I wished to tell Noah first," came the soft reply.

Julianna sank to the floor and buried her face in her hands. "Oh God, Olivia, this is all my fault."

Lady Lawrence's puzzled frown went unnoticed as her daughter poured out the story of the previous night's happenings, in spite of Olivia's weak protests. The older woman's astonishment gave way to resignation as she laid a soothing hand on her daughter's bent head. "What is done is done, Julianna. Pray compose yourself so that we may make Olivia comfortable." She turned to her son's wife and asked gently, "Shall I send for Noah, my dear?"

"No, no. Let us see what Dr. Davenport has to say."

The doctor was reassuring when he had made his examination. "I am persuaded that Lady Olivia will not lose the child if she remains at rest for some days. She told me, in confidence of course, of the strenuous riding and driving she had undertaken, and I dare say the upset of the situation affected her; but she is young and healthy. Keep her in bed and do not allow her to become upset, and I believe she will come about."

He left some sedative salts for his patient which Lady Lawrence administered forthwith. The pain gradually diminished, and Olivia shakily accepted the warm milk which was pressed upon her. When she slept again Lady Lawrence and her daughter left her quietly with Marie in attendance.

The two women repaired to the Drawing Room in

silence but once there Lady Lawrence did not offer her daughter the homily that the latter had anticipated with trepidation. Instead she sighed and commented, "We have all been at fault in this affair—Noah, you and I. It would appear that in accepting Olivia into our family, we have done nothing but harm her. Abandoned by her husband after her honeymoon, then forced to reside with the two of us at loggerheads, the strains on her have been great; and she could not even tell her own husband that she was with child. It was not wise of her to go after you alone, though."

"I think she did it so that no one else need ever know," Julianna replied sadly. "Alexander tried to shut the door of the carriage when she was holding it open and she aimed one of Noah's dueling pistols at him. Do you suppose she knows how to use one?"

"I would not wonder at it," Lady Lawrence replied with satisfaction. "I wish Noah were here, but I suppose it would not be to the purpose to send a messenger. He has no doubt left Herstwood already."

Julianna studied her mother's face, which seemed to have aged from the previous day. There were lines there which she had never noticed before, and the graying hair was accentuated by the equally pale face. "I think you should lie down for a while, Mother," she said gently. Although Lady Lawrence protested, Julianna saw her to her room and drew the draperies before withdrawing.

Chapter Twenty-Two

Two days later Noah arrived unaware of what had been going forward at his home. He found Julianna exhausted from nursing Olivia and her mother, and attempting to reconcile herself to her own disappointment and disillusion. His mother had succumbed to a putrid sore throat and proved an impatient invalid, Julianna explained as she led him to the Winter Parlor.

"Whatever is the matter with Olivia?" he asked as he closed the door behind them.

"She came close to losing your child because . . ."

Noah interrupted her. "My child! Why was I not advised that she was with child?"

"She did not tell us either, Noah, and she had no way of informing you," Julianna replied stiffly.

"I should see her at once," he groaned, rising from the chair he had just taken.

"No, she is asleep just now. Marie will advise me when she awakens."

"And Mother?"

"I have a difficult time keeping her in bed at all. Doubtless she is awake and impatient to see you, but, Noah . . ." Julianna was unable to find a way to express her sorrow for her own role in the recent events. "Well, Mother will explain everything to you, and we can talk later. I will send word when Olivia can see you."

Noah nodded and placed a salute on his sister's

cheek. "It is good to see you, Julianna. I am sorry you have had such a rough time."

Tears sprang to her eyes, and she shook her head violently, but she could not say anything further and motioned him from the room. Noah was puzzled by her reaction, upset by the knowledge that his wife and mother were ill, and overwhelmed once more by a sense of guilt. He entered his mother's room when she bid him, to find her, as Julianna had a few days previously, looking a great deal older than he remembered.

Lady Lawrence greeted him with grave enthusiasm and indicated that he should pull the chair up to her bed. "You look well, Noah. I trust your travels have been successful."

"They have," he replied shortly. "I am sorry to hear that you have been ill and hope you are recovering."

"Julianna insists that I stay here when I should be caring for your wife," the old woman fretted. "Have you spoken with Olivia?"

"No, Julianna said she was sleeping."

"Did Julianna explain the circumstances?"

"She told me that Olivia almost lost our child."

Lady Lawrence twisted the bracelet on her wrist thoughtfully. "I think it would be wisest if you knew the whole story," she sighed, and proceeded to enlighten him.

"And what has become of Alexander?" he asked coldly.

"I only know that he is no longer in the neighborhood. His carriage was retrieved the following day by his coachman, who indicated that his master was leaving the area immediately. No whisper of the elopement has reached us, but that is not to say that none exists."

"I find it difficult to believe that Julianna could lend herself to such a stunt, or that Olivia should take it on herself to right the situation alone," Noah remarked, his face set grimly.

"You will of course discuss the matter with your sister, Noah; but I pray you will not be too hard on her for she has suffered considerably in consequence. I am at fault in the way I have handled her attachment, though I cannot believe I was wrong to disapprove of the young man. As to Olivia, if one word of reproach escapes your lips to her, I swear I will remove myself permanently from your house," Lady Lawrence said vehemently. "It may not have been wise of her to go after them, but she did so in the absence of having any other solution which would not involve word of the elopement getting abroad. To send even a trusted servant after them would have courted disaster for your sister's reputation. It was a very courageous thing your wife did, and much more than we all deserve for the way we have treated her."

"You refer to my leaving her alone."

"Certainly that," Lady Lawrence retorted with asperity, "but also that Julianna and I have been at such odds over Mr. Cutler that the house reeked with our contention. I do not intend to take you to task over your absence, Noah; that is a matter between you and your wife. No one expects you to sit in her pocket. I would urge discretion on you, however, as she is clearly hurt by rumors of your affairs."

"My affairs? What affairs?" Noah asked indignantly.

"Mrs. Beaglett offered, and Julianna transmitted, the information that you were with the Comte's attractive sister in Paris, and we were all aware that Mrs. Dyer was one of the house party at Herstwood."

"Oh, for God's sake!" Noah exclaimed, clenching his fists at his sides. "Did no one tell you of the cheeky little maid at Yzeure?" he asked sarcastically, "or the dozen other women I have encountered in my travels? Can I not speak with anyone without setting the gossips about their work? When I decide to have an affair, Mother, you may be sure I will be discreet about it; it is the only thing I promised Olivia. She has no call to complain of my behavior," he muttered hotly.

"She has not complained of your behavior, Noah. She has not, in fact, complained of anything, poor dear. We have treated her shabbily, and she merely presents a cheerful front. There is no self-righteousness about it, I assure you. Olivia possesses a dignity to which the rest of the present generation of Fullertons cannot lay claim, though I remember it in her parents." Lady Lawrence sighed deeply and straightened the coverlet.

Noah laughed suddenly. "I remember her telling me with great dignity when I had offended her, that she had known how to be a *baronet's* wife since she was ten."

"She does not put on any airs with us, Noah."

There was a tap at the door, and Marie entered to advise them that Olivia was awake. Noah excused himself to his mother and followed the maid to his wife's bedchamber, where he tried to dispel his anxiety by entering with more assurance than he felt. The sight of Olivia's pale face with its tremulous smile very nearly unnerved him, however, and he grasped her hands warmly and gently touched his lips to hers. "Dear God, how I've longed to see you again, Olivia. How are you feeling?"

"Better now. Julianna has been pampering me and your mother writes me several notes each day," she replied with a grin. "It is good to have you home, Noah."

"I understand we are to have a child."

"Yes, if all goes well." Olivia turned her eyes from him. "I did not intend to jeopardize the child when I . . . rode out, you know."

Noah squeezed her hands. "Of course you did not, my dear. I must thank you for what you did, though I wish it had not been necessary. I should have been here to look after matters myself." His voice held a faint note of apology but he found himself unable to say more about his long absence.

"Well, I promised you that I would not overlook such an occurrence," Olivia pointed out. "I wore your clothes and have not been able to check them for mud. They are in the bottom drawer of my dressing table."

"Robert can see to them," he replied absently. "I notice you have redone your room most attractively. Did Miss Stewart come to stay with you?"

It seemed inconceivable that he should not know something that had happened so long ago. "Why, yes, she was here for almost two months. And I have learned to drive a pair; in fact, the other night I had four in hand."

Noah shook his head wonderingly. "And that was the first time you had attempted it, in the dark of night on an unfamiliar road?"

"Yes, but the horses were tired and we went very slowly, I promise you. There was no choice, Noah."

"I am not angry," he protested, "merely amazed."

"I think Julianna has come to realize that Alexander is not what she wished him to be, but it is a difficult time for her. I pray you will be gentle with her, Noah."

"You and Mother make me out a veritable ogre," Noah replied, disgruntled. "I have no intention of ringing a peal over her, but it will be necessary for me to discuss the matter with her. I am not insensible to the distress she must be feeling now, Olivia."

"Of course you aren't," she agreed with a hesitant smile. "Have you concluded your business satisfactorily?"

"Yes. It should not be necessary for me to be away so long again."

She nodded silently. "Dr. Davenport said I may get up in a few days if I progress well."

"You are to do exactly as he says. I want no harm to come to you, my dear." He traced the lines of her nose, cheekbones and lips with a gentle finger. "It distresses me to see you so pale. Tomorrow we will ask the good doctor if you can sit in the garden if I carry you there."

"I would like that," she admitted. "And you must convince Julianna that she need not sit with me so often. She is beginning to look fagged."

"I shall take my dinner with you if I may." Her blush of pleasure heartened him and he bent to kiss her. "I have brought some books for you and . . . well, you shall see at dinner."

When Noah had changed from his traveling clothes with the assistance of his valet, whom he had sorely missed during the last few months, he asked that his sister join him in his library. Before she arrived he seated himself leisurely and stretched out his feet onto the leather hassock which Olivia had given him as a wedding present. He was smiling slightly when Julianna nervously poked her head around the open door and asked if she might come in.

"Yes, of course," he said as he rose to seat her. "Mother and Olivia have both urged restraint on me, dear girl, and you need not look so apprehensive. I would like to understand exactly what happened, though, and why."

Haltingly, Julianna recounted the progress of her romance, her eyes focused throughout on the letter opener Noah toyed with as she spoke. When she had completed her recital, there was silence in the room for some time.

"I did not mean to cause so much trouble," she offered in a quavering voice. "You and mother were right in your assessment of his character, I dare say, but I was very fond of him and could not see."

"Have you still a fondness for him, Julianna?" he asked kindly.

"I cannot honestly say. There is an aching . . . a pain when I think of him, but the whole seems to have happened a long time ago. I see it almost as a memory." She gave a despairing shrug. "It is not easy to explain."

"No, of course not. I should have condoned your marrying him when you came of age, you know, Julianna, for I would want no break in the family. After this incident . . . well, it would be difficult for me to do so, but I would try."

"There is no longer any question of my marrying him, Noah. A part of me still wishes it were possible, but a far larger part knows that it is not. Olivia spoke with me a little that night. She pointed out that Alexander had not acted honorably, and that you would never act otherwise. I own I would not wish to be married to someone I could not respect."

"It was my understanding," Noah spoke carefully, "that all of you, including Olivia, have found my absence reprehensible."

Julianna's eyes flashed. "And so it has been, Noah."

"But you are indicating that Olivia held me up as a model of integrity."

"Not precisely. That is, Olivia pointed out that you

had offered her the protection of your name and your position—a convenient marriage. She thought I would not be content with a marriage where Alexander was using me. I . . . I had taunted her that you were using her," Julianna admitted in a whisper.

Noah regarded her soberly. "Did Olivia feel that I was using her?"

"No, she thought it was hard of you to leave her so soon, but that you had not promised her . . . those things which might be expected in a different type of marriage."

"I see." Noah placed the letter opener carefully on the table. "I think you are wise to learn that you must be able to respect your partner in marriage, Julianna. We are often tempted by other assets which are not nearly so important over the span of years. I hope you will come to me, or Mother, or Olivia with your . . . concerns another time. We all love you dearly and do not wish to be alienated from you."

When he rose from his chair, Julianna flung herself into his arms and sobbed, "You have all been too kind to me. I would have disgraced us all with my willfulness."

He laughed gently. "It is the prerogative of the young to learn from their mistakes, Julianna, not be hounded by them. Dry your tears now and go to assure Mother that I have not imprisoned you in your room on bread and water."

When Noah returned to his wife's room, she was immensely surprised to see him laden down with bundles and packages. His eyes danced at her expression and he carefully dumped the lot at the foot of her bed so that he would be free to kiss her properly. After he released her, she blushed rosily and said shyly, "Now I feel married again."

"I should hope so," he replied with mock sternness. "You must not think that I have forgotten you while I have been away, Olivia. Far from it. There were so many things I wanted you to have, but I could not travel with them all."

"Those are all for me? What of your mother and sister?"

"They shall each have a gift later this evening when

you are asleep." He drew the closest of the packages toward her. "This one I found in London and I could not resist it."

Olivia unwrapped the Staffordshire salt-glaze figurine of a young woman obviously on her best behavior and Noah commented laconically, "I thought you would especially appreciate it."

"You mock me, sir," she laughed as she set the figurine on her bedside stand. Noah placed a larger parcel in her hands and warned her to open it carefully. She found within four Beilby goblets with a fine opaque-white twist in the stem and a design of grapes and vines on the bucket-shaped bowl. "How beautiful!"

"Yes, I thought they were exquisite," he agreed, "and I hope you will keep them here in your room for special occasions, such as tonight. We could have our wine from them."

Their meal was brought in then and set out before Noah dismissed the servants. He found that Olivia had not the appetite she had previously displayed but he did not urge her, knowing that she was not well as yet. When she had consumed as much as she wished, she entertained him with accounts of her activities during his absence and news of the estate and village. Her eyes occasionally wandered to the pile of packages at the foot of her bed and he teased her with being as eager to open them as a child on her birthday.

"I have never had many presents," she answered seriously. "As often as not my brothers were not even at Stolenhurst, but the housekeeper always remembered me, and Miss Stewart."

"Then we shall get on with the opening straightaway," he declared lightly, though he found himself rather shocked by her admission.

There was a burgundy gown from Paris, and a hammered gold ring, a number of books in French and English, a pair of silver candlesticks, and a sheer gold negligee. By the time she had finished, the array that was spread on her bed was truly staggering to her. "You are far too generous, Noah. Any one of them would have pleased me beyond reckoning, and the whole is almost incomprehensible."

"Since I could not be with you, it gratified me to search for special things I felt sure you would enjoy." He took her hand and spoke seriously. "I *could not* be with you, Olivia. That is difficult to understand, I know, but it was very necessary that I go." In her eyes he could see the struggle to trust him, to believe him. Why should he expect that of her? "It was an errand for the government, and it took longer than I had expected. Really, it is a secret, and I should not tell you more, but . . ."

Olivia swallowed painfully. "No, if you should not speak of it, then do not. I missed you, and sometimes I was angry with you for leaving me alone, but I had no right to expect you to dance attendance on me."

"It was unfortunate that everything conspired to happen at once so that you should be alone here. I know Miss Stewart proved an agreeable companion, but it is not the same as having one of your family about. I doubt it could happen again." Noah saw that her eyes were heavy with fatigue and he apologized for keeping her from a good night's sleep. The presents were removed carefully from the bed to various tables and stands about the room before he sat down beside her.

"We will talk more in the morning, my dear, but now I will send in your maid." He kissed her gently and drew the bedclothes about her, then disappeared from the room leaving her surrounded by all the beautiful tokens of his . . . what? Affection? Guilt? Olivia was too tired and pleased to give the question more than a cursory consideration. He was home.

Chapter Twenty-Three

Lady Lawrence did not recover as well as she should have from her illness, and Dr. Davenport spoke privately with Noah about the possibilities of his mother taking the waters at Bath. "It would not harm your sister, either. She is looking haggard after her weeks of nursing." Dr. Davenport very properly neglected to mention the young woman's romantic disappointments. Even he was aware that Alexander Cutler had eloped with Esther Draskin; it was the *on dit* of the countryside as well as of London.

"And Olivia? Would you recommend Bath for her as well?"

The doctor shook his head, his lips pursed. "No, I think the journey would be most unwise. She should remain quietly at the Towers. I do not say that she is not recovered, but there is no sense in taking such a risk. The jolting of the carriage ride . . . well, I would not advise it."

"Then she shall not go," Noah said with finality.

Convincing Lady Lawrence of the necessity of her going to take the waters was not an easy task. She adamantly refused to leave Olivia and her home, but Olivia took a hand in urging her to do what was necessary. "You would not wish to be at less than your best health when your first grandchild is born, Lady Lawrence."

"I am sure that I shall be; there is no need to go

jauntering off to see my health restored," the older woman grumbled.

Ignoring her, Olivia continued, "I think the change of scene would do Julianna a world of good, as well. You might return before the weather turns bad, and you would be here for the holidays and the confinement." Olivia grinned at her obstinate mother-in-law. "And I would not mind being here alone with Noah when he returns from escorting you."

"I dare say. Well, I shall think on the matter," Lady Lawrence conceded.

The combined efforts of her family eventually held sway, and she and her daughter began packing for their journey. Noah had spent the three weeks since his return home in a circle of attendance on his wife, his mother and his sister, interspersed with efforts to attend to the backlog of estate business which he alone could handle. In addition he had been given a commission by his friend the Comte de Mauppard to purchase a small estate in England in the event it should become necessary for him to remove from his homeland.

As Olivia's strength returned, she enjoyed short excursions into the neighboring countryside with her husband in this pursuit, though she was not at all sure she wished to have the lovely Francoise as a neighbor. Noah never denied the gossip concerning his relations with the young woman; he considered it refutation enough to lavish attention on his wife. After all, he knew he had no guilt on his conscience in that direction, or any other. His pride did not allow him to discuss the matter.

"I may be gone two or three weeks, you know," he remarked one afternoon as they returned to the Towers. "I should like to see Mother and Julianna settled in before I return. They have not been to Bath before and neither of them is so strong right now as to undertake the venture without some assistance."

"I hope you will stay as long as you wish, Noah."

"I do not like leaving you alone again."

"But, Noah, I am quite recovered now and look forward to seeing to the nursery. It has not been used in many years and is in need of a thorough cleaning and redecoration."

He reined in his pair in the shade of a leafy oak, out of the hot sun. Olivia turned to him inquisitively and he put his arms around her and pressed her to him. "Lord, how I want you," he murmured into her black tresses.

"But, Noah, I am perfectly all right now. I have been . . . surprised that you did not . . . come to me," she said softly, her eyes lowered. "I thought perhaps because I am all swollen now you did not . . ."

"You could never be less than desirable, my dear. Never think it." He gently touched the swelling in her middle. "Did Dr. Davenport not speak with you then? No, I suppose he would not. He told me it would not be . . . advisable for us to have relations."

"Oh. I didn't know." Olivia was relieved that there was an explanation for her husband's behavior. "For how long?"

"He would not commit himself precisely. It would be safest to wait until the child is born."

"But that is months away," she protested, "and I feel quite strong now, Noah."

"I know," he sighed, as he twisted a black ringlet about his finger.

"Could you not speak with him again? I must be much better than when he made such a statement," she said somewhat indignantly.

Noah laughed. "Indeed. I will speak with him, Olivia, but you must not be disappointed if he does not change his advice. He is rather conservative in his treatments."

"And you would nonetheless follow his advice?"

"It is for your own welfare, my dear, and that of the child." Noah kissed her again before resuming their drive. He glanced at her stubbornly set face and chuckled. "Perhaps when I return from Bath."

"Humph."

* * *

Two days later the carriage set off for Bath with Lady Lawrence, Julianna and Noah. Lady Lawrence had very nearly refused at the last moment, but the rest of her family had overruled her objections and hurried her into the carriage. Olivia stood waving them off until they were out of sight, then she returned to the house rather forlornly to begin working on the nursery.

Lady Lawrence wrote from each posting inn, and usually there was a post script from Noah or Julianna. On their way through London they learned of the army revolt at Nancy and of the Marquis de la Fayette's intervention to put it down; all this intelligence was casually transmitted to Olivia. Although it held little importance for her, it was of some moment to Noah, and he perused the news coming from France more carefully than before. The loss of prestige to the Marquis de la Fayette, when the populace called it a massacre, was significant to his supporters, including the Comte de Mauppard.

Soon after his arrival in Bath, Noah wrote to Olivia instructing her to complete the purchase of the last piece of property they had inspected for the comte. On the day his letter arrived there was also a letter directed to him from France and Olivia immediately dispatched it to her husband, with an assurance that she would conclude the purchase for him.

Noah's letter from the comte advised that the situation in Paris was less amenable for him now that the Marquis de la Fayette was discredited in some circles. The comte was a practical man and foresaw the necessity of transferring more of his resources out of the country, citing the difficulties of several of his colleagues. With sufficient delicacy he hinted that Noah could be of service to him at this time, but that he would not wish to impose on his friend if it were not convenient for him to journey to France. Noah had a strong desire to tear up the letter and pretend that he had never received it, but he was too conscious of the kindness and assistance so recently offered him. So he wrote that he would be free to journey to Paris in a week or two.

The letter Olivia received informing her of this news she did tear up in exasperation and burned in the grate of the Winter Parlor. Really, it was too much. So what if he

211

would stop in London on his way, to see if Miss Stewart was free to come to the Towers? Miss Stewart's company was scarcely a substitute for that of her husband. And she probably would not be free to come in any case, Olivia thought with annoyance. To say nothing of the fact that Noah was perfectly willing to drop everything to rush to Paris. What did he care if he deserted his long-suffering wife again? There were attractions enough in Paris for him. His abject apologies burned very well, Olivia thought fiercely as she watched the smoke curl up the chimney.

Miss Stewart was able to come, as she informed Olivia in a letter immediately preceding her arrival. Her friend was again traveling and would be from London for at least a month, should her stay need to be that long. Olivia had no idea how long a stay Miss Stewart need contemplate, and she did not wish to consider the subject.

"God alone knows when Noah will manage to return to the Towers," Olivia remarked with asperity. "He will no doubt return with a portmanteau full of presents for me and expect that I shall ignore his habitual absence." She grimaced pitifully. "On the other hand, he may be interested in meeting his child one day, so I shall not give up hope of seeing him again. Let us forget him, Miss Stewart. I am involved in a new project which will interest you, I know, a great deal more than my opinion of my husband's wanderings."

Miss Stewart was indeed fascinated by the possibilities of decorating the nursery, but she took Olivia's distress to heart and transmitted her sorrow to her own loyal correspondent. Such a careless fellow as Sir Noah was proving to be, she wrote, and his wife deserving much better. It was inconceivable to Miss Stewart that her former pupil should not be held in the highest regard by any man lucky enough to marry her, and did not her correspondent agree?

There were letters from Noah this time, and although Olivia still longed to consign them to the Winter Parlor Grate, she did not. He was delayed, the comte had not been able to make the necessary arrangements. Paris was a strange mixture of ferocity and gaiety; the streets were not altogether safe; the balls not entirely pleasing. He wished that Olivia could be with him and he hoped that her health continued well. Olivia in her turn wrote to him, precise little epistles telling of her daily activities with no expression of her anger, loneliness or fondness. Had she not accepted his explanation of his first absence with no rebuke? And what did he do but go straight off again. Let his mother assure him that he was always in her thoughts and affections. Olivia refused to accord him the satisfaction.

September hastened into October and October drifted past. Lady Lawrence wrote that she was feeling inordinately better and that Julianna had acquired a new beau, which had done wonders for her. They were looking forward to returning to the Towers soon and only waited for Noah to return to escort them. Their expectations were not disappointed, for Olivia soon heard from Noah advising that he was at last leaving for England where he would journey first to Bath.

Miss Stewart, who was on the point of departure, felt an immense relief at this news. She had been debating the wisdom of leaving Olivia alone, and, much as she wished to return to town to see her friend, she almost felt a duty to remain behind with her young companion. As it turned out, there would only be a matter of days before the party from Bath returned, so she held to her plans with a clear conscience.

It was the day after Miss Stewart left that Olivia had a surprise visitor. She was reading in the Winter Parlor, snug against the cold and gathering gloom, when Jarette announced James Evans.

"Lady Olivia, how kind of you to receive me without notice," he commented as he entered, his curly black hair gleaming in the candle and firelight.

"I am delighted that you should pay a call, Mr. Evans. What brings you to our neighborhood?"

"I have been cataloguing Lord Cranston's library. His seat is just beyond Attleborough, and I recalled that

Sir Noah resided in the vicinity of Thetford. I could not resist calling on you when you were so close. Is Sir Noah at home?"

"Not just at present. I expect him in a few days, with his mother and sister who have been in Bath," Olivia replied casually.

Mr. Evans smiled warmly. "It is thoughtful of him to escort them, even though it does take him away from you for a few days." He evidently noticed for the first time that she was with child. "At this particular time you must wish him close at hand."

"Yes," Olivia sighed, "it would be pleasant."

Although their discussion ranged over a wide variety of subjects, Olivia found herself continually in a position where she had to make excuses for her husband's behavior. No, he had not been here when she was redecorating her rooms. No, it was not he who had taught her to drive a pair. No, he had not been with her when his mother and sister came back from the London season. Well, no, he had not actually been with her while Lady Lawrence and Julianna were in Bath. If she had not known better, Olivia would have suspected him of harrassing her on the subject, but clearly he was merely startled and sympathetic.

"Could you stay to dinner, Mr. Evans? It would be nice to have company. My former companion, Miss Stewart, has just left and I am bereft of companionship."

"I would be delighted, Lady Olivia. I have already taken a room at the Bell in Thetford, but I had not bespoken my meal, and I could not expect to find such charming company there." He grinned engagingly. "In my work I frequently travel, and it is a rare treat to spend an evening out of London with an acquaintance."

"Excuse me a moment, if you will, and I will inform the cook." Olivia hastened from the room and, noting that there was probably time for the change, urged the cook to supply a more elaborate meal than she had previously ordered.

When she returned she found Mr. Evans examining the candlesticks Noah had brought her from Paris. "These are most unusual," he remarked. "Not English, I think."

"No, my husband brought them to me from Paris last summer."

"He went to Paris without you?" Mr. Evans asked, obviously appalled. Then he noticed her chagrin and hastened to add, "Perhaps it is for the best, however, as I understand there is a very rough element abroad in the French capital. And no doubt Sir Noah was not there long."

Olivia, at the limit of her tolerance in defending Noah, blurted, "No more than three months, I should think."

Mr. Evans pursed his lips and said nothing. His unspoken censure accorded well with Olivia's grievance, and she warmed to him. Always he had kept his tongue, even when she was most exasperated with her brothers. She could feel that he sympathized with her now, as he had then, and her need to tell someone her aggravations was great. Miss Stewart had not provided the proper encouragement, believing the less said the better. And Olivia would never, never voice her complaints to her mother-in-law or Julianna. She was far too proud for that, if not to drop a few astringent words in Miss Stewart's ears. But here was a heaven-sent opportunity to discharge her anger without any recriminations. Mr. Evans was the soul of discretion.

"Sir Noah," she said, giving in to her need for an encouraging listener, "has not spent two months with me since we were married last March."

"How can that be?" Mr. Evans was shocked.

"Oh, he always has the best of excuses, I dare say, but really, it is too much. You must understand, Mr. Evans, that I did not look for him to be forever with me. No, no. I think I am a very reasonable person. Certainly he should go off, as he always has, to seek his own enjoyments. I would not object to that. But I know for a fact, from things his mother has said, and Julianna, too, that he has not been in the habit of absenting himself for such long periods of time. There are any number of things here which required his attention."

Mr. Evans nodded his understanding, his face grave and his eyes warm with sympathy.

"What am I to think?" Olivia continued, bolstered by his obvious interest. "It is true that he was kind to offer for me under the circumstances, but when all is said and done, it was his fault that I was in an awkward situation in the first place. You remember the night he came to claim my assistance with . . . a sick guest at Stolenhurst."

"Yes, and how unselfishly you accompanied him," Mr. Evans assured her, admiration lighting his eyes.

"Just so," she sniffed. "Had I taken my maid with me, there would have been none of that ridiculous talk. But he wished me to come alone . . . because of the delicacy of the situation. Well, I was happy enough to comply, as I took my duties as hostess very seriously. I still do . . . or would if there were any need of me as a hostess," she grumbled.

"You are a very gracious hostess."

"Thank you, Mr. Evans. I should like to be able to show Sir Noah that I can handle that role in his home, but he is never here to observe. He was supposed to take his mother and sister to Bath and return here. He did not. He went racing off to Paris again at the slightest word from his friend." Her voice fell to almost a whisper. "His friend has a very beautiful sister."

Mr. Evans's voice was full of concern. "Surely he wouldn't . . . but, Lady Olivia, your husband has a beautiful wife at home." He stopped in confusion.

She waved a deprecating hand. "This Francoise is a mature, sophisticated lady, just such as Sir Noah admires," Olivia returned, thinking of Mrs. Dyer. "To my husband I seem a child. Why, even his sister is several years older than I am. There is nothing I can do about my age, and if I were to act older and more sophisticated, I do not doubt he would laugh at me."

"Does he not appreciate the freshness of your youth and candor? Can he possibly prefer the hardened worldly wisdom of ladies bored with society and life?" Mr. Evans protested.

Olivia regarded him wonderingly. "That is what I had hoped, you see, but alas it does not seem to be Sir

Noah's choice. It was naive of me, no doubt, but I had thought he might like a wife who was not so entirely *set* as these ladies who have been about in society for so long. Not that they are old! I do not mean that, Mr. Evans. It did occur to me, though, that they would not be so adaptable, perhaps, and I assure you I had every intention of adapting to Sir Noah's likes and dislikes, his interests and his aversions." She regarded her hands sadly. "I don't even know his likes and dislikes."

"He does not discuss such things with you? And find out your own preferences?" Mr. Evans seemed greatly annoyed with this intelligence.

"He tells me very little of himself," she confessed, "but at first he did listen to my reminiscences and my hopes. There has been little opportunity of late to discuss anything with him."

Mr. Evans said nothing, only his eyes offered consolation. One hand was balled in a fist on his knee and his mouth was set in a grim line.

"Oh, listen to me," she chided herself contritely. "You would think I had some right to expect it otherwise. Noah was very kind to offer me his name when I had nowhere to turn. I am wallowing in self-pity, which is ridiculous. It was far worse at Stolenhurst, where no one cared for me at all. Here Julianna and Lady Lawrence are very solicitous of me, as is Noah, when he is home. Forgive me for my outburst, Mr. Evans. I am ashamed of myself." She dropped her eyes from his intent ones and was surprised when he took her hand.

"Nonsense, my poor lady. You are the daughter and sister of earls, and as such deserve far more observance than you have had. Your condition, too," he said hesitantly, almost, it seemed, with embarrassment, "necessitates an even greater attention to your needs." He stared at his hand as though he could not imagine how he happened to have gained hold of hers. "Forgive me! That I am moved by your plight is no excuse for my taking liberties. Would that I were your equal that I might comfort you as a friend should. Would that it had been I you could have turned to when you had nowhere else to go," he said fiercely as he turned from her and clenched his fists at his sides. "I have never felt so cursed with my insignificance!"

"But, Mr. Evans," Olivia protested, shaken, "you are a most admirable young man, and very talented. I . . . I am grateful for your friendship and do not regard the difference in our positions, I promise you."

Chapter Twenty-Four

Jarette entered to announce dinner before Mr. Evans could reply to his hostess. He placed her arm on his and led her into the dining room with his accustomed ease of manner. Olivia sat in her usual place at the foot of the table and had him seated to her right. Their discussion of but a few minutes past was set aside, and he entertained her with tales of the households he had visited, ever discreetly withholding family and place names.

"Last year when I was with a family near Edinburgh, I visited the Scottish capital and heard the tale of a store-farmer in Caithness who had large tracts of land under lease from the gentleman whose library I was cataloguing. The store-farmer, a Mr. C., would sell his wool for a good sum and pocket the price to go down to town and waste it at law. He was one of the mad litigants for which Edinburgh is so famed.

"On his way to town he would pay twice the cost of each meal, so that when he had nothing on his return, he might have one free. Forever attired in his Highland trews, with a gray or tartan jacket and a bonnet on his head, he would arrive at the Parliament House with a tin case almost the size of himself, which contained the plan of his farms. He was used to declare that he and his laird were close to agreement—there was only some *ten miles* of country debated between them now!"

Olivia laughed appreciatively, but asked, "Why is it

that some men are forever suing their neighbors? Surely such a man must know that he could not afford to spend all his earnings on so wild a venture."

"With some it is a matter of principle, I think. However, it is often the fear of being bested by one's neighbors, and having people snigger at you behind your back that motivates such an action. Few gentlemen can tolerate the thought of being laughed at. And some are so sensitive that they see persecution where none exists. When I catalogued a library at . . . in the north, the gentleman called me into his sitting room one day to berate me for having several of his books in my room. The maid had told him of it. You may remember that I told you I take the opportunity to read those works in which I am particularly interested while I am resident. I pointed out to this fellow that the books were already on the lists he had received and I had no intent of absconding with them, but he would not listen and ordered me from his house."

"Poor Mr. Evans. Did the matter get straightened out?"

"Oh, yes. A member of his family interceded for me, and a servant was sent to bring me back from the inn where I spent the night. The appearance of guilt is almost worse than the commission of it with some people. When I was a child I used to bring bunches of heather to my mother when I had been into some mischief—broken a window with a cricket ball or muddied my best clothes by the pond. It took me some time to realize that I was proclaiming my guilt rather than propitiating it," he laughed.

Although Olivia shared his amusement, she was sobered by her reflection of Noah's gifts to her on his return from France. Was he, too, proclaiming his guilt?

"Not that I have never made a mistake in my work," Mr. Evans was continuing. "I assure you I have done so on many occasions. Well do I remember the time I thought I had found an original handwritten Farquhar. It was *The Recruiting Officer,* which he wrote in '06, you know. There were crossouts and additions; certainly it could be none other than the author's own work, I thought! Imagine my surprise when I very solemnly presented my find to the lord of the manor only to have him tell me that his great uncle was known to have copied that gentleman's work any number of times in the mistaken belief that he himself was Farquhar."

Olivia was enchanted by his easy acceptance of his own fallibility. There was in Mr. Evans a modesty of manner which did not exist in Noah, whose pride made him unapproachable and uncommunicative at times. She was encouraged to relate some of her own scrapes, and they sat laughing over their meal. The intimacy of the setting reminded her of the time she had spent with Noah at Frobess Grange on their honeymoon. Mr. Evans was every bit as attentive to her as Noah had been, and a good deal more forthcoming about himself. It was charming to be in his company, to be admired as his eyes frankly told her he did. Olivia drank more than she should have.

Mr. Evans did not wish to leave Olivia alone to stay at table for his claret. "I would rather forego it than desert you, Lady Olivia," he said with mock gallantry, his eyes twinkling.

"You are too civil, Mr. Evans," she laughed. "Jarette will see that it is brought to the Drawing Room."

Jarette clearly disapproved of this order, but Olivia was oblivious to his haughty gaze. When they were seated in the Drawing Room and the tray had been brought in, Olivia dismissed the servant and motioned Mr. Evans to serve himself. "I should not drink alone," he insisted. "May I pour you a small glass?"

"I believe I will, thank you."

Mr. Evans raised his glass to toast her in the traditional manner: he looked fixedly at her, bowed his head and then drank with due gravity. Somehow it was not quite a traditional glance, however, for Olivia read depths of meaning in it and flushed slightly under his scrutiny. After she had sipped from her own glass she suggested, rather more loudly than she meant to, that she play for him. Not waiting for his answer, and unable to meet his eyes, she hastened to the harpsichord and sifted through the music she found there.

"Would you play a favorite of mine?" he asked deferentially.

"Of course," she offered with a nervous smile. "What is that?"

"Robin Adair."

Olivia nodded mutely; she did not need the music for the hauntingly beautiful song which was a favorite of hers as well. It seemed rude to stare at the harpsichord, but when her eyes locked with his she was wholly disconcerted. As though he realized her discomfort he turned slightly and studied the portrait of Noah's father on the opposite wall until she finished the piece. "Thank you," he said softly without turning, "that was beautiful."

With an unintelligible murmur for reply she placed the music for a sonata on the stand. Without hesitating she launched into the new piece and Mr. Evans courteously stood behind her to turn the music for her, his hand occasionally brushing against her black locks. Whenever she glanced at him, he was studying her with an alarmingly tender expression. As she continued to play one piece after another, she could feel the tension mount between them, and she was unable to speak. During the pause while she selected the next number, she felt the child within her move vigorously and she burst into tears.

Immediately his arms were about her and he asked in an agonized whisper, "Whatever is the matter, my dear Olivia? Have I done something to upset you? Only tell me and I will endeavor never to do so again!"

"No, no," she sobbed. "You have been everything that is kind, Mr. Evans." Her body shook with her sobs and he held her to him whispering gentle encouragement.

"Hush now, my dear. It cannot be good for you to cry. Here, let me dry your eyes." He drew a handkerchief from the pocket of his waistcoat and turned her face up to him. Her eyes, swimming with tears, visibly affected him and he impulsively bent to kiss her.

Olivia had wanted him to kiss her for some time now, and she responded warmly to his lips, but another movement of the child froze her and Mr. Evans abruptly released her, apologizing profusely. He tucked the handkerchief in her hand and stiffly strode away from her, to stand rigidly across the room. Unsure how to handle the situation, Olivia dabbed forcefully at her face and eyes before she gulped down the last of her sobs.

"It was not your fault, Mr. Evans," she said at last, barely loud enough for him to hear. "My condition tends to make me emotional, I fear. Pray do not regard it."

"How can I not?" he groaned. "Please believe that I meant nothing . . . did not mean to insult you, Lady Olivia."

More composed now, Olivia waved her hand in a disparaging gesture. "You have not insulted me, Mr. Evans. It is I who am at fault with my whining self-pity and careless disclosures. I beg your pardon."

"Never do so," he cried adamantly. "I will leave now, provided you are sufficiently recovered. I can only thank you for overlooking my lapse so graciously." He tugged the bell cord himself before he took her hand and gripped it gratefully. "I hope you will call on me in any necessity; I stand your friend, if you will allow me to do so."

Jarette entered and Olivia said only, "You are very kind, Mr. Evans."

When he had left, with one last humble bow, Olivia remained alone in the room, distressed, ashamed. There was no excuse for her behavior, no extenuating circumstance could explain it. It made no difference that she had been neglected. Surely she should have strength enough to surmount such a minor inconvenience. Nor did it matter that her husband felt free to dally as he wished. She was a married woman, a woman with child.

Noah had returned from France laden down with his presents, thinking that he would take up where their honeymoon had left off—in bed. He had been patient when he found that he could not, but he had left soon enough, Olivia realized. Was that the only virtue she held for him?

"No, I will not believe that," she whispered aloud. "For all his insensibility, all his carelessness of me, all his pride, I do love him."

*   *   *

Olivia was not as sure of her devotion to her husband the next morning, when she received a letter from him. Noah wrote from Bath that Julianna's young man had invited them to his home near Salisbury to meet his family. It was not that Olivia could not rationally see the wisdom of their accepting such an invitation; she was delighted for Julianna. There would certainly be no other time soon when such a visit could be made, with the holidays approaching and Olivia's own confinement. It was the most practical solution imaginable, and Olivia was furious. Another delay which she had to accept with good grace. For a ha'penny she would have sent a message to the Bell to see if Mr. Evans had already departed for London!

Instead she ordered the gig brought round and bundled herself warmly against the chill November day. There were baskets of foodstuffs and medicinal concoctions to be delivered to the tenants, a visit to be paid at the vicarage. Perhaps she would also stop in Welling for another length of wool. One more cover for the crib would do no harm.

As she guided the gig through the gates she saw a rider approaching, and knew before she could see his face that it was Mr. Evans. A feeling of panic seized her momentarily, but she drew the horse to a halt and stoically watched his approach.

His smile was hesitant and conciliatory. "I could not leave without assuring myself that you are well this morning, Lady Olivia. I am truly vexed with myself for adding to your distress."

Olivia returned his smile uncertainly. "I appreciate your concern, Mr. Evans, but you find me in the pink of health. The day is most invigorating, and I am just going about some errands."

"Should you go about alone in your . . . that is, did you not wish to take a groom to handle those baskets?"

Her laugh tinkled on the frosty air. "There is never any need for me to lift the baskets, Mr. Evans. No sooner is my gig spied from the window than half a dozen children crowd round to assist me. I cannot doubt it would be so even were I to go abroad on the wettest of days."

He surveyed her dubiously. "Nevertheless, I would be honored to accompany you and be of what service I could."

"Very well, if you wish to spare the time. Are you not expected in London?" she asked curiously.

"My time is not regarded as that of a clerk," he replied stiffly, a frown creasing his forehead. "I am at leisure to come and go as I choose."

"Now I have offended you," Olivia cried contritely. "I did not mean to disparage your independence, Mr. Evans. It would give me great pleasure to have your company."

The frown gave way to a sheepish grin. "Perhaps I am too sensitive on the subject. Where are you headed?"

He rode beside her and questioned her on the neighborhood. Olivia was relieved to stay on neutral topics and expanded on her answers enthusiastically. Each time they made a stop, the children did in fact gather round, but Mr. Evans handed her down from the gig with a solicitousness which would have made her laugh in Noah, but was very flattering from her companion. The visit to the vicarage she considered unwise under the circumstances, and the wool from Welling was decidedly unnecessary, so at the end of her rounds she invited Mr. Evans to join her for tea at the Towers.

His reluctance was apparent and she felt a slight twinge of apprehension herself, but having made the invitation, she pressed him to accept, which he eventually did. The warmth of the Winter Parlor was welcome after the morning cold and she held her hands to the blaze on the grate after ordering tea. Mr. Evans purposely avoided watching her as she moved about the room, and she was poignantly reminded of the previous evening.

When they were seated she introduced the topic of the library at the Towers and Noah's just pride in it. Mr. Evans was forced to meet her gaze as they talked and he cautiously maintained a respectful countenance, accepting

225

the cup of tea she handed him without allowing their hands to touch. The cook had provided a delectable selection of tarts and cakes, biscuits and bread with butter, and Olivia found herself ravenous after her drive. They did justice to the tray of goodies, laughing at their appetite, and Mr. Evans at length wondered if he might see the library before he left.

Olivia promptly rose to lead him there, and frowned on finding Jarette in the hall outside the Winter Parlor. The old man asked, "Will Mr. Evans be leaving now?"

"No, he will not," Olivia snapped. "I will ring for you, Jarette, when you are needed."

"Very good, ma'am."

She shook her head exasperatedly and continued to the library, where Mr. Evans unerringly chose to comment on the hassock. "Yes, it is rather handsome, is it not? I gave it to Noah as a wedding present."

Mr. Evans murmured something about it being a shame Sir Noah had had so little chance to use it, but Olivia chose to ignore his remark. "The foreign language books are on the west wall—Latin, Greek, German, French, Italian, Spanish. Noah reads most of them in the original, though heaven knows where he picked up the knowledge. The south wall is devoted mainly to an extensive collection of volumes on estate management, farming, animal husbandry and such. It dates back hundreds of years. Technical works, biographies and art books are on the east wall, and fiction on the window wall. Most of the volumes here are older; more recent additions are kept in the book room next door. Noah showed me several volumes inscribed by the authors to his father and grandfather. Let me see," she mused, her eyes moving along the rows, "I believe this is one of them."

When she attempted to reach for a volume above her head, Mr. Evans objected indignantly and set her aside firmly. "I can reach it very well myself, Lady Olivia. You have no business exerting yourself so."

"In my condition," she finished playfully, laughing up at him.

"Yes," he said ruefully, "in your condition. If you were my wife . . ." He stopped abruptly.

"You would not allow me to lift a finger. I would be pampered disgracefully and become quite unbearable," she suggested, assuming the demeanor of an old tartar.

"You mock me. It is only right that you should be treated with the tenderness due your . . . condition, your station and your own particular radiance." His face was earnestly serious and he thrust his hands out in a gesture of helplessness.

Shyly, Olivia clasped his hands. "You refine too much on what I have said, Mr. Evans. Really, I am tolerably comfortable and need want for nothing."

"Except the attention of a loving husband," he said fiercely and pulled her protectively against him where she rested unprotesting. "I find it . . . intolerable."

"No, no," she whispered against his coat. "It is just that sometimes I am unbearably lonely. I had foolishly thought that I need be no longer when I left Stolenhurst."

He kissed her then and she felt a desire rise within her which clouded her reason. But, as before, the child moved, as if to release her from her bewitched state. Mr. Evans felt the movement as well and he reluctantly dropped his hands from her waist, raising one to rub his brow bemusedly. "I obviously cannot be trusted with you, Lady Olivia. Please do not think too hardly of me. I will go now, but I pray you will remember that I am yours to command in any contingency." His searching eyes scanned her confused face. Only when she had nodded did he bow and turn abruptly on his heels to leave.

Her confusion did not abate with his disappearance, rather it grew until her head ached and her hands shook. She slumped on the hassock and feebly beat her hands against it in an excess of emotion. How could she act this way with Mr. Evans? How could she encourage him, be attracted to him, need his comfort when she loved her husband? I am indeed the child Noah thinks me, she decided. I will take comfort from whomever offers it. There is no strength of character about me at all. Thank God Mr. Evans will be in London, for I do not seem to be responsible for my actions when I am with him.

Olivia rose slowly and went to her room, where she informed Marie that she wished no luncheon and would rest for some time. Emotionally exhausted, she fell asleep immediately to awake only when the pale daylight was failing. She rose then, full of determination to make the best of her situation, and, even seated in lonely splendor at the dining table, she did not waver in her resolve.

Chapter Twenty-Five

For a week Olivia kept her hands and mind occupied with any task which suggested itself to her. When she was presented with the next letter from her husband she braced herself before reading it for another delay. Noah informed her, however, that they would be back at the Towers by Friday, only four days away. In light of this, Olivia dutifully considered the various emergencies which could arise to prevent its achievement. One of the three could become ill; the carriage or one of the horses could be injured; the road might be impassable. Any number of unlikely occurrences might prevent them, she thought gloomily. She advised the staff just as though there were no doubt in her mind but she expected, right up to the moment the carriage drove up to the oak door, that she would receive a message announcing some delay.

Noah thought his wife looked more astonished than pleased to see him. "I did tell you we would be here Friday, did I not?" he asked, puzzled, when they were alone in the library.

"Why, certainly you did, and everything is quite in order," she replied distantly.

"I don't think you look so well as you did when last I saw you." There was concern in his voice as he studied her.

"But that was so long ago I dare say you are mistaken. Dr. Davenport is altogether satisfied with my progress."

"Are you not pleased to see me, Olivia?" he asked, half serious, half teasing.

"Of course I am, Noah. Your mother and Julianna look well. Do you approve of her young man and his family?"

"Yes, but there is nothing settled as yet. I wish you will talk to her to be sure this is what she wants, Olivia. It follows the Cutler episode rather closely."

"I hope she will confide in me. Is your mother satisfied?"

"I believe she is. There is certainly no reluctance over the young man himself, a most suitable fellow, but she feels a certain uneasiness as I do over the suddenness."

"Yes, I can understand that. I should go and see that they are settled," she said as she rose.

"Surely there is no hurry," he protested. "You haven't told me what you've done while I've been away."

Olivia paused perplexedly. "I did as I always do, Noah. I managed the house, took walks and drives with Miss Stewart, did some embroidery, redecorated the nursery, and called on tenants and the vicar." She moved toward the door.

"Olivia!"

"Yes, Noah?" She turned patiently with a look of query.

His thunderous eyes were not belied by the even tone of voice in which he spoke. "If you are angry with me, you will have to explain why. I have but just arrived home and cannot think how I have offended you."

"Then I am sure it is not possible that you have done so."

He grunted exasperatedly. "I understand women in your condition are given to a certain moodiness, but I am not accustomed to handling it, Olivia."

"I know, Noah," she said softly, and slipped out the door.

When Olivia had checked to see that her mother-in-law needed no assistance, she went along to Julianna's room and found her friend gazing out the window at the few snow flurries falling there.

"It is fortunate that you arrived home when you did," Olivia observed. "By tomorrow the weather may be much worse."

Julianna turned slowly and smiled at her friend. "Noah insisted that we make only a stay long enough to satisfy propriety. He was anxious to be home."

Olivia chose to ignore the inference made by her sister-in-law. "Did you enjoy your stay with the Monroes? Tell me about your young man." She curled up in a chair opposite and watched Julianna.

"I was introduced to John at an assembly by one of Mother's many acquaintances there. After our stays in London I should not have been surprised that she knew so many people, even in Bath. You would think that she had spent her entire life going to such watering places and building up an assortment of friends. Perhaps it is all the letters she writes and the family connections with which she is familiar," Julianna mused.

Olivia laughed. "I am sure Lady Lawrence knows half of England, Julianna, but you are not telling me of John."

The young woman flushed. "Well, it is not easy to explain how we happened to become such friends, Olivia. He is not at all the beau, you know, though he is well enough looking and dresses just as he should. At the first assembly he was attentive to me, perhaps because he had once met Noah years ago, but there were several other young men whom I had met in London who were far more arduous in their interest."

She sighed and turned her head away. "The others knew of . . . Alexander's elopement with Esther Draskin, of course, and how it affected me, or so they thought. It was comforting to me that John was not privy to that knowledge, you see; and he did not associate very freely with the London beaus, so he was not likely to hear of it." She turned abruptly to her sister, her eyes sad. "I felt humiliated with the others, Olivia, thinking that they were laughing behind my back."

"Oh, my poor dear," Olivia murmured as she took her friend in her arms. "I can see how it must have been."

"If I had thought to encounter people I knew there, I am not sure I would have had courage enough to go," Julianna admitted, "but it had not really occurred to me. At first I felt desperate to attract someone's special interest so that I would not feel so unprotected, so exposed. The whole of the season in London there was always Alexander at hand; I was never left on my own to face the embarrassment of the dowagers rushing about to locate a partner for me." She shuddered reminiscently. "You have no idea how awful that can be, my dear, and it happened often enough the first two seasons I spent in London."

"But you are an attractive young woman," protested Olivia.

"I was rather shy in society at first and had nothing to say to the young men who stood up with me, so they were not eager to return. Only when I knew Alexander was there behind me, watching me, waiting for our dances together, was I able to forget my awkwardness. It gave me confidence, Olivia," she admitted, her voice soft and urgent. "Can you understand that?"

"Yes, of course I can, my love."

Julianna sighed. "Well, there I was in Bath with no Alexander. As I said, I had not thought about the change in situation, and when I did, I wished to rush from the room. I felt that all the men were staring at me, whispering among themselves of my humiliation. Oh, they asked me to stand up, tossed about their compliments and politely never mentioned Alexander. It was awful." She sat silent for a minute regarding her hands. "Mother came to me after a while and told me, without any preface mind you, that I was a Lawrence and should be proud of it. I think she very nearly told me to keep my chin up, Olivia." She gave a painful laugh.

"And did you?"

"It is strange, you know, but I did. I told myself that I was well rid of Alexander, that I could be every bit as much at ease without him, and that I intended to enjoy myself. I pretended that you and Noah were watching me from the side of the hall," she confessed, slightly shamefaced.

"I wish we had been."

"I had to force myself to be clever and charming with those young men I knew, but with John I could relax. There was no need to be evasive, to be forever *not* mentioning Alexander. And John is so confident himself that it is impossible to feel clumsy with him. We became friends over those weeks. He took Mother and me to the Abbey and escorted us to the pump room, and we rode sometimes.

"It was only when he left Bath that I realized how attached I had become to him. He went to his home near Salisbury for two weeks, and although I found myself still courted at the assemblies without his support, I was not happy. But I still believed that I missed him as I would miss you, Olivia, deprived of the company of a friend. After all, it was not midsummer moon with me as it had been with Alexander." She laughed deprecatingly. "My intellect did not feel the least disordered, I assure you. Mother said nothing, did nothing to promote or prevent the relationship. How was I to know that you did not have to be at odds with everyone to be fond of a young man?"

"You goose," Olivia laughed. "What happened when John returned?"

Julianna grinned mischievously. "He was very exasperated with me and my chatter. Well, naturally I was delighted to have my friend restored to me, and I had ever so much to tell him about what we had been doing and whom we had seen. There were the books I had read to be discussed and your letters, of course. He told me he was taking me for a drive. He did not ask me, mind you; he told me."

"Sensible man."

"Yes, I suppose he was, for although I was surprised at his being so high-handed, I agreed to go. When we were outside of town in a woods he stopped the phaeton

233

and sat staring at me for the longest time. I was quite put out of countenance, and thought that I had done something to offend him. When he . . . kissed me," she said with a blush, "I realized what a dolt I had been."

Olivia smiled tenderly at her friend. "I am so delighted for you, my love."

"I thought it necessary to tell him about Alexander and everything that had happened."

"The midnight ride as well?" Olivia asked gently.

"Yes, for I could not withhold anything from him. He knew most of the rest, as he was not as unfamiliar with the London gentlemen as I had thought. We are more or less engaged, but there is to be no announcement for a while. John wishes to give me sufficient time to know my mind, and Mother and Noah are concerned at such a rapid change of heart. I do not blame them, you understand; I am amazed myself."

"But you are sure that you wish to marry him?"

Julianna's eyes glowed in the wintry light. "Very sure, my dear. I have none of the doubts and fears I had with Alexander. John is the kind of man you wished for me, Olivia, a man I can love and respect."

Despite the aching in her own heart, Olivia hugged her friend warmly. "You must have been very annoyed with Noah for dragging you back to the Towers so soon."

"Not really, for I wished to be with you when the child is born. John is to visit us early in the new year, and I think Noah will be satisfied then of my resolve."

"He is pleased with your choice, Julianna. I shall look forward to meeting John."

"I am anxious for you to do so. Now do not let me keep you longer, Olivia. You must wish to be with Noah."

Olivia rose slowly and nodded before pressing her friend's hand. "We will talk more later."

When she returned to her room, Olivia was surprised to find Noah there. He was pacing the length of the room, tight-lipped and grim-faced. At the sound of the door closing he swung about to face her.

"Did you wish to speak with me, Noah?" she asked softly, rather shaken by his visage and his presence.

"I did, madam," he said coldly. "I would like an explanation of one Mr. Evans's visit to you."

"Just what would you like me to explain, Noah?" she asked stiffly as she seated herself rigidly on the Hepplewhite chair.

"I would like to know," he said sarcastically, "who he is, why he visited you, how you came to receive him unchaperoned, and what went on between you."

"I see. Very well, I shall endeavor to satisfy your curiosity." Olivia achieved a more comfortable position on the chair and folded her hands nonchalantly in her lap, because she knew it would infuriate her husband. "I believe you have met Mr. Evans—at Stolenhurst. He was cataloguing my brother's library when you were present for Peter's birthday celebration. You may not have been introduced, but he and Miss Stewart were with me when you summoned me to Mrs. Dyer."

Recollection, and something more, dawned on Noah. "I vaguely recall the young man."

"Yes, well, recently he was performing his cataloguing services for Lord Cranston at Attleborough, and he very kindly thought to pay a call on us, since the Towers lies almost on his route to London. How could he be aware that I was alone here? Who would expect such a pass for a young bride with as much family as I now have?" she asked impertinently. "In any case, I saw no reason to have him denied. Miss Stewart had left the previous day and I welcomed the opportunity to renew my acquaintance with Mr. Evans. He is a most engaging young man and a delightful conversationalist."

"I am informed that he did not merely make the usual half-hour social call, Olivia. He stayed to dinner and most of the evening. In addition, you went out the next morning alone, and returned with him some hours later."

"Gossiping with the servants, are you, Noah?" she asked coldly. "Jarette could barely resist putting his ear to the door, I dare say, and was just bursting with the news when your valet returned with you. Let me see, you have been home almost two hours now. Hardly a record for the servants, I imagine," she sighed.

"There is no need to be flippant, Olivia." He stood, hands on hips, glaring down at her. "I notice you have not answered my last question as to what went on between you."

Olivia steeled herself against the blush which threatened to spread over her cheeks. "Do you wish for me to elaborate on our discourse, Noah, or will an abbreviated version do for you?"

"So long as you do not omit anything of importance, an abbreviated version will do," he snapped.

"As you wish. We chatted for some time on matters of mutual interest, and then I invited him to stay to dinner. He was very sympathetic to my pitiful description of being abandoned for most of my married life." Olivia ignored his muttered oath. "Over dinner he was most solicitous and regaled me with anecdotes from his travels and his youth. I drank a bit too much. After our meal he had his claret in the Drawing Room with me. It reminded me of our honeymoon," she said smoothly, "except that he was more forthcoming about himself than you ever were. Then I played several pieces for him, burst into tears and he kissed me, apologized and left."

Noah regarded her with astonishment, unable to speak. Olivia continued, "In the morning I had your letter kindly explaining that you would be delayed *again,* as you were taking your mother and sister to Salisbury. I was unaccountably angry," she shook her head wonderingly, "but proceeded on my usual tasks. Mr. Evans was just riding up as I left the gates and he accompanied me on my drive to several of the tenants. He was concerned that *in my condition* I should wander about alone and took painstaking care of me. I felt it only fair to invite him back to tea, of course. We discussed your library, and I took him to see it. Jarette was most disapproving, you will be happy to note. Such a well-built room, though, I doubt he was able to hear anything."

She regarded her irate husband casually. "Mr. Evans expressed once again his sorrow at the treatment I received as your wife, and I admitted that I was sometimes lonely. Overcome by my plight he held me and kissed me, and assured me that he was mine to command. Then he left."

In a voice shaking with fury, Noah gasped, "And you dare to tell me such a thing?"

"But, Noah, you asked me. Julianna has but recently convinced me of the efficacy of disclosing the whole truth."

"You told Julianna of this?" he yelped.

"Of course not. Whyever would she be interested?"

He sat down on her bed and regarded her uncomprehendingly. "Olivia, do you consider that you behaved properly with Mr. Evans?"

A judicious consideration of his question brought a vigorous shake of her head. "No, I should not have told him of your neglect of me. That is a family matter and should not be discussed amongst strangers. It was very wrong of me, and I apologize."

"For God's sake, Olivia, is it possible that you do not think it improper for you to *kiss* Mr. Evans?"

"Ordinarily I might," she said thoughtfully, "but, as I recall, when we decided to marry we did not endeavor to maintain such a rigid faithfulness. Now I imagine I would disapprove of Julianna acting as I did when she is married to Mr. Monroe."

"Well, *I* disapprove of *your* acting as you did," he grumbled disconcertedly. "This is not Devonshire House. I did not intend that you should take my words as giving you permission to have liaisons."

"Were you reserving them for yourself alone?" she asked innocently.

"No, yes. God help me, you are distorting the whole situation, Olivia. You should be ashamed to have acted as you did."

Olivia bowed her head and whispered, "I am, Noah."

Startled, he rose from the bed and came to take her hand. "Then why did you do it?" he asked gently.

"I'm not sure. Perhaps because I was hurt and angry with you. Perhaps because Mr. Evans was so very attentive to me, and I was flattered. You know that it is easy to manipulate me, Noah, you said so yourself. When I spoke with Julianna just now, I thought I understood it a little better."

"What did she say?"

"Oh, we spoke of confidence, and embarrassment and pride, a number of things. I could not explain it, I fear, but at the time I thought my actions made more sense. Not that I was right," she hastened to add. "You see . . ."

A tap at the door interrupted her and she bid Marie to enter. "Begging your pardon, ma'am, but Robert said Sir Noah must have this straight-away. A special messenger brought it." She curtsied and presented Noah with a sealed, crested letter. When he had thanked and dismissed her he sought Olivia's leave and broke the seal. She could tell by his expression that it was bad news and she braced herself.

At length Noah raised his eyes from the single sheet. "I will have to leave for France immediately."

"Oh, no. Please, Noah, not again. Don't you care at all about me and the baby? What have I done to deserve such treatment from you?"

"You don't understand, Olivia," he protested, his voice urgent. "I don't want to leave you. The letter is from Viscount Mortley advising me that the Comte de Mauppard is in serious trouble. His sister Françoise intimated to the wrong person that Jacques was involved in a plot to spirit the King out of Paris. Mortley offers me his assistance in getting Jacques out of France, where he is in hiding now. His life is in danger, Olivia."

"But why would your friend have tried to get the King out of Paris?"

"I doubt that he actually planned to do so, unless there was an emergency. He and his friends discussed the matter when I was last in Paris. Their goal is a constitutional monarchy, but there are elements in France who would like to see the King dead, and a republic established. No doubt Françoise was not privy to their discussions but overheard some talk of how to rescue the King if necessary. What a needless dilemma!" He took her hand and pressed it. "Olivia, my friend has been of service not only to me but to our country. There is no one else who can help him just now. Lord Mortley assumed I would be willing and able to do so."

"Then of course you will go."

"I must, Olivia," he said helplessly. "Wait here a moment."

She watched him stride to the door of his dressing room and vanish within. The murmur of his voice, giving instructions to his valet, was not distinguishable as words. Dear Lord, he had not been home but a few hours, only long enough to hear of her stupid behavior. She had not even told him of the letter from Miss Steward. In a trance she watched him return to her, an old pad of foolscap tucked under his arm.

"It will be dangerous for you in France, Noah, as a friend of Mauppard's."

"Yes," he admitted reluctantly.

"I will see that their estate is prepared." She moistened her lips before asking hesitantly, "Do you suppose that you will be back before the child is born?"

"I will do everything in my power to be here," he promised. "I am to sail from Great Yarmouth with the morning tide; Mortley will have a ship there."

"Then you had best be away, Noah." Determinedly she gulped down a sob.

"Olivia, do you remember the day we dug up my treasure chest, the day after you agreed to marry me?"

She nodded.

Awkwardly he presented the pad of foolscap to her. "This was in the chest. A journal I kept then, as a boy. Perhaps . . . you would be interested in looking at it. You needn't, if it would be boring. No one else has ever seen it, probably no one ever wanted to."

Olivia was too choked to say more than, "Thank you, Noah. I would like it of all things."

"You do not think Mr. Evans will be in the area again soon, do you?"

"No, I am sure he won't."

"Good." His relief was apparent. "When I return I will try to make up to you for all the time I have had to be away." His valet appeared to announce that all was in readiness for his departure. Noah nodded a curt dismissal and turned to his wife. "Please give me a chance to make you happy, Olivia." He drew her into his arms and kissed her tenderly. "Take care of yourself, my treasure."

"I will, Noah. God-speed."

Chapter Twenty-Six

"I cannot believe he has left her again!" Julianna exclaimed exasperatedly to her mother. "Why, he was eager to get home to see her, I would swear to it. And he didn't even come to take leave of me."

"He was in a hurry. A message arrived informing him that the Comte de Mauppard's life was in danger."

Julianna frowned. "Then it isn't safe for Noah to go there, Mama. Why would he do that when Olivia is to have her baby in only a month or so? Surely the worry cannot be good for her."

"He is aware of it and instructed me most earnestly to distract her mind from such thoughts. You must not let her see that you are concerned." Lady Lawrence sighed. "Noah operates under his own code of honor, as all men do. He could not abandon his friend, even with Olivia so near her time. Thank God we are here and can do our best to help her."

"I will go and sit with her now, Mama."

When Julianna entered Olivia's room, she found her friend seated by the fire with an old pad of foolscap on her lap, her cheeks wet with tears. "Dearest Olivia, don't cry. Noah will be back before you know it and there must be a thousand things to do before the baby arrives."

"If there are, I cannot think of another one," Olivia confessed, "but I must see that the estate purchased for the Comte de Mauppard is put in readiness for his arrival."

"No, I should like to consider that my project, but you may help me if you wish. It would be good training for me, Olivia. John will be very impressed when I write him."

"Yes, I can see that." Olivia set aside the pad of foolscap and went to her escritoire. There would be plenty of time to continue her reading of Noah's youthful thoughts and adventures. He could have done nothing which comforted her more than make her such an offering. Delightful as all the gifts he had brought her on his first return had been, they were nothing compared with this simple—yet extraordinary—gesture. Did he then have some special affection for her after all? Or was it the only way he could think of to combat her attraction to Mr. Evans? Was it his pride speaking again, a pride which could not allow his wife to turn to another man for comfort?

Brushing these thoughts aside, Olivia picked up a pen and dipped it in the standish. "We will make a list of the necessary work to be done, and decide how many servants must be hired for the household, Julianna. Do you think the comte and his sister would prefer to have a carriage at their disposal immediately, or choose their own when they arrive?"

There were, of course, no letters from Noah. He was in France incognito, in search of a man wanted by the more revolutionary element, and he had to be circumspect in his travels and his enquiries. The information Viscount Mortley had given him was out of date by the time he arrived and he traveled to Romilly only to find that Mauppard and his sister had moved to another, safer location.

From Romilly Noah left by barge for Rouen, and if it was a scenic way to travel and less conspicuous than hiring horses or carriages, it was not particularly swift. As the waterman poled the gaily-colored craft along the Seine, Noah found that he was spending long hours thinking of his wife. It was true that he had not spent much time with her since they were married, but it had not been his choice. Did she not realize that he wanted nothing more than to be with her? He was staring moodily at the sluggish water when he made a startling discovery.

It was no longer a simple matter of pride which dictated that he endeavor to make his wife happy. And it was not a sense of outraged propriety which made his blood boil when he thought of her with Mr. Evans. He was jealous of the smooth-talking library cataloguer who had so easily attracted his wife's confidence. Noah wanted Olivia to love *him,* as he loved and cherished her. The Françoises and the Lilas were all very well, but they did not gaze at you with those big trusting gray eyes of Olivia. They did not find the world an adventure and eagerly share with you their stumbling way through it.

Would Olivia have read his journal when he returned? Would she have been interested in his own stumbling progress in the world? He experienced a moment's unease at the thought of someone reading his candid view of himself, though he knew that Olivia would not laugh. But when she understood him better, would she like him?

Noah's thoughts continued to circle about his wife until he finally reached Rouen, where he forced himself to put them from him and concentrate on the problem of getting Mauppard and Françoise out of France. He had barely had a chance to greet his friend when Françoise burst into the room and pointed an accusatory finger at him, declaring, "This is all your fault."

"Is it? I had no idea," Noah replied equably.

Mauppard attempted to silence his sister but she would not heed him. "It is for associating with you, an Englishman, that we are forced to leave our home. And it is because the Vicomte de Preslin is annoyed with you that he will not . . . He would have married me."

Noah and Mauppard exchanged mournful glances which only further inflamed Françoise. "It is true! You have ruined everything! Preslin is very angry that I brought you to his home. Now I shall have to live in England where it is cold and wet all the time, and the people are not civilized."

243

When she had slammed her way from the room, Mauppard turned to his friend with a grimace. "She will not be an easy companion in our travels, I fear."

Such superb understatement needed no elaboration in the days that followed. Françoise complained of the clothes she had to wear, the food she had to eat, the cart she had to ride in, and the beds in which she slept. When she refused to move after a stop for bread and cheese, Noah, exasperated, said, "My wife would not be so poor-spirited."

The French woman glowered at him, but flounced to her feet. She did not miss the amused glance which passed between her brother and his friend, and she vowed to avenge herself on Noah. By the time they reached Oostende and the ship, she was speaking with neither of them and went directly below to repair her ravaged appearance. Her pride wounded, her dignity assailed, she determined that she would make Noah regret his rash words which belittled her in deference to his wife. She was not one to accept that she alone had precipitated the whole crisis; had turned all of their lives upside down for the chance to gossip about something she should not have eavesdropped on in the first place. Françoise held Noah responsible for her own rejection by the Vicomte de Preslin, and she would repair her vanity at his expense.

Christmas Day dawned on a very unsettled household at Welling Towers. Although unexpressed, the fears of each of the three women had risen as the time lengthened since Noah's departure. Olivia expected to be confined shortly and her apprehension for her husband was great. The gifts were left unopened at Julianna's suggestion. "We will wait until Noah can be with us," she suggested with a forced smile.

They were seated at their dinner when Noah arrived, exhausted but exhilarated, with the refugees. He went directly to Olivia, whispering, "I see I am in time."

"Thank God you are safe, Noah. We have been so very worried and felt helpless to do anything." She smiled radiantly before turning to be introduced to the comte and his sister.

"We can never express our gratitude to your husband, Lady Olivia," the comte assured her, "nor to you for your patience with all our trials. No one was ever more fortunate in his friend than I."

"I am relieved that you are all safe. Now our Christmas can truly be joyous," Olivia said happily, including the beautiful Françoise in her remark.

The Frenchwoman tossed her head haughtily and said only, "I would rather be in France."

"Yes, it must be upsetting to leave your country. Noah's mother is arranging for your rooms, and Julianna has seen to the preparation of your brother's new estate. It is but twenty miles from here, and no doubt you will be anxious to become acquainted with it."

"Not I. I have traveled enough for a lifetime these last weeks, and I refuse to go another inch until I have sufficiently recovered," she purred in her lilting English, as she laid a proprietary hand on Noah's arm.

Startled, Olivia murmured, "Yes, well, we shall be happy to have you stay with us."

When they were all seated about the table, Olivia and Julianna plied Noah with eager questions about his adventure, and he attempted to answer them, but Françoise kept interrupting him.

She gazed about the room and said, "I would not have satin draperies here. They should be velvet, and a darker green, don't you agree, Noah?"

He frowned at her. "No, I am very fond of this room and find it entirely to my taste."

In spite of her brother's damping glare, Françoise continued in the same vein. "Surely, Noah, you would prefer a marble mantelpiece to that painted wooden one with all its lumps of fruit and vines."

"It is an Adams mantel, and a fine example of the style," Noah retorted. He turned to Olivia with a smile. "I presume the nursery is changed out of all recognition. Will you show it to me later?"

Olivia beamed. "Oh, yes. Miss Stewart embroidered the most colorful . . ."

Apparently unaware that he was in the midst of a conversation, Françoise spoke again. "You must have a carpet brought over from France, Noah. This one has none of the subtlety of color of those in Jacques' house."

Her brother was seated next to Lady Lawrence and unable to give Françoise the kick he felt she deserved, and he did not wish to cause a scene at his friend's table, so he sat silent but grim-faced. Polite at first, Noah became increasingly impatient with the young lady's ploy. He had no doubt of her intention; he was familiar enough with her character to judge that she wished to embarrass him before his family for the wrongs she wished to believe he had caused her, and his callous disregard of her dignity on their escape from France.

Noah could see that Olivia was becoming more and more uncomfortable as the evening progressed. When they all gathered in the Drawing Room, Françoise heralded her own performance on the harpsichord, insisted that Noah stand by her to turn her music and stayed at the instrument for almost an hour. When the comte tired of hinting to his sister, he ordered her to leave the harpsichord, which she did with ill-grace.

"I shall play for you more another time, Noah, as I know how much you enjoy it," she said.

His patience gone, and tired from his journey, Noah ignored her and made a remark to his friend, directly cutting her.

Piqued by his action, Françoise turned to Olivia and said loudly, "I see we have something in common, Lady Olivia."

"And what is that?" Olivia asked curiously.

"We are both with child by your husband."

Chapter Twenty-Seven

Stunned silence reigned in the Drawing Room. Olivia's face drained of color and for a moment she thought she would faint. In an instant Lady Lawrence and Julianna were beside her, the older woman flushed with anger and the younger horrified. Without a word they assisted Olivia to her feet and out of the room.

Although Noah wished nothing more than to be with his wife, he was faced with Mauppard's careful scrutiny, and Françoise's triumphant gaze. "Is this true?" the comte asked, his face rigidly set.

"It is totally impossible," Noah replied formally.

"What could it benefit her to make such an accusation? You are married and it must shame her to admit she is a fallen woman."

Noah regarded the young lady with cold fury. "You have only to look at her to see there is no shame in her. She has tried the whole of the evening to discomfort me before my wife and my family, and she has achieved her goal, at my wife's expense."

Mauppard was indeed perplexed by his sister's pleased countenance. "What have you to say, Françoise?"

"I am with child by Sir Noah as I have said. Of course he would deny it, Jacques. He treated me most dishonorably as you must see. By promising to divorce his wife, he overcame my reluctance and seduced me in your own house. He did not tell me that his wife was with child." She continued to regard Noah victoriously.

"If your sister is with child, it is not mine. I have never made so much as a personal remark to her, Jacques, let alone bed her." Noah shrugged his frustration. "I cannot prove I have never touched her. It is her word against mine, and you have mine as a gentleman. If she is with child, which I doubt, then she has left her lover in France and is grasping at straws."

Mauppard considered him gravely. "You give me your word as a gentleman that you have never touched her?"

"Yes."

"Then I believe you, my friend, and with the loan of your carriage we will leave your home immediately. I am grieved to be so shamed before you."

Françoise leaped to her feet and struck her brother viciously across the face. "How dare you believe his word against mine? I am your sister, one of your own blood. Sir Noah is nothing but an Englishman." She stood panting before him.

"Ah, yes, my dear, but he is an honorable man. You have proved to me on several occasions that you are not an honest woman. Though I find it difficult for even you to so degrade yourself, there is no question in my mind as to who tells the lie. I would have done better to leave you in France," he said sadly.

"He might have seduced me!" she screamed. "I am a beautiful woman and the two of you have jeered at me and dragged me about the countryside until my complexion is nearly ruined. He deserves to be humiliated before his family for his disregard of me."

Lady Lawrence was standing at the doorway and she beckoned to Noah. He went to her immediately and learned that Olivia's time had come and that Dr. Davenport had been sent for.

"I will come straight away," he said tersely before he returned to his guests. "Jacques, my wife's confinement has begun and I must go to her. You are welcome in my home at any time, but your sister cannot be forgiven for the pain she has caused my wife. I will have my mother see you are provided with a carriage. If you will excuse me . . ."

Noah found his sister with Olivia in the bedroom. "Julianna, I would like to speak with Olivia."

Julianna stamped her foot and cried, "Is it too much for your pride, my dear brother, to confirm or deny what that woman accused you of?"

"It is not true, Julianna, as Mother has heard." He rubbed a hand wearily over his eyes. "Please leave me alone with Olivia."

Julianna glanced toward the bed where she received a confirming nod from her friend. Noah stood silently by his wife until they were alone in the room. "I cannot tell you how sorry I am for the scene Françoise created, Olivia. I swear there is no truth in it, as she has managed in her anger to convince her brother and Mother as well. She is a disagreeably vain young lady and was vexed that her dignity suffered before me and her brother in our travels."

"Are you telling me that she is not with child, Noah, or that you have not . . ."

"I have done nothing with her, nothing. I have not been with any other woman since we became engaged," he admitted.

"You forget your visit to London when I was at Stolenhurst," she reproached him.

"No, Olivia," he said gently, taking her hand in his. "I confess I had intended to continue my liaison with Mrs. Dyer, but she had other plans."

"I see. Well, it is all most noble of you, but I did not expect such a sacrifice."

"Nor did I expect to make one, Olivia, but I find I have no desire to be unfaithful to you."

"But why?" she asked pitifully.

"Because I love you, my dear." He seated himself beside her with her hand in his while she suffered a painful contraction. "Dear God, I have so much I want to tell you, but I should not burden you with my feelings at such a time."

She smiled wanly at him and murmured, "It could never be a burden to have you tell me that you love me, Noah."

"And do you think that in time you could come to

love me? I have not Mr. Evans's ease of manner, perhaps, but I am sincerely attached to you."

"Ah, Mr. Evans. There was not time during your last brief stay to finish explaining about Mr. Evans." She smiled impishly at him, forgetful of her discomfort. "Before you arrived I had a letter from Miss Stewart informing me of a most shocking state of affairs. It appears that the reason she left Stolenhurst was that she had allowed Mr. Evans some liberties with her that night. Nothing serious, you understand, but quite enough to frighten her away. In her distress at your carrying me off in the middle of the night, she allowed Mr. Evans to comfort her. He is very good at that."

Noah regarded her ruefully. "You knew all this when I brought Mother and Julianna home?"

"Yes, and I would have told you but that you had to leave so abruptly. Miss Stewart was then courted by Mr. Evans in London, and in her correspondence with him she revealed a great deal about our relationship. He could not resist the temptation to renew our acquaintance, armed as he was with such a superfluity of detail. But it appears that Mr. Evans is already married, and has been for any number of years. His employer has been forced to dismiss him finally after several complaints from the households where he has catalogued libraries. Mr Evans is unable to resist the temptation to seduce any woman who comes in his way."

She regarded her husband with wide, anxious eyes. "You must not think that the knowledge of his activities in any way makes me feel less ashamed of myself, Noah. I could not help but think you did not care for me, and I assumed you were seeing other women. You certainly did not deny it, though you were aware that all of us thought it to be true."

"I did not think it necessary to deny it," he said stiffly, but her sad smile made him relent. "Oh, Julianna is quite right. I was too proud to admit it to you. And perhaps I thought to make you care for me by arousing your jealousy."

"I was horridly jealous of Mrs. Dyer."

"Do you care for me, Olivia?" he asked, amazed.

"Of course I do, Noah. I have loved you since our honeymoon, though I have often suffered from your absence. I was never so lonely at Stolenhurst as I have been here without you."

"I will be here with you now, Olivia," he promised.

Dr. Davenport, with impeccable timing, arrived then and ordered Noah from the room.

Epilogue

Olivia sat before the glass, satisfied that her figure had returned to normal and that the hair she brushed was as thick as ever, in spite of all the tales she had heard that it came out in handfuls after one gave birth. She responded to the tap at her door and, in the glass, watched Noah stride over to her and place his hands on her shoulders. "Julianna made a beautiful bride, don't you think, Noah?"

"Charming, my love. They suit one another extremely well, and I cannot doubt they will be content."

"If John is not forever wandering off," Olivia remarked pertly as he led her to bed.

"I have not left the Towers since Jason was born, wench."

Olivia regarded him seriously. "You must not think I expect you to be forever in my pocket, Noah. When you wish to go to London or to Newmarket, I hope you will do so. Nothing would upset me more than to think you feel constrained to stay by me if you would rather be off enjoying yourself. My idea of a felicitous marriage does not necessitate our being always within sight of each other."

"I plan to go to London in a few weeks."

"Then I hope you will go and enjoy yourself without thinking that I resent your absence." She pressed his hand in an effort to assure him of her sincerity. "Julianna's wedding has kept you here well into the season."

"So it has, and you and mother have been run off your feet what with that and the boy, Olivia."

"Yes, it will be a welcome change to be here quiet for a while."

"Only for a few weeks, my love, as I said. Then I intend to take you all to London with me."

"With you?" Olivia could not hide the eagerness which crept into her voice, but she stemmed the tide of her enthusiasm and looked down at their linked hands. "Although I would really like to go, Noah, I cannot feel that you would altogether enjoy yourself with such a house full of us. Perhaps you have not considered that in addition to your mother and me and Jason, there would have to be the nursery maid and an inordinate number of servants."

"I have considered it."

"I fear it would mean taking a house, you know, and with the season under way that may be very difficult."

"I have already taken a house, Olivia."

"You have been *planning* to take us?"

He rumpled her hair and kissed her. "Of course, goose. How am I to enjoy myself when you are not around to plague me?"

Olivia's eyes sparkled with delight. "And we will go to the theatre, and the opera, and to Ranleagh, and Sadler's Wells?"

"Certainly."

"And to Vauxhall and Astley's?"

"Yes, love, and to the Royal Academy if you wish."

"You do not think perhaps there will still be gossip of me there?" she asked anxiously.

"No, I do not," he replied firmly.

"And I shall see Miss Stewart and her new beau?"

"For God's sake, Olivia, if you were so eager to get to London, why didn't you tell me? I thought it would be a treat for you, but I had no idea it was well nigh imperative to your happiness." Noah gazed at her with mock exasperation, and made to take her in his arms. "Where are you going *now?*"

"I have left the snuffers on my dressing table."

He caught her wrist and gently drew her back. "I am quite capable of taking care of everything."

"I know, my love," she replied with a grin.

ROMANTIC ENCOUNTERS